Kelly Elliott is a *New York Times* and *USA Today* bestselling contemporary romance author. Since finishing her bestselling Wanted series, Kelly continues to spread her wings while remaining true to her roots and giving readers stories rich with hot protective men, strong women and beautiful surroundings.

Kelly has been passionate about writing since she was fifteen. After years of filling journals with stories, she finally followed her dream and published her first novel, *Wanted*, in November of 2012.

Kelly lives in central Texas with her husband, daughter, and two pups. When she's not writing, Kelly enjoys reading and spending time with her family. She is down to earth and very in touch with her readers, both on social media and at signings.

Visit Kelly Elliott online:

www.kellyelliottauthor.com
@author_kelly
www.facebook.com/KellyElliottAuthor/

Adore Me

NEW YORK TIMES & USA TODAY BESTSELLING AUTHOR
KELLY ELLIOTT

piatkus

PIATKUS

First published in Great Britain in 2019 by Piatkus

1 3 5 7 9 10 8 6 4 2

the ... ... ed
i

ISBN 978-0-349-42243-5

Printed and bound in Great Britain by
Clays Ltd, Elcograf S.p.A.

Cover photo: Shannon Cain, Photography by Shannon Cain
Cover design: RBA Designs, www.rbadesigns.com
Interior Design & Formatting: Christine Borgford
Developmental Editor: Elaine York, www.allusiongraphics.com
Content Editor: Sarah Weber, Yellow Bird Editing
Proofing Editor: Hollie Westring, www.hollietheeditor.com

Papers used by Piatkus are from well-managed forests
and other responsible sources.

Piatkus
An imprint of
Little, Brown Book Group
Carmelite House
50 Victoria Embankment
London EC4Y 0DZ

An Hachette UK Company
www.hachette.co.uk

www.littlebrown.co.uk

Adore Me

One

BLAKE

THE MOMENT I stepped into the dark bar, I had to adjust my eyes. It was loud with the sounds of music playing, shot glasses hitting together, and voices coming from one side of the large room. As I inhaled the mixing smells of old wood and beer, I smiled, and the tension in my shoulders melted away. I could have gone to Sedotto. It was one of the hottest bars in Austin, and it happened to be owned by one of my best friends, Tucker. But I needed to be alone in my own thoughts. This bar was my escape—the place I could be and let go without having to explain to anyone why I needed to get shit-faced. This was the one time of year I attempted to smother the guilt, hurt, and anger. The one day I simply wanted to forget that night. When I moved from Austin to New York after college, I missed this place. After only a year, I had secretly flown back to Austin during *that* week, and I'd been making the annual pilgrimages to my favorite bar ever since. This was my first time in since I'd made the move back to Texas.

I missed Butch, the owner of the bar. At least that was what I told myself. Even though I only saw him once a year, he had become a friend. I guess Butch was a part of the therapy I needed to keep the demons from that night from coming back to haunt me. That and caving. I made my way to the bar once I caught sight of the old man.

"This is what I need," I mumbled as I walked toward the bar. I needed a place where I knew no one would judge me or throw in a few jabs at my expense. Everyone thought I was someone I wasn't. Blake the manwhore. Blake the player. Blake, the guy who only wants to have a good time. It was an easy part to play, and it kept all the questions about when was I ever going to find someone to settle down with at bay. It wasn't that I didn't want to settle down and get married someday, but there had only been one woman who had even come close to making me think for the briefest moment that it might be possible. And at the time, she was out of my reach. Hell, she still was, if I wanted to be honest with myself. I carried two dirty little secrets with me. One I never wanted to talk about, and the other . . . The other was another torment. I had a thing for my best friend's sister. Ever since the first time Nash brought her around, I couldn't stop thinking about her. Now when I was near her it nearly killed me to pretend I wasn't attracted to her.

I knocked on the bar as I sat on the old leather stool. I was positive Butch hadn't changed them since the 1970s. The time-hardened leather barely gave way as I sat on it.

Butch made his way over. He smiled and set a glass of draft beer and a shot of whiskey in front of me. With a smile, I picked up the shot and downed it. I had found this bar when I was out walking one night and stumbled upon it. It was the anniversary of her death, and like each year when that day came around, I'd been attempting to escape the memories. That was when I found Butch's Place.

"You read my mind, Butch."

He let out a rumbling laugh and then coughed. The years of working in a smoke-filled bar were catching up with the old man.

"Bullshit," he said, refilling the shot glass. "You and I both know why you come here, and it's not for my winning personality."

I held up glass again and smirked. "Amen. Nothing like a good shot of whiskey to drown the problems."

He nodded. "Good whiskey like this is scarce."

"A lot of good things in life are hard to come by."

Lifting a brow, he asked, "You still haven't found you a girl to settle down with?"

This time I laughed. "No, Butch. That is the last damn thing I am looking for."

Leaning over the bar, he stared at me like he had all the answers in the world. "Blake, one day it will hit you, and you won't know what to fucking do when you meet the one."

I forced a smile. I had to keep myself from telling him it had already hit me a long time ago. "Is that right? How do you mean, old wise one?"

Butch took a step back, crossed his arms over his large chest, and smirked. He was an ex-military man. His son had also been in the military and had committed suicide, nearly destroying Butch. He didn't talk much about him at all. The only thing I knew was it had happened around the same time as my nightmare. We had both agreed a few years ago that neither nightmare was something we cared to speak about.

"I mean you'll know when the right one comes. You'll feel all these confusing feelings all at once, and you won't know what to make of 'em. She'll make you think you're going crazy. You'll discover that you would rather die than see her hurt. You'll spend a small fortune to simply hear her laugh and see her smile."

I laughed again. "Yeah, sometimes I don't think that was ever in the cards for me, old man."

He shrugged. "You haven't looked into the right set of eyes." He lifted a brow. "Or maybe you have, and she got away."

I took a drink of my beer and decided it was time to change the subject.

"What have you been up to?"

With a shake of his head, Butch took the hint and moved on. "Running a bar. What about you, Blake? How's life treating you now that you've moved back to Austin?"

"You know I only moved back so I wouldn't have to fly here once a year to see your sorry ass."

This time it was his turn to laugh. For some strange reason, Butch's deep rumble reminded me of the Santa Claus my mother used to take Dustin and me to see at the country club every year.

"I believe it. Like I said, winning personality."

I rolled my eyes. "I've been busy trying to live the perfect life. Working, spending time with friends, and working some more. About the only thing that keeps me sane these days are my friends."

He nodded. "Good friends are hard to come by. Don't ever let them go."

Something caught Butch's eye, and he turned. He held up a finger and yelled at someone at the other end of the bar. "Stay away from her. Do you hear me?"

When I glanced over to see who Butch was pointing to, my mouth nearly dropped to the bar and my heart felt like it stalled in my chest.

Holy fucking shit. Could it really be her?

"Morgan?"

Butch turned back. "You know Morgan?"

Sighing, I pushed my fingers through my hair.

Jesus. How in the hell do I answer that *question? Yeah, Butch. I know Morgan. She's the girl who stole my heart years ago, and she has no fucking clue.*

"Yeah, I know her. She's my best friend's sister."

I turned back to Butch and asked, "How do you know Morgan?"

"She was Mike's girlfriend."

My heart dropped to my stomach. "Is that why she's here? Is today . . ." I let my question slip away.

Nodding, he faced Morgan again, and I followed his gaze. "Yeah, today's the day. She comes in here once a year and gets shit-faced, just like you. I'm surprised the two of you haven't run into each other yet, doing the same damn thing year after year."

I swallowed hard as I continued to look at her. What were the odds Morgan and I would be coming to the same bar each year, during the same time? How had we not run into each other? I felt the heat of Butch's stare and knew he wanted to say something but was having a hard time. We were both quiet for a good minute before Butch spoke again. This time his voice had a hint of sadness in it.

"She blames herself for his death."

"Why?" I asked.

"Probably the same reason I do. I let her have her day without any questions, the same as I do for you. Then I make sure she gets home. We used to meet once a month for dinner, but I've started backing off of it. She needed to move on, and I felt like that was her way of hanging on to one last piece of Mike."

I refocused on Morgan.

"You know her well then, I'm guessing, since she's Nash's sister?" Turning back to Butch, I nodded. "You know Nash?"

"I do. We met long ago. Mike and Morgan dated in high school."

My face heated after I realized what a stupid question that had been. Of course he would know Morgan's family. Hell, she was engaged to his son.

"I, um, met her in college. Nash had brought her to a party and introduced her to everyone. We're friends, but for a while I really only saw her when she was with her brother or were at the same party or something. She never hung around with us in college, but her best friend—Kaelynn—is engaged to Nash now, so she comes around more often."

"Yeah, she told me about that. I'm happy for Nash."

My eyes swung back over to her and I watched as she downed the rest of the beer she was drinking.

"Damn, Nash wouldn't be too pleased she was here alone."

Butch didn't argue. His bar wasn't the place people like Morgan—or, hell, even people like myself—hung out. It was in an older area of Austin, not a bad area, just not a place where people our age hung out. The patrons here were mostly vets who served with each other or had heard about the bar from other friends.

"Why would she do that to herself?" I asked, feeling a bit guilty I hadn't known about the silent suffering she was putting herself through.

Butch scoffed. "She's doing the same thing you're doing: trying to drown out the pain."

I swallowed hard again then looked from Morgan to Butch. "You don't know how to sugarcoat things, do you, Butch?"

"No. I do not."

My eyes landed back on Morgan. She was two sheets to the wind, and my heart ached for her. Morgan came here to feel closer to Mike. That had to be hard on Butch as well. He'd already had to deal with his son taking his own life six years ago. Mike had PTSD and had recently gotten out of the army. Now it all made sense. I knew Morgan had dated a guy named Mike who had been in the army. I knew he killed himself, and I knew that was what had driven her to go into counseling. But I couldn't believe that her Mike was Butch's Mike.

I rubbed the back of my neck. *Jesus, Greene. Way to be so fucking self-absorbed.*

"How did she get here?"

"Luber."

Jerking my head back to look at Butch, I asked, "Huh?"

"Wuber?"

"Uber?" I asked with a slight chuckle.

"Whatever it's called. She always has them drop her off, then I make sure she gets home, whether I drive her or Lucy does."

Lucy was Butch's daughter. She worked behind the scenes of the bar, managing everything. By Butch's own admission, this place wouldn't have been able to stay afloat had it not been for her business sense.

The guy who had been trying to talk to Morgan walked back up to her, and Butch looked like he was about to lose his shit.

I held up my hand to stop him. "Let me take care of it, Butch."

He reached across the bar and grabbed my forearm. "She's important to me, Blake."

The look in his eyes made me pause for a moment. It felt like he had looked deep into my soul and could see the secret feelings I had harbored for Morgan. I laughed at his comment, attempting to play it off. "You don't scare me. Her brother on the other hand—he scares me. He'd probably have me killed and dumped into a foundation so he could have a skyscraper built over me."

Butch grinned. "He probably would."

Making my way over to Morgan, I nearly sent Nash a text, then stopped. This might not be something Morgan wanted her brother to know about. I could respect that. I shoved the phone back into my pocket.

"Hey, fancy meeting you here," I said, sitting on the stool next to her and giving the guy who was trying to talk to her a dirty look. He took the hint and quickly walked away.

Swinging her body around, Morgan stared at me for the longest time. Something in those sky-blue eyes made my breath hitch for the slightest moment. I wasn't sure if it was because I saw the same lost look in her eyes that I saw in mine every morning, or if it was because she was looking at me like she never had before.

"Blake?"

Her voice was low and very drawn out. She was drunk. Very drunk.

"How's it going, Morgan?"

She smiled, and I couldn't help smile back at her.

"How'd you me know here?"

I leaned in closer. "What?"

Morgan giggled and then lifted her glass. "Butch! Another one, and two for my good-looking friend here."

My brows lifted, and I glanced over to Butch. I was hoping he would say no. He looked at me with the strangest expression before turning back to Morgan.

"Sweetheart, you've had enough."

She huffed and attempted to fold her arms over her chest. "Party pisser."

"Pooper . . . I believe you meant to say," I said with a laugh.

When her head swung back at me, she attempted to steady herself. "You have to go poop?"

I shook my head. "No, Morgan, you said . . . never mind. Listen, how are you getting home?"

"Home? I don't want to go home." She spoke slowly, appearing to be thinking a little too hard.

"Butch cut you off. He said it was time to head home, princess."

Her lower lip came out in the most adorable pout. God almighty, how in the hell had I never noticed how blue her eyes were? They were the color of the sky after a spring rain. Her blond hair was piled up on top of her head in a sloppy mess of a bun, with pieces falling down and framing her face. I knew it was wrong, but I didn't give a shit. I let my gaze rake over her body slowly.

She was hot as hell. Her body was perfect. Not too skinny, with curves and tits any man would want to squeeze in his hands.

Oh hell, knock it off, you idiot. Stow the dirty thoughts, and remember who this is. She's the goddamn reason why you left Texas.

My entire body heated, but I quickly put the flame out by remembering this was Morgan.

Nash's sister.

His baby sister.

"Butch, what's Morgan's bill? I'll pay it."

Walking over to us, he tapped on the bar. "She drinks for free in here."

I smiled. "Looks like we both enjoy benefits from knowing the owner."

"You knows Butch?" Morgan shouted as she clapped her hands and damn near fell off her stool.

Reaching out to steady her before she tumbled off the stool, I said, "Whoa. I think it's time we get you home, princess."

Her teeth dug into her lip as she gazed up at me with those lost eyes that also looked like she was wanting something more. I ignored the way she felt in my arms and cleared my throat.

"What's your address, Morgan?"

"Um . . . I don't remember!" she said with a giggle. "I just moved in!"

I turned to Butch, and he shrugged. "I have no clue. She recently bought a little house in town."

With a sigh, I reached over and grabbed Morgan's phone. If she was anything like her brother, she would have her address in her phone somewhere.

Searching through it, I smiled when I opened her notes and saw it.

My new address.
1123 South Iron Street
Austin, TX 78745

With Uber pulled up on my phone, I typed in Morgan's address and hit enter. There was a car five minutes away. "I'm taking her home, Butch."

"Thank you, Blake. That means a lot to me."

It shocked me how drunk Morgan really was. It was one thing for Butch to let me get drunk, but for him to let Morgan get this wasted sort of pissed me off. I already knew Nash would be livid as fuck if he knew.

"Why in the hell would you let her get this shit-faced?" I asked as he held the door open for me to get her out.

He stared at me, not saying a word, and I knew why. The same reason he let me. It was a vice we both used to deal with our issues. The numbness did a hell of a job drowning out the guilt. At least for a little while.

"Never mind."

"Thought you would say that."

We exchanged a knowing look as I pushed Morgan's phone into my pocket. Wrapping my arm around her, I guided her out to where we waited for the Uber. When it pulled up, the driver shook his head.

"If she throws up, I'm charging you a cleaning fee, bro."

"Fair enough," I said, helping Morgan into the backseat.

Twenty minutes later the car pulled up to a small bungalow on the west side of Austin. The driver jumped out of the car and ran around to the back to help me get Morgan out.

"Dude, your girl is wasted."

My heart panged for a moment. She wasn't my girl. "She's just a friend, and I know she is. Today's a tough day for her."

He nodded. "I get it. Enjoy your evening, bro."

"Yeah, you too."

As we walked up to Morgan's door, I paused. I hadn't seen a purse on the bar back at Butch's place.

"Morgan? Princess, where are your keys?"

She looked up at me. "I feel sick."

Oh great. "Keys to your house?"

"In pockets."

Glancing down, I held her with one arm as I reached into her pocket and felt for her keys.

"God . . . it's been a long time since a guy touched me."

I groaned internally. It was one thing to innocently look for her keys, but something completely different when she talked about me touching her.

"I'm not touching your body, Morgan. I'm getting your keys."

"Oh. Bummer."

I ignored her comment and unlocked the door. I decided it was easier to just pick her up and carry her. Morgan let out a yelp as I lifted her and walked into the dark house.

"Bedroom?" I asked, looking around for a light.

"What kind of girl do you thinks I am? Right to sex, Blake? Not even kisses? That's not fair. I've always thought you would be a good kisser." She pursed her lips and made kissing sounds.

I didn't have time to think about that.

"Morgan, we're not having sex. I'm not kissing you, and I don't want to touch you."

Her body sagged against me, and she buried her face into my chest.

After opening doors into an office and a spare room, I finally found her room. Walking in, I gently placed her on the bed. When I pulled back, I froze.

"Morgan? Why are you crying?"

"You're not attracted to me."

Staring at her like she was nuts, I watched her pull her covers over her head. I sat on the bed and pulled them back down.

"Why would you say that?"

Morgan tossed her hands up in the air and then let them fall to the bed. "You said you didn't want me."

I laughed. "No, I never once said that. I said we weren't having sex, and I . . ."

She raised a brow and gave me a hopeful look. Then she ran her tongue over her lips, and I nearly died on the spot.

"Let me go get you some water."

She smiled. "Yum."

Covering her back up, I made my way to the kitchen and got a glass of water. Then I found some Advil in her bathroom and poured out three, then I grabbed the small trash can from under the sink in case she needed to get sick. When I walked back into her bedroom, Morgan was snoring. Loudly.

Thank God.

I set the water on the side table along with the Advil. Glancing down, I couldn't help but smile. Even drunk and snoring, she was the most beautiful woman I had ever laid eyes on.

Leaning down, I went to kiss her forehead and stopped myself. My eyes moved to her soft lips, and I ached to kiss her. I pulled back. With a whisper, I said, "Sleep well, princess."

Morgan smiled in her sleep and mumbled something. I headed to the office, grabbed some paper and a pen, and quickly wrote her a note.

Morgan,

I hope you took the Advil. Drink some orange juice mixed with the V8 you have in the refrigerator. Trust me on that one. Nasty as hell, but a miracle hangover cure.

Hope you wake up feeling all right. You were pretty toasted, princess.

I took your house key so I could lock your doors. I didn't feel comfortable leaving them unlocked. Call me tomorrow and we can work out a time for me to swing by and give them to you.

Blake.

P.S. It impressed the Uber driver that you didn't throw up, considering how drunk you were.

P.P.S. It's Blake Greene, in case you know another Blake.

I let myself out and locked the door behind me.

As I waited for another Uber to come, I couldn't help the way my mind kept flashing to Morgan looking up at me, silently pleading for me to kiss her. Damn, Morgan Barrett drunk out of her mind and wanting me to kiss her, touch her.

Fuck. I tried to ignore that familiar little ache in my chest. A part of me wanted to go back to Butch's Place and finish what I had started. Another part wanted to go home and replay every touch and look from Morgan.

I sighed and rubbed the back of my neck. I'd go home, drink myself to sleep, and forget about this night. Little did I know those blue eyes would haunt my dreams.

Two

MORGAN

ROLLING OVER, I felt my head pounding behind my eyes. I attempted to open them without screaming out in pain from the headache that had already settled in.

Why do I do this to myself?

I drug in a deep breath and slowly opened one eye, then another. It was still dark in my room. My body relaxed instantly, and I let out the breath I had been holding in. I could hear the birds in my backyard singing, and it made me smile. I might have a massive hangover, but that sound calmed me instantly.

"At least I was smart and kept the curtains shut."

With slow movements, I sat up. My eyes adjusted to the room before I swung my legs over the edge of the bed. Catching a glance at the side table, I saw a glass of water and three Advils.

"I cannot believe I had the whereabouts last night to set those out," I mumbled as I reached for the water and pills. With one quick movement, I tossed them into my mouth, then I drank the whole glass of water. It felt amazing. Especially since my mouth felt dry as all get out. I couldn't even remember leaving Butch's Place. Maybe Butch left the water and

Advil? Or Lucy?

After taking a few deep breaths, I stumbled my way to the bathroom and into a hot shower. I would have to call Butch and thank him or Lucy for getting me home safely. I gave myself one day a year to lose control, and yesterday had been that day. It didn't matter, though. No amount of drinking in the world could take away the guilt I felt or the emptiness I couldn't ever seem to get used to.

Tears pricked at the back of my eyes. I caused myself even more pain when I attempted to hold them back. They won, like they always seemed to do. I covered my mouth in hopes that I could keep the sobs back. I lost that battle. Tears mixed with the hot water as I slowly slid down the tile wall and dropped to the floor. I pulled my knees into my chest, and I lost it.

What would people think if they knew how many times I had broken down in the shower? Or lying in bed? The girl who counsels others through their grief and pain can't seem to control her own.

"Six years! It's been six years, God. Why can't I let the guilt go?" I shouted.

After a good cry, I picked myself back up and finished my shower. With a towel wrapped around my hair and my fluffy robe on, I headed to the kitchen to make myself a cup of tea, already feeling loads better.

Kaelynn's voice filtered in through my thoughts as I walked toward the kitchen. She was my best friend, and she was also engaged to my brother Nash. They had had a whirlwind romance and were now not only planning a wedding in a few months, but planning on being parents as well come October third. Kaelynn was still early on in her pregnancy, and I guess since she was settling down into a happy married life, she thought that meant I had to as well.

"Maybe you should think about dating again, Morgan," Kaelynn had said over and over.

I groaned at the thought. My last attempt at dating was Rich. It was fun; the sex was okay, but that was all it was. The sex was just a tool I used to try to forget about all the crap that rattled around in my head day in and day out. There was absolutely no emotional connection between Rich and me. I was closed off to him, and he saw it. I wouldn't allow him in, and he wanted more than sex. I didn't though, and it wasn't fair to him.

We broke up, but we remained friends.

Sighing, I closed my eyes and leaned against the counter. It wasn't like I didn't want to find love again. But the last time I was in love it left me confused, lonely, and guilty.

When I opened my eyes, I saw a note sitting on the island. It instantly made me smile. Butch was probably giving me orders about how to prevent the dreaded hangover. Unfortunately, my headache was still hanging on.

My smile faded when I saw the handwriting. That wasn't Butch's handwriting or Lucy's. My eyes swung down to the signed name.

Blake.

Wrapping my arms around my body, I stared at the note. That warm familiar feeling I got whenever Blake was around filled me from head to toe.

"Blake? As in Blake Greene?" I whispered, trying not to notice how my body trembled slightly at the thought.

With shaking hands, I picked up the note and read it. I couldn't help but smile at the reference to who he was at the end. Why was Blake at Butch's bar, and how in the world did he end up being the person to take me home?

Setting the note down, I headed to the refrigerator. I sighed in relief when I saw both orange juice and a V8. Trying not to gag as I mixed them together, I plugged my nose and drank the entire glass in one long gulp.

I put the glass on the granite countertop and dragged in a few deep breaths.

"Oh. My. God. That was gross!"

My body shuddered, and I reached for the note again. My phone was sitting next to it, plugged into the charger. The way my chest squeezed at the kind gesture surprised me. I hadn't felt that feeling in a very long time. It was nice having someone care about something so silly. Of course, it didn't hurt that I had a secret crush on Blake as well.

Dialing his number, I sat on the bar stool and tried to figure out what I would say about my behavior last night. Blake was one of my brother's best friends, and they'd known each other since college. Hell, I'd known him since college. At least, until he'd moved away right after he graduated.

I closed my eyes and said a prayer that Blake hadn't called Nash last night. I didn't really want to explain to my brother why I went once a year on the anniversary of Mike's suicide and attempted to drink away my guilt and sadness. Six years was too long for me to be holding on to this, that much I knew. I counseled people almost every day on how to handle grief, anger, guilt, and loneliness. The irony of that wasn't lost on me.

"Hello?"

His voice sounded like he was panting for air, as if he had been playing between the sheets with someone. Knowing Blake, he probably was, and that instantly made me feel jealous.

I swallowed hard as the image of a naked Blake popped into my head. My lower stomach pulled with desire.

What in the hell! Oh my gosh! Morgan!

The urge to throw my phone and squeeze my eyes shut hit me like a brick wall. I had never thought of Blake like that. Ever!

Okay, that was a lie. Blake was hot, and I had more than once let my eyes wander over his body while trying not to let Kaelynn or Nash or any of our other friends see me doing it. When I met Blake in college, I thought he was cute—very cute—but I was already with Mike. And besides, Blake hadn't ever really seemed to think twice about me as anything other than Nash's little sister. When he moved back to Austin, I had to admit, it was hard not to want a handsome guy like that to pay attention to me. I clearly wasn't his type, though, because he never so much as flirted with me.

"Hello? Morgan, are you okay?"

He knows it's me!

My mouth opened to speak, but nothing came out. I rolled my eyes and cursed myself.

Of course he knows it is you, Morgan. He has your number!

We had exchanged numbers when I drove with him to Nash and Kaelynn's new property on the night my brother surprised my best friend by asking her to marry him. Kaelynn had surprised Nash as well by announcing she was pregnant.

"Um, yeah. Sorry, Blake. I'm running on slow this morning. Did I . . . ah . . . interrupt anything?"

He laughed. "I bet you are running slow. You were trashed last night.

And no, I was out for a run."

I sagged in relief and tried not to think of Blake hot and sweaty. My tongue ran over my lips as I let the imagine flit across my mind.

Lord, what is wrong with me this morning?

"Please tell me you didn't call Nash."

"I didn't call him. How are you feeling?"

Smiling, I replied, "I think your nasty concoction is helping. How did you know I had V8?"

"I saw in your refrigerator. You're the one who turned me on to that nasty shit, if you don't remember. I came up with the concoction one morning when I was hungover and I accidentally mixed the two together and drank it. I think I was still drunk, to be honest with you."

I laughed, and man, did it feel good.

"Thank you, Blake. For making sure I got home safely."

"Of course. Nash and Butch would kick my ass if I hadn't made sure you were just that. Safe."

"You know Butch?"

"I do. So I need to give you back your house key. How about we talk over breakfast? Give me thirty minutes, and I'll swing by and pick you up."

My stomach growled in agreement. "Food sounds fantastic right about now."

"Perfect, I'll see you soon, princess."

My breath hitched in my chest for the briefest of moments before I managed to say, "Okay. See you."

The call ended, and I sat there unable to move. I'd never had a guy call me by any sort of endearment. Mike hadn't even done that, and we had dated since high school and even been engaged.

Why had Blake calling me princess stolen my breath away like that?

I did not understand why and really didn't have much time to debate it with myself. I headed to the bedroom and tried to make myself not look like I had the worse hangover of my life.

༺ঙৎ༻

THE DOORBELL RANG, and I jumped. I took one quick look at myself in the mirror and blew out a breath, causing my cheeks to puff up.

"Well, at least I don't look like death."

I had pulled my blond hair up into a ponytail and put on jeans and a light blue T-shirt. A bit of mascara, and I was ready. I never had been much of a makeup kind of girl.

"Okay, Morgan. This isn't a date. It's Blake. You've known him forever, so stop acting like this. It's a crush. He's a good-looking guy, and it's natural to be attracted to him."

Taking a deep breath, I quickly rushed to the door and opened it.

"Hey!" I said, trying not to let my eyes drag over his body. He had obviously come straight over from working out, and I had to force myself to keep a casual smile on my face as I quickly took in the sweatpants and the tight black T-shirt.

Okay, so the T-shirt showed off his upper muscles nicely, and I was definitely staring.

I dragged my eyes away and looked up at him. Blake on the other hand, wasn't hiding the fact he was looking me over. My cheeks burned slightly as I motioned for him to come in. Maybe it was because we were alone that we both felt like we could give each other a good once over.

"How do you feel?" he asked again.

"No worse for wears, I suppose. Want some water? Looks like you came straight over from your run."

He smiled and something deep inside my stomach pulled slightly . . . again.

Whoa. Okay . . . what in the hell is happening? It's been a while since I've had sex, but this is insane.

"Yeah, I figured you might need your house key."

Glancing down at the key in his hand, I spoke. And the words that came out of my mouth were not what I meant to say.

"Oh, I have a spare. You could have kept it."

I paused, hearing myself, and looked at him. Fortunately, he laughed.

"So am I your new designated driver when you get smashed? Is that it?"

I worried my lip before turning and grabbing two water bottles. Refocusing, I faced him again.

"Listen, I'd like to explain that over breakfast."

He held up his hands. "Morgan, you're a grown woman. You don't have to explain anything to me."

The corners of my mouth rose slightly. "I appreciate it, but I think it might do me good to talk about it."

The way his face went from happy to serious told me he might already know the reason.

"Magnolia Café?" he asked, grinning again and giving me a wink that made my knees feel slightly weak.

So maybe what I felt for Blake was more than a crush.

Oh dear. Oh dear, oh dear . . . oh shit.

With a much-too-excited pitch to my voice, I answered, "Sounds perfect!"

"I'll drive, if that's okay with you."

With a nod, I reached for my purse and the bottle of water and motioned with my hand for him to lead the way. As we got to the door, Blake handed me my house key.

"Thanks!" I said, still sounding a little too chipper. I locked the door then pulled up the security app on my phone and set the alarm.

"Good thing that wasn't set last night."

I giggled. "Right? You might have had to call Nash for bail money."

Blake placed his hand on my lower back and guided me toward his car. My mind went fuzzy for a moment as the feel of his hand on my body sent a zap of energy through me. Forcing down my desire for more of him, I looked at the car in front of me and whistled. The white Audi R8 Coupe was beautiful.

"When did you get that, Mr. Greene?"

"Last week." He was suddenly grinning like a kid in a candy shop. "You'll be the first one to take a ride in it."

Did he mean to make that sound so sexual, or was it me? My gaze turned from the Audi to Blake, who was still smiling at the car. Yeah. It was just me.

"Come on," he said, this time taking my hand and pulling me to the car. I laughed and shook my head.

"I'll never understand how someone can get so excited about a car."

He opened the door to reveal sleek black leather seats. Lifting his hand to my mouth, he brushed a kiss over the back.

"I only get excited about two things, princess. Cars and sex."

Swallowing hard, I forced a smile. *This* was Blake. He flirted all the time, yet never with me. I'd seen him in action before, so this shouldn't surprise me in the least, but it felt different. His flirtatious joke had sounded more like a promise than a tease. My body shuddered, part of me wanting to drag him back into my house. That was pure insanity on my part.

"Good to know," I replied with a wink before slipping into the seat. When he shut the door, I quickly pulled in a deep breath and let it out just as fast. I had flirted back.

"I'm starving. I didn't have any dinner last night," I added as he climbed into the driver's seat, hoping it would wipe away my last comment.

I looked at him, taking in his profile. Good Lord, the man was good looking. I mean, I had noticed how handsome he was before, but today it was like I was seeing him in a whole new light. My fingers itched to reach over and touch the unshaven hair on his jawline. I balled my fists and placed them in my lap. Before I could look away, Blake turned and looked at me. Then he frowned, and I couldn't help but wonder if it was because I had been staring at him like a lovesick teenager.

"You haven't eaten since lunch yesterday?"

Wait. Was that genuine concern in his voice?

"No," I said softly before clearing my throat. "Um, no. Honestly, I had just woken up and taken a shower when I called you."

"I was tempted to stay last night with you."

Thud.

My stomach dropped.

"What? Oh my God. What did I say to you? Did I ask you to have sex with me? I'm so embarrassed."

"Morgan."

"I mean, I know I was drunk. Truth be told, I don't even remember seeing you at the bar, or you taking me home. Putting me into bed. If I came on to you, I'm so sorry."

"Morgan."

"It's just been a really long time since I've had sex, and you know how it is when you get drunk and you get horny. I mean, you say things to people you wouldn't ever normally say things to. Like, *hey, you're so damn hot, and I really want to have sex with you*. I mean, that could really go horribly wrong and—"

"Jesus, Morgan, please stop talking!" Blake cried out.

My mouth shut instantly. "Sorry."

He gripped the steering wheel and took a few seconds to stare out the front window before facing me again.

"You didn't come on to me in any way, and I didn't take advantage of you."

I gasped. "Blake! It never even crossed my mind you would do that."

He grinned. "Good, I'm glad to hear that."

Chewing on my lip, I peeked over at him. "Did I say anything embarrassing? I mean, besides what I said a second ago?"

With a shrug, Blake answered, "Not really. I mean, you told me I had a big dick when you felt me up in the Uber."

My eyes widened with shock, and my hand came up to my face. I could feel my cheeks growing hot with embarrassment. "Oh. My. God." His face was void of all hints he was kidding. I wanted to crawl into a hole and stay there for the rest of my life.

How. Embarrassing. And how messed up is that? I touched Blake, and I don't even remember it! That's a bummer.

Blake had pulled out and was on his way to the restaurant, which was only a couple of blocks away.

"I'm so embarrassed. I don't even know where to begin to apologize to you." Blake shrugged. "I hope you know I would never do that if I was . . . well . . . if I was in my right mind. I'm not that type of person."

Clearly I was that type of person around Blake.

He pulled into the parking lot of Magnolia Café and slipped easily into a spot. I focused straight ahead and wondered if he would be mad if I asked him to take me back home. There was no way I could sit across from him now.

When he reached for my hand, I couldn't ignore the way it made my entire body prickle with goose bumps. I took a quick peek over to him, but he seemed to be unaffected by the touch.

Damn. That sucks.

"Morgan," he softly said before placing a single kiss on my wrist. My breathing picked up, and I prayed he didn't notice. "I'm kidding. You didn't do or say anything last night."

I let out a breath and closed my eyes. "Thank God."

"Now, if you do want to feel me up, I won't complain. At all."

Jerking my hand from his, I snapped my eyes open to see him giving me the most brilliant smile I'd ever seen. His dimple was on full display. My chest tightened, and there was no way I could ignore the way my lady bits tingled at the idea.

"You asshole! You made me think I did that nearly the whole drive here!"

He laughed, making me smile as I pushed his shoulder before climbing out of the sports car.

"Sorry! I had to, princess." Blake reached for my hand and intertwined his fingers with mine. We walked hand in hand into the café. My heart was pounding as I searched through my memory for a time when he held my hand before. Never! But again, we'd never been alone together before.

Had Rich ever held my hand? Of course he had, but it had never made my heart feel like it was about to beat out of my chest. Mike had, in the beginning. In the end, he hardly touched me.

I erased all thoughts of Rich and Mike and thought to the few times I had been with Blake. The day he picked me up to drive out to Nash's for the proposal. Had he taken my hand at all? He hadn't. We'd talked like we were the best of friends, though, during the entire drive out there. It was so comfortable. Not a moment of awkward silence.

"Morgan? Hello? Where are you?"

Blake's fingers snapping in front of my face brought me back to the moment. "S-sorry. I was thinking about something and got lost in the memory."

He winked, and I focused on the hostess. "Table for two?" she asked, letting her eyes roam over Blake.

With a sweet grin, Blake replied, "Yes, ma'am."

As we made our way to the back corner, he placed his hand on my lower back again and gently guided me in the direction the hostess had gone. My head was spinning, and it confused me beyond belief. Why in the world was Blake having this effect on me? What was happening? Was I that much in need of sex? And not just sex, but sex with Blake?

Blake pulled out the chair for me, and I slipped into it. As he sat, I took him in. The way he brushed his fingers through his hair. The way he grinned at the young girl and thanked her. The way his eyes flickered up and met mine. The idea hit me all over again, all at once.

Sex with Blake.

That was what I wanted. A onetime, casual hookup with a man I knew, was attracted to, trusted, and clearly had a connection with. How easy was that?

He smiled, and I returned the gesture.

Now, how do I present this plan to him without him laughing his ass off? That is the burning question.

Three

BLAKE

FLEXING MY HAND, I tried to ignore the way it tingled after touching Morgan. I tried to ignore the way my heart felt like it stopped each and every time she smiled. Or laughed. Or looked at me. Or fucking took a breath.

Get it together, Blake. Now. And stop flirting with her.

Hell, this woman was one of the reasons I'd moved out of the state. There was no way I could let it happen. Not then, and not now. Not with Morgan. We were friends. She was Nash's sister. And she was staring at me like she wanted me too.

Morgan was deep in thought again, and the way those blue eyes seemed to look into my soul scared the bejesus out of me. I had worked hard to not show any interest in her, but she was clearly picking up on the sexual connection between us, thanks to my teasing. I knew she felt it. Every time I touched her, her body trembled, and it sent a shock straight to my cock.

I smiled, and she smiled back.

Stop picturing her naked, you asshole. Stop dreaming of what her skin feels like. Or how she would feel wrapped in your arms.

I couldn't help but wonder what Morgan would be like as a lover. Would she be a shy, inexperienced lover? Maybe she was a devil in bed and could teach me a thing or two. No fucking way. Not Morgan. And truth be told, I was leaning on the side of hoping she was shy and would need me to teach *her* a few things.

Clearing my throat, I focused back on the menu. Nash would cut my balls off if he knew what I was thinking about.

"I know what I'm getting. You?" Morgan asked, setting her menu down and snapping me out of my dirty thoughts. I already knew what I was getting. The same thing I always got when I came here.

"Yeah, I know."

My voice sounded strained, and I took a long drink of water to cool myself after I had let my thoughts go wild.

The waitress came over and looked at Morgan first.

"Know what you want, sweetheart?"

"I do. I most certainly do."

My eyes lifted to see her staring at me again. My throat bobbed as I attempted to swallow when she pulled that lower lip between her lips and bit down on it.

Is she flirting with me?

The idea of it nearly made me laugh. No freaking way.

She ordered, but I didn't hear a damn thing she said.

"And for you, handsome?" the waitress asked.

Clearing my throat yet again, I pushed aside the idea that Morgan was coming on to me. "Yeah, I'll take the Mag Scramble."

Morgan giggled. "You're ordering the same thing as me?"

The waitress took my menu and headed toward the kitchen. "It's my favorite thing on the menu."

"Same here."

"We have good taste," I replied, flashing her a grin. When her smile turned into something more purposeful, I glanced around the restaurant.

"Blake, I have a proposition for you."

"What's that?" I asked, glancing at the boxer lying under the table outside on the patio.

Maybe I should get a dog. I could see myself with a dog. Someone to hang out with. A running partner. A warm body to snuggle up to at night.

Snuggle up to at night? Jesus, what is happening to me?

"It's a onetime, no-strings-attached kind of thing."

That piqued my interest as I looked her directly in the eyes.

"Okay, is it a party or something you need a date for?"

The corner of her mouth rose slightly. "We could make it a party . . . for two."

Drawing in my brows, I let out a confused chuckle. "What?"

She leaned in, letting her tits sit all nice and pretty on the table as if they were on display.

Eyes, Blake. Stay focused on her eyes.

Then she said the word. The magical word that had my entire body coming to her full attention.

"Sex. You and me. One night together with as much sex as we can fit in. After that we go back to this . . . to being friends." She motioned between us with her hand and flashed me an innocent smile.

I coughed, which led to a full-on coughing fit, which had everyone in the place looking at me. One man stood up and came over to see if I was okay. He patted his hand on my back a little too hard. I was pretty positive he had overheard Morgan's . . . proposition.

Lifting my hand, I said, "I'm fine."

Morgan sat there, leaning back in her chair, arms folded across that perfect chest of hers, a smirk on her face.

Once I could form words, I glared at her. "That was not funny. And it was mean, too."

Her brow quirked. "It wasn't meant to be funny. Why is asking for a night of sexual pleasure mean?"

I wasn't sure how many times I opened and closed my mouth to speak. Ten? Maybe even twelve. Possibly twenty. It felt like an eternity before I finally could answer. Morgan ended up talking first. Saving me from looking like a complete fool.

"Thank you for taking me home last night and making sure I was safe. I should have started with that before I told you I wanted a night of sex."

I reached for my water, finished the entire glass, and set it on the table. Someone was there instantly to refill it. When they walked away, I leaned in and narrowed my eyes at her.

"Do you hear what you're saying? Are you still drunk?"

She laughed and leaned forward. "I am very sober, and I'm being serious. I need sex, Blake. I haven't been with a guy in a long time, and I'm tired of using . . . other means . . . to make myself come."

I groaned and closed my eyes as I buried my face into my hands. It was like both a dream come true and a nightmare. This was my karma coming to cash in on my ass.

"Who better to ask than a friend? Someone I know. Someone I trust. Someone I'm attracted to. A guy who will take care of me in all the right ways."

"Fuck," I mumbled. "Morgan. Stop. For fuck's sake, you were just in a bar last night drowning the memory of your ex."

Her eyes dropped to her hands. It had probably been a dick move to bring that up, but it was true. "If the drinking couldn't drown him out of your thoughts, I don't think one night of fucking me will do it."

Morgan's eyes lifted to meet mine. "My reasons for last night are not what you think. When Mike killed himself, it devastated me. But something strained things between us in the end. I think . . ."

Her voice cracked and she sat up straighter. "I give myself one time a year to mourn his death and let myself drown in guilt."

"Guilt?" I asked.

She nodded. "I couldn't make him happy. I couldn't see he was hurting. I never saw the signs. He told me in his note he had been having an affair. I couldn't seem to get anything right when it came to Mike. So forgive me for giving myself one night a year to get shit-faced over it."

I scrubbed my hands down my face. "I'm sorry, Morgan."

She turned away, trying to get her emotions in check before she focused back on me.

Morgan lifted her chin and said, "Be honest with me. Are you not interested in me that way?"

Dropping my hands to the table, I stared at her like she was an idiot. "Not interested in you?" I laughed. "If you only fucking knew." I looked away and then back to her. "I've already pictured you naked and imagined my mouth exploring every inch of your body."

She squirmed in her seat as she bit her thumb.

"Don't do that." I growled.

"Do what?" she asked, her breath a little husky sounding.

"Don't sit there and squirm like you're horny."

"What if I am, and even more so since you so graciously gave me that visual? What else would you do to me, Blake?"

My dick grew hard, and I had to reach down to adjust the fucker.

"What?" I asked in a cracked voice.

"Tell me what else you want to do to me, Blake. I want to hear."

Widening my eyes in shock, I looked around the restaurant then back to Morgan as she smirked.

Okay, so she wanted to play it that way. I could play, and I could beat her. Little minx. I knew exactly how to scare her off.

"After thoroughly kissing your mouth, I would make my way down your neck to your chest. I'd suck on each nipple, giving each one plenty of attention before I moved my mouth down your stomach. Over to each hip, then down your inner thigh."

Her tongue wet her lips. "Just one thigh?"

I groaned and closed my eyes for a moment before piercing her eyes with mine again. "No. I'd kiss you down one leg, then back up the other."

Morgan stared at me. Her chest rose and fell, and I wasn't sure if she was nervous or excited. I forced myself to believe she was nervous, having realized she had gone too far.

God, if only I could tell her what I would do next. Spread her open and taste her. Lick her and play with her clit until she screamed my name over and over as she came on my face.

"Blake?"

I cleared my throat. "Then I would realize who I had in my bed and stop."

The disappointment on her face was clear, and it nearly gutted me. "You'd stop?"

The sound of her voice nearly had me taking it all back. A part of me wanted to stand up and pull her to my car. Take her back to my place and teach her a damn lesson. The other part, the sensible part, reminded me that this was my best friend's sister. A friend who I valued and didn't want to lose, even if I'd had more wet dreams about her than I cared to count.

"Yes. Morgan, I would stop. What are you doing here? Nash would kill me if he knew what in the hell we were talking about right now. It's not like it would ever happen, anyway."

She nodded slowly and looked away. I could see the tears forming in her eyes, and I had never hated myself more than I did in that moment.

I reached for her hand, and she pulled it away, placing it with her other hand in her lap.

"Morgan."

Shaking her head, she replied, "It's okay, Blake. I understand. I'm sorry I even said anything."

I exhaled loudly and jerked my hand through my hair. "Morgan, listen."

Holding up her hand, she forced a smile. "Please, let's just forget I even said anything. It was a stupid idea, and I should have known you, of all people, would never be interested in someone like me."

"Someone like you? What the hell does that mean?"

She shrugged. "Please . . . can we forget all of it? It's like you said, I was just sitting in a bar getting drunk over another guy."

"Morgan, let me—"

She gave me a pleading gaze. "*Please*. Can we forget this ever happened?"

I nodded but said nothing. Reaching for her phone, Morgan typed something in and set her phone down on the table.

"Okay, here are two Mag Scrambles. You kids need anything else?" the waitress asked.

"No, thank you," we both said at the same time.

We sat in silence while we ate. It was the first time things had ever been awkward between us, and it was destroying me. My heart pounded in my chest, and I had the strangest feeling. Almost like I had made a terrible mistake. But which part was the mistake? The part where I led her on like a dick, or the part where I told her nothing could ever happen between us? I set my fork down and was about to ask her to go for a drive. We needed to talk about this. What in the world would ever make her proposition me like that?

Shit, what if she asked another guy? Someone she didn't know. I couldn't let that happen. My head was all over the damn place.

"I'm going to run to the restroom, if you'll excuse me."

I glanced up at her as she stood. "Sure."

I needed a few minutes alone to gather my thoughts. To figure out what in the world was going on in that head of hers.

She walked off, but instead of going to the restroom, she walked up to the hostess. I frowned when she reached into her purse, took out some money, and then turned to walk out the door.

What in the hell? She's leaving?

Reaching into my wallet, I pulled out two twenty-dollar bills to toss onto the table and quickly made my way through the café.

When I pushed the door open and got outside, I saw Morgan walking to an Uber.

"Morgan!" I shouted.

She didn't bother to turn around. She opened the back door and got in.

Running toward the car, I called her name. "Morgan!"

The car pulled out of the parking lot and across Lake Austin Boulevard.

"Shit!" I cried out, scrubbing my hands down my face. "Aw, hell. Fuck!"

"Sir, excuse me, but the young lady paid for your breakfast before she left."

The hostess was trying to hand me back my forty dollars. "Tell the waitress to keep it."

She smiled and nodded. "Will do. Thank you!"

Her voice was chipper and full of life. I forced a smile before heading to my car.

I had no fucking idea what had just happened. None. The only thing I knew was that I had hurt Morgan Barrett, and I hated myself for it.

❧

"BLAKE? EARTH TO Blake?"

Lifting my gaze from the glass of beer up to Tucker, I said, "Did you say something?"

He laughed. "Yeah, I said a lot, and you haven't heard a damn thing. Dude, what is going on with you?"

With a sigh, I answered. "I don't know. I haven't really slept well the last few nights."

He frowned. "What's wrong?"

I shrugged. "I don't know. Everything, maybe? I'm hating my job. I can't seem to make my father happy. My sex life has been dead for the last few months. Fuck, I'm even thinking of getting a dog to keep me company."

Tucker stared at me with a look of disbelief on his face. "A dog?"

Looking back at Tucker, I nodded. "I know. And that isn't the worst."

"Want to talk about it?"

"Yeah. Can we head back to your office?"

"Sure. Let me let Lou know. I'll meet you in there."

I watched as Tucker walked over and let his manager know he was stepping away. Tucker had been an old friend from college who had finally followed his dream almost two years ago and opened up one of the hottest bars in Austin. Sedotto. His wife, Charlie, was the CEO of her family's billion-dollar consulting company. We'd all gone to the University of Texas together, and Tucker and Charlie had a weird relationship back then. After spending one weekend together, they'd spent the next seven years hating each other. Made it a little awkward for our group at first, but we all got used to it fast enough. Luckily, they got their heads out of their asses and got back together and married.

Five minutes later, Tucker walked into his office to find me pacing back and forth.

"You look like you're trying to solve world peace. What is so heavy on your mind?"

I stopped walking and faced him. I knew no other way to say what had happened with Morgan to not make it sound so bad, so I blurted it out.

"Morgan asked me to have sex with her, no strings attached, for one night only."

Tucker laughed. "Morgan? Morgan Barrett?"

When I nodded, he laughed more and made his way over to his desk.

"Tucker, I'm being serious. You know the bar I go to every year?"

He nodded, his smile fading. Tucker and Nash were the only two people I had ever told what had happened to me that night.

"It's called Butch's Place."

He shrugged. "You never mentioned the name. I've never heard of it."

"You wouldn't. It's an old bar, and the guy who owns it is a Marine. His son killed himself around the same time my mom passed. His son was is Mike. Morgan's Mike."

"What?"

"Yeah, she was there because—"

"The anniversary of Mike's death."

"Yes."

"It's been six years. You think she's still . . . grieving over him?"

It felt like something knocked all the air out of me. The idea of Morgan still that in love with Mike made me feel . . . sick. How fucked up was that?

"I don't know. She said something about feeling guilty. Did you know he told her in his suicide note that he'd been cheating on her?"

Tucker's eyes went wide. "No way."

"Yeah. She was saying something about not being able to keep him happy, not being able to see him hurting. I don't know. I don't know why she was there last night, but she was. And she was drunk as hell."

Slowly sitting down in the chair, I looked away, trying not to remember the look of pain in her eyes.

"Okay, let's start from the beginning."

Sighing, I stood again. If felt like I was about to crawl out of my own damn skin. "I stopped by Butch's Place to be alone and drink. I needed to get shit-faced, and that's where I always go. Morgan was there, and she was two sheets to the wind. I told Butch I'd take her home."

He narrowed his eyes at me. Tucker also knew my other dirty little secret. That the painful memories of my mother's death weren't the only reason I'd left Texas. Every damn time I saw Morgan it felt like killed me a little bit more.

I held up my hands. "Now hold on. I didn't make a move on her. I got her home, got her to her bed, and left Advil and water on her nightstand. I took her house key so I could lock up the door, and I left her a note saying I had it. She called me, and we agreed to have breakfast. Dude, you know I would never do it. When I came back to town, I promised myself that even though Morgan was single, I wouldn't do it to Nash."

"You've clearly never noticed the way Morgan looks at you, Blake."

I paused and turned to him. "What?"

He shook his head. "Keep going with the story."

"Right. Well she called, we agreed to have breakfast, and I went to her house to pick her up. We eye fucked the hell out of each other for a good minute before we moved on and went to breakfast."

"Okay. Are you attracted to her still?" Tucker said, leaning back and folding his arms across his chest.

I let out a gruff laugh. "I've never not been, Tucker. She's beautiful, has a rocking body, but . . ."

"She's Nash's baby sister."

Rolling my eyes, I replied, "His sister. Can we say that without making it sound like something sinister?"

His brow lifted. "His little sister. The little sister he is protective of. The sister he would not be happy knowing you've been pining over all these years."

"I haven't been pining over her."

"No, you've been putting on a good show and making everyone think you sleep around. Even I was fooled until you admitted your feelings about Morgan to me a few months ago."

"I needed to talk to someone."

He smiled. "Dude, I'm glad you talked to me. If you would just talk to Nash, I know he would understand."

"And break the unspoken rule?"

He sighed. "Nash broke the rule with my sister."

Nash had fallen for Tucker's younger sister Lily and had been secretly dating her for a few years before she had admitted to having an affair. It shook Nash hard, and it took him a while to get over her. Kaelynn coming into his life had helped things along in that department, no doubt.

"*Anyway*, so we're sitting there, and she all of sudden busts out and says she wants one night of no-strings sex. A lot of sex, because she hasn't had sex in a long time. Then the next morning I can go on my way and we can be friends again."

Tucker stared at me. An incredulous look on his face. Finally, he spoke. "Morgan? Morgan said that to you? Was she still drunk?"

I tossed my hands up in the air. "Dude! I asked her the same thing! Then I thought she was screwing around, so I flirted with her a little. When I realized she was serious and my flirting was going too far, I told her it could never happen. There was no way it would happen."

"I'm glad you think a one-night stand is the wrong thing to do."

"Yeah, well, she took it like I wasn't attracted to her, and she said some bullshit about me not going for a woman like her. She was already about to cry, and then I might have mentioned that she'd been pining over Mike the night before. That didn't go over well."

"I imagined it didn't. What did she mean about you not going for a woman like her?"

I shrugged. "Hell if I know. I tried to explain it wasn't about me not being attracted to her, but she wouldn't let me. She told me to forget she'd even brought it up. Next thing I knew she said she was going to the restroom, and she walked out the front door and got in an Uber."

"Shit."

"Yeah. Shit. Now I don't know what in the hell to do. Do I call her? Do I go over to her place to try to explain why us hooking up would be terrible? Tucker, what do I do?"

He sat there, contemplating his answer. "You have two options. One, do like she said and forget she ever said anything."

"And the attraction?"

"Ignore it. Hope it goes away."

I dropped back in the chair. "That's never going to happen. Especially now that I know she's attracted to me too."

Tucker smirked and leaned forward. "Dude, it's fucking time you admitted the truth—not only to yourself, but to Morgan and Nash too."

"And what if I end up losing them both?"

"She's got to be worth the risk, Blake. I mean, a guy doesn't leave town because he simply has the hots for his buddy's sister."

I looked away, knowing exactly what was coming.

"Blake, it's time you faced the truth: you want Morgan."

I shot him a dirty look. "No kidding, asshole. What is option two?"

He shrugged and replied, "Tell Nash you're attracted to Morgan."

Closing my eyes, I dropped back down into the chair and whispered, "I am so fucked."

Four

MORGAN
MARCH

TWO WEEKS HAD passed since the dreaded moment I asked Blake to have no-strings sex with me. Kaelynn was sitting across from me in the booth, talking about her morning sickness while we waited for Nash to join us for dinner. I was excited for her and my brother, but if I was being honest with myself, I was also jealous. Kaelynn had found her happily ever after, and I seemed to be stuck in the past. Why was it that I could help other people move on when I refused to follow my own words?

I smiled, but she must have seen it was forced. She took my hand in hers.

"Hey, are you okay?"

"Yes! My patients were exhausting this week. I'm just emotionally drained."

She must've seen right through my lie, because she didn't let go of my hand. "Are you still thinking about Mike?"

I squeezed her hand. "Sometimes. It's always hard around this time of year."

She took in a deep breath, then slowly let it out. "Have you thought about going on a date?"

With a halfhearted laugh, I shook my head. Little did she know. I imagined my best friend would be shocked to find out I had asked Blake to sleep with me. Casual sex with no strings attached. What had I even been thinking? Would I honestly have been able to sleep with him and walk away? After the way I had felt with him that day, I was even more confused than ever.

"I've been on dates," I said defensively.

She frowned. "Maybe you need to . . . you know. Have some no-strings, fun sex with someone."

My eyes jerked up to her, and I almost confessed.

Her mouth dropped open. "Oh my gosh, have you? Had no-strings-attached, hot sex with a guy you met at the grocery store aisle as you both looked at what type of cereal to eat?"

I stared at her. "What?"

"Sorry." Kaelynn shrugged. "It was in a romance book I read the other night."

Rolling my eyes, I laughed. I would be mortified if she knew the irony of what she had suggested, and I could feel the heat building on my cheeks.

"Oh my gosh, Morgan, have you? Have you had fun sexy time?"

"No, I wish."

Kaelynn's body sagged. "Well, darn, I thought maybe you had, the way you blushed."

I buried my face into my hands and groaned before I dropped them and looked at my best friend. "God, I'm so embarrassed. Kaelynn, I asked a guy for no strings sex, and he turned me down."

Her eyes widened in shock. "You asked a guy for casual sex?"

I nodded.

"And he turned you down? Is he gay?"

With a chuckle, I replied, "Nope. He's very much straight, but I guess I'm not his type."

She pulled her brows in tight. "Who is it?"

"No one who matters."

Reaching for my hand, she gave it a light squeeze. "Screw him, then. Morgan, you're a beautiful, intelligent, amazing woman. Any man should want to give his left nut to spend a night with you."

I stared at her for a few moments before we both dissolved into laughter.

"What's so funny?"

Glancing up, I saw my brother, Nash. He leaned down and kissed Kaelynn sweetly before sliding into the booth next to her.

"Nothing. Girl talk," I replied.

"Staying clear of that," Nash stated.

"How was your day?" Kaelynn asked.

He smiled, and the way they looked at each other had me glancing away for a moment.

My eyes caught a guy sitting at the counter. He must have sensed me looking at him, because he looked up. He smiled, so I smiled. He was cute. Looked like he had a nice body. I couldn't see a ring on his finger. I wonder if he would turn me down, too, if I asked him to take me in the bathroom stall of this restaurant. Maybe I could squeeze my eyes shut tight and pretend he was Blake.

Blake. Ugh. Get out of my head!

I groaned internally. What in the world was wrong with me?

"Hellish. Dad is giving me shit about a project. Then I had to deal with Blake."

My head snapped to the left, and I looked at Nash. "Blake? What about him?"

He shrugged, and Kaelynn gave me a suspicious look. I ignored her and focused on my brother.

"I have no damn clue. He's been acting weird the last couple of weeks. He stopped by work a few days ago and said he needed to talk."

Holding my breath, I tried to calm my heart beat. He wouldn't dare tell Nash about my proposition.

"About what?" I asked, trying to sound casual.

"No clue. He was talking in circles and not making any sense. He's been in a hell of a bad mood too. Today he nearly bit off the waitress's head for bringing him the wrong drink. I think he's in a slump."

"A slump?" Kaelynn and I asked together.

"Yeah, no sex. He's been working long hours, and I know he hasn't been going out like he used to."

"Maybe he's just settling down," Kaelynn said, glancing to me with a raised brow. How in the hell was she putting this together? It had to be the pregnancy hormones sharpening her intuition.

I adverted my eyes.

Nash sighed. "I have no idea. Something is going on with him, though. He mentioned something about going out tonight. Let's hope his dry spell ends."

A pain shot right through the middle of my chest, nearly taking my breath away. Clearing my throat, I stood. "I remembered I have to write up notes on my two patients today. I'll catch up with y'all later."

They both stood for hugs. Nash pulled me in first, placing his mouth near my ear and asking in a low voice, "Are you okay?"

Drawing back, I looked him in the eyes. It had always been hard hiding things from my brother. With him, I seemed to always wear my emotions on my sleeve.

"Yes. Just a rough time of year."

He kissed my cheek. "I love you, sis."

My heart suddenly felt full. "I love you more, Nash."

Kaelynn took her turn, wrapping me in a tight hug and whispering, "Is something going on with you and Blake?"

I laughed and drew back. "You're crazy. I'll talk to you soon."

"Bye, Morgan. Call me, please," Kaelynn said as she waved.

Hurrying away, I replied over my shoulder, "I will!"

The faster I got home and into my pajamas with a bowl of ice cream, the faster this day would be over.

⁓✿⁓

BUT INSTEAD OF going home, I found myself at Butch's Place. This was new for me, and I expected Butch to question why I was there. He didn't. He simply hugged me when I walked in and placed a beer and a shot in front of me. This time I wouldn't let myself get shit-faced.

"You want to talk about it?" Butch asked.

"Not really."

He nodded.

"You know he would want you to move on, Morgan. He wouldn't want you to blame yourself."

"I have moved on, Butch. I dated Rich for a while."

Butch laughed. "Okay, if that's what you want to call it."

Rolling my eyes, I picked up the shot and downed it. It burned my throat but warmed my entire body.

"This isn't about Mike. I mean, maybe it is. Why can't I seem to keep the men in my life happy?"

"Morgan."

"It's true."

"He was my son, and I miss him every day. But Morgan, you deserve better. You deserve to stop feeling guilty for his death. It wasn't your fault."

My chin quivered. Before I opened my mouth to reply, the air in the bar changed. My body tingled everywhere, and I knew . . . I knew it was Blake who had walked in.

"What brings you here."

I stilled as he sat down next to me.

Butch rapped on the bar with his knuckles. "Blake, the usual?"

He shook his head. "No, Butch. I need something stronger."

The old man raised his brows. "Stronger?"

"Yes. Make it a goddamn triple."

Turning to look at him, I stared in disbelief. He looked like shit. Like he hadn't slept in days.

He glared at me. "This is supposed to be my place."

"*Your* place?" I asked.

"Yeah, Morgan. The place I go to get shit-faced and drown my sorrows without worrying about anyone judging me. You've invaded it."

I laughed. "Maybe you should find another place."

"Why are you here? Butch said you're only here once a year when . . ."

His voice trailed off, and he had the decency to look sorry for what he was about to say.

Butch placed four shot glasses down in front of Blake and filled them up. Blake picked up each one and downed them one after another. When he got to the last, he shook his head.

"Damn, Butch."

His voice sounded strained, and his face was red.

"You asked for something stronger."

When Butch walked away, Blake turned and faced me. He lowered his voice and spoke. His hot breath hit the side of my face, causing me to still. I didn't even dare breathe. His soft brown eyes held me captive.

"Nash is my best friend. Do you know what he would do if he found out we fucked?"

"Nice."

"What? That's what you wanted from me, Morgan. A night of mind-less fucking. No strings attached. That is what one-night stands are, are they not? There is no lovemaking, no whispered sweet nothings. It's just fucking."

I swallowed hard. I wanted to argue with him. Tell him he had a crude mouth, but I couldn't. He was right. That was exactly what I had asked him for, and it was clear that was what was bothering him. The idea of me only wanting him for one night.

"I think you're just afraid," I said.

"Me? You're one to talk. Seems I'm not the only person hanging out in a bar drowning my emotions. You make a living helping other people with their issues, and from what I've heard, you're damn good at it. You know one night of sex won't change anything. It won't make you forget whatever it is you're trying to forget."

"I know that!" I spat out. My eyes darted to the end of the bar. Butch was lost in conversation with another patron. Refocusing on Blake, I closed my eyes and took a deep breath before I spoke again.

"I'm not here because of Mike. I'm not trying to fuck him out of my mind. I might have been doing that with Rich, but I'm here because I . . . I . . ."

My mouth snapped shut. How did I tell him I was there because I felt worthless? Like no man would ever love me or look at me like the way Nash looked at Kaelynn, or Tucker looked Charlie. The way Jim practically melted on the spot when he looked at Terri. But even Mike had made me feel like I was never enough. How did I make Blake understand that the one time I put myself out there with a man, one I truly was attracted to, he turned me down?

"Because why?"

"It doesn't matter."

"It matters, Morgan."

I pulled out a twenty and laid it on the bar. "I'll leave you be so you can enjoy your time alone."

Blake reached for my wrist, causing me to stop. "Morgan, tell me why you're here. Please."

Tears burned my eyes. "Why do you care, Blake?"

"Because you're—"

"Nash's sister. We've established that." I jerked my arm to free it. "Let me go."

"No. I care about you, Morgan. Now fucking tell me why you're here."

My gaze darted to Butch again. He wasn't paying any attention to us. He probably thought I was okay, since it was Blake.

"You want to know why I'm here? Fine, Blake, let's get it all out on the table. I'm here in this bar because I foolishly opened myself up to a man I was attracted to, only to have him reject me. I stupidly offered him a piece of myself in exchange for one simple night of pleasure. One night where I could stop thinking about everything wrong in my life. Stop remembering. Stop blaming myself. A night where it felt like someone wanted me, even if it was just for sex."

Blake opened his mouth, then shut it.

A tear slipped free, and I quickly wiped it away. "A night where I could feel like I was doing something crazy and fun. I wanted to feel . . . adored. Wanted. Needed."

"Morgan," Blake whispered as he tried to place his hand on my face.

Holding up my hands, I shook my head. "I get it. I'm not your type, Nash is your best friend, and all the other reasons you pushed me aside."

"What?"

"Enjoy your evening, Blake."

Stepping away from him, I looked at Butch and plastered on a fake smile. "I'm heading out, Butch. See you around."

Although his face showed concern, Butch lifted his hand and let a small smile pull at his mouth. "You call me if you need anything."

"I will! Bye."

Turning on my heels, I headed to the door. The desire to turn back and look at Blake nearly had me doing just that. Instead, I pulled out my phone and picked up my pace.

Five

BLAKE

I SAT THERE like an idiot while her words replayed in my head.

"Everything okay?" Butch asked, pulling me out of my daze.

"No, I need to go after her."

"Took you long enough to figure that out."

Standing, I pulled out a twenty. "What?"

"Never mind paying. Your money is no good here. Make sure she's okay."

I headed toward the door.

"Blake."

Turning, I looked at Butch. "You hurt her, I'll kill you."

All I could do was nod and rush out the door.

Morgan stood there with her back to me as she waited on an Uber. I watched as the car drove up and she opened the back door and slid in. I was right behind her.

"Change of plans," I said, pushing her farther into the car.

"Blake, what are you doing?" she cried out.

Smiling at the driver, I said, "Do you know a place called Jax's?"

He smiled. "Hell yes, I do."

"Jax's? The underground club for members only?" Morgan asked.

With a smirk, I replied, "Just the place you need, princess."

"Just the place I need? If you think I will hook up with some random guy, you are crazy."

The driver's eyes jerked up to look at us in the rearview mirror before he pulled out into traffic.

I laughed and leaned back, giving Morgan a quick look. She stared at me.

"I'm going home." She crossed her arms over her chest. My cock jumped at the sight.

"You're not going home, Morgan. We're going out. You want a night to forget everything? Fine. I'm giving you a night to forget everything."

I could practically see the steam coming from her ears. "Fuck you, Blake. I don't want your pity fuck."

"Oh damn," the driver said.

"How is taking you to a dance club a pity fuck?"

Her cheeks turned red, and she looked out the window. Shit. She thought I was turning her down again. God, this was why I avoided this with her. I would end up fucking things up.

"Jax's is a pretty cool place. It's only for the wealthy, so I hope you have connections," the driver said.

With a wink in Morgan's direction, I said, "I know the owner."

Morgan groaned and rolled her eyes.

The driver answered before I could. "Dude, if you have connections, I wouldn't mind a hookup."

Her eyes met mine. "It's a dance club? What makes it so special?"

I shrugged. "I guess that not everyone knows about it. It's under a condo building downtown. You'd never know it was there."

"I'd rather go home, thank you."

"That's your problem, Morgan. You're a homebody and too afraid to take a chance at fun."

Laughing, she glared at me. "I'm the one who is afraid? That's great coming from you." Turning to the driver she said, "Do you now I offered this man a night of no-strings sex and he turned me down? He says it is because my brother is his best friend."

The driver frowned. "Yeah, I've got to side with him, lady. That could be some deep shit. Or the dude really likes you and is afraid of losing both of you if you hooked up and things went south."

Morgan and I stared him.

Looking away, Morgan said, "He'd never find out."

"I'd feel guilty lying," I countered.

She huffed and recrossed her arms over her chest. I couldn't help let my eyes swing down and stare.

Fuck me. I wanted to bury my face in those breasts of hers.

Clearing my throat, I started to talk, but the car came to a stop.

"Here ya go."

"Drop us off, and then swing back around. I'll leave your name at the door."

The driver smiled. "For real, dude? You have that type of connection?"

I nodded. Once the driver told me his name, I got out of his car then reached back in for Morgan's hand.

She declined and got out on her own side and slammed the door.

"Good luck, dude. I have a feeling you will need it with that one."

"Yeah, me too."

I shut the door and stepped away from the car. I walked over to Morgan and placed my hand on her lower back. The instant rush of warmth raced through my hand and straight into my body. If my touch affected her, she hid it well tonight.

"Come on, it's this way."

As we walked through the lobby of the building, the security guy glanced our way. I smiled and turned Morgan to the left and down a hall. After walking through a door, we came to an elevator, and I hit the down button.

"This is the entrance to the club?" she asked. "How do people who live here not find it?"

"They tell you about the club when you buy a condo here."

Her nose wrinkled up in the most adorable way. "And how do you know?"

With a smirk, I replied, "Because I own a condo here."

"You do? Why didn't you ask the driver to take you home then?"

Laughing, I said, "How do you think you would have reacted if I'd said I was taking you back to my place?"

She bit down on her lip and looked away.

"Exactly."

The doors opened, and we instantly heard and felt the bass from inside.

After another short walk down a hall, we came to a stop in front of a bouncer.

"Lou, how are you tonight?"

"Good evening, Mr. Greene. How are you tonight, sir?"

"Doing good."

He held open the door for us, and as we walked into the club, I gave him the name of the Uber driver and told him to let him in free.

Reaching for Morgan's hand, I navigated our way through the crowd and to the bar. I tapped on it and Jim, the lead bartender, turned to face me. "Mr. Greene! Great seeing you. Your usual?"

I could feel Morgan's eyes on me. "Yes, and a vodka cranberry for the lady."

Her body pressed against mine, and I felt my breath catch in my throat. "How did you know that was what I liked?"

"I pay attention to things, Morgan. You've ordered it every time I've been out with you."

"Oh."

That was all she said. It was soft, and the heat of her breath hitting me on the neck made its way down to my dick. I had to focus on it not going hard as a rod in my pants.

Turning, I handed her the drink. "Come on, follow me."

She took my hand again, and I tried like hell to ignore the way her touch made my stomach dip.

After making our way through the crowd and up a small flight of stairs, we walked over to an empty table tucked back in a dark corner. It had a sign on it that said reserved.

"Blake, this is reserved."

"I can see that."

She narrowed her eyes at me. "Smart ass. We can't sit here."

"We can."

Pointing to the sign, she said, "No. We can't."

A waitress walked by and Morgan stopped her. "Excuse me, who is this table reserved for?"

The girl looked at the table, then me. The look she gave me said she was confused. "Good evening, Mr. Greene."

I nodded and smiled.

Morgan glanced from me to the waitress, waiting for her to answer. "The table is reserved for the owners, ma'am."

"See!" Morgan nearly shouted at me.

"Will you bring us a bottle of my favorite champagne?"

The waitress nodded and flashed a bright smile. "Right away, Mr. Greene."

Morgan watched the girl walk away. The confused look on her face was cute as fuck. I slid into the booth and set my drink down. When Morgan turned and looked at me, her hand came up to her mouth. It had finally dawned on her.

"Are you just going to stand there, or are you going to sit down?"

Dropping her hand, she quickly slid in. "You own this place?"

"I'm a partner in it."

"So you own it. Does Tucker know?"

"He knows. I'm more of a silent partner. A good friend of mine from college approached me about investing in the club since I lived in the building. He wanted to make it different from the other clubs in town."

"How is the club different?" she asked, taking a sip of her drink.

"He wanted to put a sex club in the back."

She choked on her drink. "What?"

Laughing, I added. "I wasn't into that scene, so I passed. Instead, he came up with the whole underground secret dance club for the wealthy. That was an idea I could get on board with."

The waitress brought over a bucket of ice and the champagne. I took the bottle and said, "I'll open it, thank you."

I watched Morgan as she took everything in while I filled her glass. She slowly sipped on it while her eyes moved around the club. The vibe was exactly what we needed. You could practically feel the sexual tension in the air.

"Want to dance?" I asked.

Chewing on her lip, she finally smiled and said, "Yes! I want to dance."

We slid out of the booth and headed to the dance floor. I had no idea what song was playing, but it was a fast beat. Morgan, or course, was an amazing dancer. I had seen her a time or two at Sedotto the few nights she went out with our little group, which wasn't often. I had the feeling Morgan hardly hung out with us because didn't like feeling like Nash's little sister—along for the ride.

After two fast songs, things finally slowed down.

"I'm dying of thirst," Morgan called out.

We headed back to the table, and I refilled her champagne while she ordered another cranberry and vodka. When that arrived, I informed the waitress we wouldn't be needing her for a while, hoping Morgan and I could have some privacy. The waitress slid the two side curtains almost closed, only leaving a small gap open so we could see out.

Morgan downed both drinks and turned to face me. "So tell me why you really brought me here, Blake."

I smirked. "It's the one place I know we won't run into any of our friends."

Her brows lifted. "Why does that matter?"

Morgan's eyes were getting glassy, and I knew the alcohol was catching up. I had no idea how much she'd had over at Butch's Place.

"It matters a lot. But I need to know how much you've had to drink tonight, Morgan."

With a roll of her eyes, she looked away.

"Morgan, Nash is like a brother to me, and I would never do anything to hurt him or risk my friendships with either of you."

She nodded, still not looking at me.

"But. . . ."

Focusing her attention back on me, she repeated me. "But?"

"I haven't been able to stop thinking about you since that morning I showed up to take you to breakfast. Hell, if you only knew the half of it, Morgan. You're fucking crazy if you think I don't want you."

Her tongue swept over her lips. Those blue eyes turned dark with seduction, and I could feel my dick getting hard. The table we were at was set back into a dark corner, and with the curtain closed, it would be nearly impossible for anyone to see what we were doing, especially if I pulled her farther back.

"For the last two weeks, I can't sleep, I can't eat, I'm miserable."

"W-why?" she asked.

I let out a soft chuckle. "Thinking about you not thinking I want you, for one. Knowing I hurt you, because that is the last thing I would ever want to do. Then that bullshit you said about not being my type. Morgan, I've wanted you for what seems like forever."

The corners of her mouth turned up slightly.

"What are you saying, Blake?"

I lifted her hand up and turned it so her wrist was inches from my mouth. "I'm saying . . ."

Bringing it closer to my lips, I let the tip of my tongue slide over her skin, causing her to suck in a breath.

"That if you want a night to forget, I will give you a night to forget everything. But I need to know what you drank over at Butch's Place."

My lips pressed against her wrist, kissing her.

"Um, only half a beer."

I grinned and kissed her wrist again, watching her entire body shake slightly.

"Now, imagine that kiss all over your body, princess."

Her lips parted, and I thought I heard a moan slip free. I'd held off for as long as I fucking could. Grabbing her, I pulled her onto my lap. Morgan straddled me, her fingers pushing into my hair, our mouths inches from each other. My heart was pounding in my chest, and I wasn't sure if it was from the anticipation of her mouth on mine or the sensation of her body finally on top of me. Or maybe it was knowing I was about to have sex with my best friend's sister and I had yet to tell him how I felt about her. Before I had time to think any harder on it, Morgan pressed herself against my hard length and covered my mouth with hers.

Nothing else mattered in that moment except for the way my body instantly caught on fire. Fuck everything and everyone else.

Morgan was the only thing I cared about.

Six

MORGAN

THE FEEL OF Blake's erection against my throbbing core nearly had me coming on the spot. Then, when our mouths collided in a kiss, I melted into him. The man could kiss. My God, the man could kiss.

I was lost.

Everything slipped away, and all I could feel were his hands on my body. His tongue danced with mine. The taste of whiskey mixed with the sweet champagne. When he grabbed my ass and squeezed, I moaned into his mouth. His hips lifted, and the sweet friction his jeans caused drove me mad. I'd done nothing like this before. Knowing I was on his lap, making out with him in a public place, was surging my desire on. And it was Blake. God, it was Blake I was sitting on. Blake I was grinding against. Blake, who I desperately wanted to have inside me.

"More," I whispered. "I need more."

His hand moved to the front of my body and when he touched my bare stomach, I jumped. He stilled, and I pushed down harder against him, pulling out a groan from him that vibrated through my entire body.

His fingers moved across my skin, leaving a path of tingles that shot straight to the throbbing between my legs.

"Yes," I hissed when he rubbed my nipple through my lace bra.

He pulled his mouth off of mine, our chests heaving. "Just tonight. We can only do this for one night."

"That's all I want. Just tonight."

I ignored the way my body, mind, and even my heart screamed that tonight would never be enough. The way I was feeling was unlike anything I had ever experienced before, and I wasn't sure one night with Blake could soothe my desire for him.

He pushed my bra up and exposed both breasts. I turned to look over my shoulder, remembering we were in a very public place. But I knew no one would see us unless they stopped and looked through the curtains. Even then, Blake had pulled us farther back into the darkened corner.

What in the world are you doing, Morgan?

Blake's tongue swept over my nipple, then he blew on it, causing my body to tremble.

"No one can see us."

"Anyone who walks by can see if they look hard enough."

"That makes it all the more fun."

The thought made me wet. It was so out of character for me. The thought of being seen terrified me, but it excited me at the same time.

Blake lifted my shirt and buried his face under it. I moaned when I felt his hot mouth on my nipple. He flicked his tongue over it in a teasing manner. Then, he sucked and bit down gently as I slapped my hand over my mouth. Pleasure shot through my entire body, causing me to rock against his hard length. That I still had all of my clothes on made my mind swirl. I'd never known this sort of pleasure before. Never.

Oh my gosh. I'm about to come, fully clothed, in a public place.

I wanted this more than I wanted my next breath.

"Blake," I panted out. He let go of my nipple with his mouth, rubbing and twisting it with his fingers instead. He looked up and smiled. I rocked faster against him.

"I'm so close."

His fingers went into my hair, and he pulled my lips to his. We kissed passionately, and I let myself go. I felt every single thing this man was doing with his mouth, his fingers, and his hips rocking up to meet mine.

Then he pulled his mouth barely off mine and urged, "Come, Morgan. Come."

The sound of the bass rattling through my body, my heartbeat racing, and the way Blake looked at me sent me falling over the edge. Stars exploded before me, and I closed my eyes. His mouth was over mine, drowning out my moans of ecstasy.

I didn't care how it might look. I was writhing on top of this man. Shamelessly grinding into him while he swallowed my moans. The sweet relief of my orgasm felt amazing, and the second it was over, I wanted more. I needed more.

Blake dropped his head against the back of the booth, his breath fast and hard.

"I'm so sorry," I whispered as I adjusted my bra. "I lost control, and it's been . . . a long time."

He lifted his head and stared at me. "Don't you dare say you're sorry for that. I never thought I'd have one of the most erotic moments of my life fully clothed in a bar. It felt like I was back in high school making out in the back of my dad's car."

I groaned and buried my face into his neck. I inhaled the woodsy smell of his cologne. The way it relaxed me and made me feel so safe should have been a warning sign. Instead, it was a drug that made me fall a little more for this man. It was more than physical, but I pushed that silly feeling to the back. I'd deal with it later.

"Blake, I want you."

With one quick movement, he moved me off him so fast the room spun. Blake slipped out from the booth and came around to my side. He took my hand, helping me out. Then we started for the back-left corner of the bar. My heart was still racing. Where in the world was he taking me? For a moment I panicked. What if there really was a sex club back here? I almost pulled him to a stop before I saw an elevator with a sign that read Private.

Blake pulled out a black key card and swiped it over the panel. The doors opened, and he pulled me in. He hit the top button, and the moment the doors shut, he pushed me against the wall of the elevator, his mouth covering mine. The alcohol and the way he kissed left me feeling dizzy.

The doors opened, and Blake picked me up. I wrapped my legs around his body, and our mouths crashed together once again. He walked us through a room and down a hall. Blake pulled out his key again, pushed a door open, and then walked us down another hall. He walked into a room, and I drew away from his addictive kisses to see that we were in a bedroom.

"Where are we?" I asked.

"My bedroom."

"You have a private elevator that takes you from the club to your condo?"

"Penthouse, and yes."

My eyes widened as I took in the room.

"This is your last chance to back out of this, Morgan. Once I put you down, I'm taking these clothes off of you. Slowly. Then I'm burying myself inside you all fucking night."

I focused back on him. Our eyes met, and I could see he wanted me as much as I wanted him. "I want this. I want you, Blake."

Closing his eyes, he slowly let me down. Then he cupped my face in his hands. The way he stared at me made my entire body tremble. It almost felt like his next set of words pained him.

"Just for tonight, princess," he whispered, pulling my T-shirt over my head. His gaze felt heated as he took me in. I reached behind my back and unclasped my bra, letting it fall to the ground.

"Jesus," he whispered, lifting his hands and rubbing each nipple with the pad of his thumbs. "You're perfect. So beautifully perfect."

Heat flooded into my cheeks, and I tried to look away, only to feel his finger on my chin, forcing my eyes upward to meet his gaze.

"You. Are. Beautiful."

My eyes burned with the threat of tears. I had never imagined Blake to be so sweet. I figured he would have ripped my clothes off and fucked me against the elevator. Hell, I figured we would have sex in the club or the bathroom. I never dreamed he would bring me up to his own bedroom. Everything about him surprised me, and yet none of it surprised me.

His hands moved to my skirt, and he slowly pulled it down along with my panties. He dropped soft kisses as he dropped to his knees.

When he placed a kiss just above my throbbing clit, I gasped out, "Oh God. Wait. I need to know something."

He kept kissing above my clit. When he looked up and our eyes met, I couldn't believe I was about ask what I was about to ask.

"How many women have you had in your bed?"

"I've never brought a woman here before, Morgan."

His confession made my stomach flip, and I liked that I was the only woman he'd ever been with in his bed. I liked it more than I wanted to admit.

His eyes were pools of lust. "I need to taste you."

The moment my fingers went into his hair, I heard him moan. Then he stood, lifted me into his arms and gently placed me on the bed.

"I will explore every single inch of this body. If I only have tonight, I want to memorize it all."

Blake stood back and quickly undressed. My eyes took in every inch of his glorious body. He pulled his T-shirt over his head, and my mouth watered at the sight of the well-defined V dipping into his jeans. I slowly lifted my gaze to his broad, perfectly sculpted chest. On the way, I noted his six-pack abs were so defined I felt like I was looking at a picture.

"Lord almighty, how much do you work out?" I asked, not even caring that I was looking at him like I wanted to devour him. I might have even wiped drool from the corner of my mouth.

"A lot. Especially lately."

My eyes jerked up to his. "Why?"

He shrugged as he moved his hands to the button of his jeans. "Stress reliever. I haven't had sex in a while and need an outlet."

I wasn't sure why knowing Blake hadn't had sex in a while made me feel all tingly. I wanted to ask him when the last time was, or why he hadn't had sex, but now was not the time to dive into his subconscious.

Then, off went his pants and boxers in a quick movement. My mouth fell open at the sight of his hard length resting against his solid rock of a body.

"Oh my," I breathed out. "I'll be feeling the aftereffects of you for days."

With a chuckle, Blake climbed back onto the bed and did exactly what he promised he would do. He started at my neck and slowly placed kisses all over my body. When he paused to pay attention to each nipple, I nearly came again.

"God, it's been a long time," I gasped between breaths. My fingers laced through his dark hair as I let myself get lost to him.

"I'm going to take care of you, princess. Just relax, and let me make you feel good."

Feel good? I was feeling much better than good. I was in heaven. Lost in a world of absolute euphoria. No man had ever paid this kind of attention to my body. Not even Mike.

For a moment guilt ripped through my body. How could I be lying here comparing Blake to Mike? Pushing my thoughts aside, I grabbed the sheets and froze when I felt his hot breath between my thighs.

"Stop me now if you don't want this, Morgan."

"I . . . I want it, Blake. Desperately." I hadn't realized until that moment how long I had wanted this. Wanted him.

The moment his mouth touched me, I arched off the bed. The room spun, and I cried out his name within minutes. Seconds, maybe. I'd never had an orgasm that felt like that. It was so intense I had to wiggle away from him to make it stop. My body felt like it would combust as each ripple raced from my toes to my head then back around again.

"How was that?" Blake asked while placing soft kisses up my stomach.

"Can't. Think."

He laughed lightly, then took my nipple into his mouth while twisting the other with his fingers. Then his mouth was on my neck, his fingers were pushing inside me. It was all too much. His touch, his kisses, the way he whispered every word. I knew I wouldn't be walking out of here the same person.

"I've wanted to do this for so long, princess. You're so beautiful. I want to hear you cry out my name. God, you feel so good."

It wasn't lost on me when he said he had wanted to be with me for so long. How long was so long? Two weeks? Two months? Years? How long had I wanted him? Maybe since the first time I first saw him all those years ago. Every word, every touch made me feel like I was free falling into a black hole, and I had no idea whether I would be able to simply walk away from him tomorrow morning like nothing had happened.

I had to, though. I had promised Blake one night of no-strings sex.

"Morgan," he whispered as he pressed a kiss to the base of my neck and slipped his fingers back inside me.

Squeezing my eyes shut, I made a promise to myself.

I'll walk away tomorrow. I have to.

Seven

BLAKE

"BLAKE."

The way she whispered my name and lifted her hips as her body clenched around my fingers nearly had me losing my control, which was already hanging on by a thread.

Slow down, Blake. Christ almighty, slow the hell down.

My hand slipped from her warmth and teased her swollen clit. I wanted to hear her cry out my name again and again. See her tremble while her orgasm raced through her body. I knew the moment I slipped inside her I would lose my shit. There was no doubt in my mind that tonight would leave me half of who I had been. I'd never experienced what was happening with any other woman before in my life.

"You are so beautiful, Morgan." I whispered as I kissed along her jaw. "I want you so fucking badly I can hardly think straight."

Her fingers dug into my back. "I'm yours. Completely yours."

The tightness in my chest was something new. I wanted those words to be true. Not just something she said in the heat of passion.

One night. It's only one night. Then you'll see it was lust. That's it.

Lust my ass. Everything about Morgan and tonight is different.

My knee pushed her legs apart, and she spread open for me. Grabbing me by the ass, she pulled me to her, silently begging me to push inside her.

"Blake, stop teasing me. Please, I need to feel you."

Reaching across the bed, I opened my side drawer and pulled out a few condoms.

"Wait."

Her voice instantly made me stop.

Fuck me. She's changing her mind.

Turning to face her, I asked, "Did you change your mind?"

Her eyes widened with surprised before she laughed. "God, no. It's just . . . well . . . since this is a night of doing things I don't normally do I was thinking. Well, what I mean is. I guess I wanted to . . ."

Frowning, I shook my head. "Tell me, Morgan."

Her eyes jerked to mine, and I could see the doubt in them. I'd give anything to take that way.

"Never mind. It was stupid."

The mood in the bedroom instantly went from hot to cold. Like someone had thrown ice water on both of us.

"Please don't do that. Tell me what you were trying to say, princess. I'm trying so hard to go slow and not just push inside you and fuck you until you scream out my name."

Her teeth dug into her lip. "I think I would like that."

With a low growl, I replied, "I would too. But not our first time. You're worth more than a quick fuck."

The emptiness left her eyes, and I could see a sparkle shine through.

She swallowed hard and spoke barely above a whisper. "I'm clean, and I've never slept with anyone without a condom. Are you clean?"

Goddamn it. I can't believe I was so insensitive to not talk to her about this before I started this. "Yes. I've never had sex without a condom. I was tested a few months back just to be safe. I honestly haven't had that many partners."

She gave me a disbelieving look. "You? I figured you'd been with a lot of women."

I shook my head. "No."

She gave me a slight grin. "Good."

I grabbed the condom, only to have her grab my wrist.

"Blake, I want to have sex with no condom."

My stomach dropped, and I pulled back away from her. "What?"

Her cheeks turned red. "I told you it was stupid and irresponsible. It's a silly fantasy I played out in my head."

"With me? You fantasized having sex with me? I mean, with no condom?"

Morgan nodded and then turned her head, not wanting to look me in the eyes. Placing my finger on her chin, I drew her gaze back.

"Talk to me."

She licked her lips and then spoke. "I've always been so careful with everything. But when I think of being with you, I want to feel everything. To know what you feel like inside me. To feel what it would be like to have a man come inside me."

I swallowed hard. "Are you, um, are you on birth control?"

"Yes."

We locked our eyes on one another. "This is a dangerous game, Morgan."

She worried her lip. "Just one time?"

Just one time. I wanted to laugh. If I had sex with her like this, it would change everything. I knew it, and I was positive she knew it.

"It only takes one time to get pregnant," I said.

"We don't have to. I'm sorry I brought it up."

My eyes searched her face, and I dropped the condom back down. The smile that spread across her face made me realize there wasn't anything I wouldn't do to make her happy. And that was a new feeling.

Pulling me back on top of her, Morgan spread her legs then hooked her right leg over me, drawing me closer to her. My cock rubbed against her clit, and we both moaned.

"Please, Blake. Give me this one thing. Please."

The tip of my cock pushed slightly inside of her, teasing me with her warmth and wetness. My eyes closed, and I prayed I wouldn't come the moment I pushed in.

"Yes," she hissed, grabbing my ass and lifting her hips, pushing me in more.

"God, Morgan. This is . . . so . . . fucking . . . good."

No. No. No. No. I had meant to say wrong. It was so wrong, yet it felt so right. If any other woman had asked me to have sex with no condom, I would have laughed at them, then probably told them to leave. But with Morgan, everything was different.

Everything.

I slowly worked myself into her until I was all the way in. We both stilled, our eyes locking on to each other. Neither one of us wanted to move. It was as if we spoke to each other through our eyes.

What are we doing? There is no turning back. Can we really stop at just tonight?

This was what she wanted. One night, no-strings-attached sex. Even if it killed me, it was what I would give her, then I would walk away. We would go back to being friends.

Bullshit. Such bullshit.

Leaning down, I brushed my lips across hers. Her hands wrapped around my neck, and I deepened the kiss as I slowly made love to her. Our tongues danced together, and our bodies moved like we had been made for one another. Never in my life had I made love or felt a connection to a woman like this. I doubted I ever would again. Maybe it was because it was Morgan. Maybe it was because deep down I knew I had been in love with this woman since the moment I saw her.

Squeezing my eyes shut tighter, I pushed the thought away and moved faster. Slipping my fingers between hers, I pushed her hands above her head. Morgan moved in perfect rhythm with me. I felt her body building with her orgasm, and she squeezed around my cock.

"Morgan, come with me. Now."

And like that, she cried out my name as we both came together. My entire body shook as my orgasm raced through me. It was like nothing I'd ever felt before. I was free falling and it was the best fucking high of my life. Feeling myself letting go inside her made my body warm, while the weirdest feeling hit me square in the chest.

I pressed my mouth to hers and kissed her like I had never kissed another woman before, all the while ignoring how my heart ached to whisper something my mind was telling me to hold back.

It was only for one night.

❧

ROLLING OVER, MY hand landed on the cold sheets. I opened my eyes to see I was alone in the bed. I dropped onto my back and stared up at the ceiling. The memory of last night came rushing back like a gust of wind.

Morgan.

We had made love twice, then around five in the morning I had found her in the shower and I did what I had wanted to do since she made that proposition in the café. I fucked her. Fast and hard. Hearing her beg me to go faster, harder, nearly drove me mad. I came so hard my damn legs nearly buckled out from under me.

It was the next morning, and I waited for the guilt to set in. It didn't. How much of a bastard did that make me? I had sex, with no condom, three times with Morgan.

Morgan.

Sitting up, I rubbed the back of my neck and let out a deep breath. She was probably in my kitchen, making breakfast. At least I hoped like hell that was what she was doing.

My phone beeped on the side table. Morgan's name popped up.

With as a frown, I picked up my phone and opened her text message.

> *Morgan: Thank you for the incredible night. I've never felt so amazing, and I will cherish it forever.*

And that was it. Nothing else. My heart dropped straight to the bottom of my stomach. Morgan was staying true to her promise. One night, no-strings-attached sex. But it had been more than that. I knew she felt it too.

Staring at the phone, I contemplated my reply. What in the hell did you say to someone after a night like that? It felt as if a part of me left with her, and I wasn't sure how to deal with the aftermath. Everything we'd said to each other. The way she'd looked into my eyes when she came. None of that could be taken back, and I didn't want to take any moment of it back.

"Fuck," I whispered.

How in the hell did this happen?

"This can't be right," I whispered with a gruff laugh. "She can't possibly think it was nothing but sex."

Or did she?

I typed out my reply, trying like hell not to overthink anything.

> Me: *It was a great night. An amazing night, Morgan. I wish you would have let me take you home or at least said goodbye before you left.*

She texted back instantly.

> Morgan: *I think it's better this way. No awkward moment at my door. I've got an early morning appointment, so I had to leave early. I'm at my office now. I'll see you around, Blake. M*

"What the fuck? She blew me off."

Laughing, I pushed my fingers through my hair and shook my head. There was no fucking way I would believe last night was just a onetime thing. That she hadn't felt what I felt. I stared down at her text.

Then a sinking feeling hit me. Maybe it was. Morgan got what she wanted and now she was moving on. I ignored the way it felt like my lungs were constricting, making it difficult to breathe. I stood and took in a deep inhale, then slowly let it out.

Making my way to the bathroom, I jumped into the shower and turned the knob all the way to cold. I needed to try to forget about everything from last night. For my sake and for Morgan's.

An hour later I was walking into my office. I came to a stop when I saw Tucker sitting in the chair.

"Tucker, hey, to what do I owe this honor?"

My heart raced as I tried to act normal.

He knew. Damn it, he somehow found out. Maybe someone from Tucker's bar was at the club.

Shit. Shit. Shit.

"I stopped by to invite you over to a dinner party Charlie is hosting for Kaelynn and Nash. To celebrate their engagement and the baby."

I dropped my briefcase onto my desk and sat. "Damn, I can't believe they're having a baby. You don't think they're moving too fast?"

Tucker shrugged. "They both seem happy. When love hits you, you sort of know."

My eyes jerked up to his, and I don't know which one of us was more stunned by what came out of my mouth next. "What does it feel like?"

Tucker grinned. "Love? Hell, like your entire world has been turned upside down, but in the most beautiful way. You can't breathe with them near you, or when they're away from you. You'd do anything to hear them laugh, see them smile. Holding them in your arms will erase all the day's bullshit. It's a crazy feeling."

His description was almost the same as Butch's.

Butch. Dear God.

If he knew what I had done with Morgan, he would probably have me killed.

"How did you know you were in love with Charlie?"

His head tilted to the side. "Why are you asking this, Blake?"

Acting casual, I answered, "I'm honestly just curious."

He grinned again. "I think I felt it in my chest first. A weird, warming, squeezing sensation. Or sometimes I felt it right in the center of my gut. Like someone had tied my stomach in knots. Sort of like being back in school, when we used to have finals or big projects due."

I nodded.

"You ever feel that way about a woman?"

Laughing, I lied. "No." He didn't need to know that was exactly how I felt around Morgan.

Tucker smirked. "What did you do about Morgan?"

Trying not to look guilty, I replied, "Nothing."

"You're just going to push your feelings for her aside?"

I stared at him, not wanting to get into this conversation. I was beginning to regret telling him how I felt about Morgan.

"When is the dinner party?"

He scoffed and shook his head, taking my change of subject with a grain of salt. "This Saturday night at six."

"Will Charlotte still be up?"

Tucker stood and gave me a smile. "You try to act like you don't like kids, but dude, my daughter's got you wrapped around her finger."

I returned his smile. "I won't argue with you on that one."

"She'll be up. She doesn't go to bed till around eight."

"Then I'll see you this Saturday at six." I stood. "You didn't have to come all the way to my office just to invite me dinner."

He gave me a look I couldn't read. "I wanted to check on you. See how things were, what you had decided to do about Morgan."

Swallowing hard, I barely nodded my head.

"See you Saturday, Blake."

"See ya, Tucker."

I spent the next few days burying myself in my work. Projects that I had pushed to the back burner were moved up to priority. Ideas for a house I had been designing just for fun became my nighttime work when I couldn't sleep. I offered to take on work other coworkers didn't want to be bothered with. I did whatever I could to keep Morgan out of my mind.

It was working too. As the days went by, I was forgetting how she smelled. What she tasted like. How the sound of her laughter made joy pulse through my veins.

I even asked a friend of mine, Rose, to accompany me to Charlie and Tucker's dinner party. She was more like a friend with benefits. We liked to have a good time together, but when we needed that occasional dinner date or companion to a social event, she was my go-to girl, and I was her go-to guy. We hadn't hooked up in almost a year, though. Hell, I hadn't been with anyone but Morgan in the last year. At the time I invited Rose, I didn't even think about Morgan being there. Of course she would be there, and I was a stupid asshole for not realizing that. It was a party for her brother and her best friend.

When she walked into the living room and glanced down at me on the floor with Charlotte, she smiled. Then she saw Rose, her entire body went rigid, and the light from her baby blue eyes dulled.

Rose stood up. "Hi! I'm Rose, Blake's date."

I closed my eyes briefly and wished like hell I had informed Rose she was just a friend tonight.

Morgan's eyes darted down to me, then back up to Rose. She played it off and smiled. I couldn't help but wonder if I was the only one who noticed it was a forced smile.

"It's a pleasure to meet you. I'm Morgan."

"Blake has never mentioned you. So how do you know Nash and Kaelynn?"

My stomach jumped as Morgan bit into her lip, trying not to show the hurt on her face.

Picking up Charlotte, I stood and cleared my throat. "Morgan is Nash's sister and Kaelynn's best friend. Morgan, Rose is a friend of mine."

"Nice to meet you, Morgan. It must be so cool having your best friend marrying your brother."

Morgan nodded. "Yes. It's fantastic."

"Morgan is an art therapist," I said, pride radiating in my voice because, dammit, I was proud of her.

Rose drew in her brows. "What is that?"

"Art therapy is a form of expressive therapy in which patients use creative processes as a way to explore their feelings. I specialize in veterans. Post-traumatic stress syndrome, things like that. They aren't normally the chatty types, so art works better."

"Wow, that is an amazing job. It must be stressful."

Morgan shrugged. "It can be. What do you do?"

Rose wrapped her arm in mine as Charlotte reached out for Morgan. I leaned out and let her take the squirming baby from my arms. Clearly, Rose didn't get the hint when I introduced her as a friend.

"I'm an architect. Same as Blake."

Morgan nodded. "I see. Have you two known each other long?"

Rose chuckled. "We met when Blake moved back to Austin. A year and a half or so? We instantly hit it off when he started working at our office."

I groaned inside. Rose was putting on a show, making it seem like we were an item. That would not sit well with Morgan. If she thought I had been seeing someone and slept with her, it would piss her off. Or hurt her. I didn't want either to happen.

Before I could say we were just friends again, Charlie walked into the living room. "Dinner time, y'all."

Scooping Charlotte out of Morgan's arms, she smiled. "I'll go put her down for the evening. Everyone, make your way into the dining room."

Tucker followed Charlie as they disappeared to put their daughter down for the night.

When we walked into the dining room, I did a quick survey of the table. Place cards. Charlie would have place cards. Holding my breath, I watched where Morgan went. They'd seated her next to Kaelynn. Across from her, though, was Rose. I sat down next to Rose and across from Jim, another best friend of ours from college. His new wife, Terri, yet another college friend, sat next to him. They had only gotten married last fall, but they had been dating since our days at the University of Texas. It appeared all of my friends were settling down and getting ready to pop out a kid or two.

"Blake, how are things going at the firm?" Jim asked.

"Good. I'm up for partner, so things have been stressful. Beginning to wonder if I even want it."

Rose squeezed my hand, and my gaze jerked to Morgan. She looked away.

"If they don't give that promotion to Blake, then they don't know who they have working for them," Rose stated as if she were the proud girlfriend.

Gently pulling my hand from hers, I gave her a look that said to tone it down. I was hoping she would know that meant to lay off happy couple gig. Everyone here knew I wasn't seeing anyone seriously.

Unfortunately, Rose didn't get my hint. She shared tales of cocktail parties, dinners gone bad, and last year's Christmas party, when we ended up locked in the elevator of the hotel.

"We were in that elevator forever. But we made good use of our time," Rose said with a smile.

"I don't know if playing games on our phones was good use of time," I added, trying to save face. Truly, nothing had happened between us that night.

Morgan sat there the entire time, smiling and laughing at each story. It seemed like she didn't care I was here with another woman. Was it possible she hadn't felt the things I felt that night? Maybe it was time I realized this stupid fantasy of being with Morgan was simply that. A fantasy. She only wanted me for the one night. That was it. The thought made my stomach roll.

Rose put her hand on my thigh and started moving it up. Seems she wasn't playing a role after all. For a moment I thought about letting her keep going, then I put my hand on hers and pushed it off. Maybe that would give her the hint. I picked up my drink and drank it all in one gulp.

Eight

MORGAN

THE FIRST HOUR, Blake had seemed uncomfortable. He would steal glances my way, then look away when our eyes met. I had to admit, the moment I had seen he had brought a date, I'd felt a pain in the middle of my gut. That night we had spent together had been beyond amazing, and I was hoping he had felt it too. When he never called or texted after the one time, I knew he must not have. I'd acted so casual the morning after, but I was confused and freaked out by the feelings I was having.

Then, seeing him here with Rose, I realized he couldn't have sent a clearer signal.

Had that night really meant nothing to him? Sure, he put on a good show. Whispered sweet words into my ear, touched me like I was the first women he had ever made love to, and treated me like a princess when it was time to fall asleep.

In the end though, it was a night of pleasure shared by two friends who'd agreed that when it was over, they would go back to being friends. No strings attached. What I hadn't bargained on, though, was that Blake was seeing someone. From the stories Rose told, they seemed to be an on-and-off couple.

I tried like hell to not let Rose bother me, the way she touched Blake or whispered in his ear. I attempted to ignore the way her hand moved under the table. At one point, though, I swore he had pushed her hand away. After that, Rose seemed to back off.

Taking a long drink of my wine, I stood to excuse myself from the table to help Charlie and Kaelynn clean up. I didn't even bother to look at Blake. Somewhere around the midpoint of dinner, he had starting knocking back more alcohol and had withdrawn into himself. I needed distance too. I thought I would be okay seeing him, and I probably would have if he'd come alone. It was seeing him with another woman that had thrown me.

"Hey, are you okay? You seem like you're a million miles away," Kaelynn said, handing me a plate to dry.

"Sorry. I've had a lot on my mind the last few weeks."

She nodded but gave me that same knowing look she always gave me. Kaelynn had a way of being able to read me when everyone else around me couldn't.

We'd washed and dried a few more plates when I heard Rose laugh. I rolled my eyes and sighed.

"You don't like Rose?" she asked.

Snapping my head to look at her, I opened and closed my mouth at least four times. It was hard lying to Kaelynn—like I said, she could always read me.

"That's not true."

She frowned and tilted her head, giving me that look that said, *Really? I know you're lying.*

"Fine, she annoys me a little. She talks so much. Do we really care if she and Blake were stuck in an elevator for three hours?"

"But Morgan," Kaelynn said in mock admiration, "they made good use of their time!"

I scoffed. "Ugh, who does that? Who brags about sex like that?"

Kaelynn shrugged. "Blake made it clear nothing happened between them. You're sure you're not bothered by something else?"

"Like what?" I asked, taking the last plate from her.

Wiping her hands on a towel, Kaelynn turned and faced me, leaning her hip against the sink counter.

"I saw the way you and Blake looked at each other when you walked in. I couldn't help notice how nervous he was when Rose talked, and the two of you can't stop looking at one another."

"You're seeing things, Kaelynn."

I absolutely hated lying to my best friend. But would it do any good to tell her Blake and I had slept together? It wasn't like it would happen again.

She stared at me longer. "What?" I asked.

"Morgan, it's okay if you and Blake like each other."

Laughing, I replied, "Like Blake? Are you kidding me?"

Nash walked into the kitchen, making both of us jump when he asked, "What are y'all talking about?"

My cheeks heated, and my pulse raced. I was not going down this path of keeping secrets. Nash had done that with Tucker when he secretly dated his sister, Lily. Things didn't work out between them when Lily ended up cheating on Nash, but Tucker had been furious when he found out Nash had been hiding the relationship. I couldn't do that to my brother.

Wait. What am I worried about here? There was no relationship. There is no Blake and me.

That thought made me sad.

"Nothing. Your fiancée is insane."

Nash smiled and wrapped his arms around Kaelynn, resting his hand over her stomach.

"Hey, you about ready to head on out?"

"This early?" Kaelynn asked.

"I don't want you getting too tired."

My heart swelled in my chest as I watched the two of them.

Someday, Morgan. Someday you'll find a man who looks at you like that. A man who adores you and only wants to make you happy.

Kaelynn turned in his arms and reached up to kiss him. "Nash, I'm not tired, and I promise if I get tired, I'll let you know when I want to leave."

He kissed her nose. "I love you."

I looked away to give them a private moment. A light outside caught my eye. When I turned back to ask what it was, Nash and Kaelynn were lost in a kiss. With a roll of my eyes, I headed out the back door and toward the light.

As I drew closer, I saw what it was. A gazebo. Tucker had mentioned they were building one, but I hadn't seen it yet.

Picking up my pace, I walked up the three steps and spun around, looking up at the beautiful architecture and the white lights that were strung along the top.

"How romantic," I whispered.

"It's meant to be."

Letting out a scream, I jumped back and covered my mouth and my pounding heart with my hands. Blake stepped up into the gazebo, a wide smile on his handsome face.

"What are you doing out here?"

He shrugged. "I saw you walking out here, so I followed you."

"Why?" I asked.

"Are you okay?"

My pulse quickened. Was he worried about me? And why was he worried?

"Yes, why?"

"I don't know. I wanted to make sure you were still good with our no-strings agreement and all. I didn't reach out to you at all after that one text, and I feel guilty."

I lifted a brow. "You feel guilty?"

He nodded.

"Not guilty enough not to flaunt your date in front of me. Please tell me you were not with her when we . . ."

"Had sex?"

I turned and looked out over the night sky. The moon was climbing in the sky, and it gave off a slight glow, making the closest trees visible.

"I wasn't flaunting her, and no, we are not—nor have we ever been—a couple."

Spinning around, I laughed. "You might want to tell her that, Blake. She sure has a lot of stories about the two of you."

"She's my go-to girl, and I'm her go-to guy."

"Go-to girl?" I asked, trying to damper down the sickness that rolled through my stomach.

"Yeah, when we need dates to functions, we call each other. A friends-with-benefits kind of thing. I honestly wasn't even thinking you'd be here, Morgan."

My body jerked. "Gosh, thanks for that, Blake."

He sighed and pushed his fingers though his hair. I ignored the fact that I thought that was sexy as hell and that I loved this habit of his.

"Hell, you know what I mean, Morgan."

"No, I really don't, but it doesn't matter. You don't owe me any explanations about why you brought a date." My voice was cold, and I hated that I sounded like a bitch.

He stared at me. "No, I guess I don't."

Those five words hurt more than I wanted to admit.

My breathing increased as he stared into my eyes. I couldn't help let my memory wander back to the other night, to the way his lips felt on my body while he moved slowly in and out of me. It had been more than sex. We had made love.

Fighting the tears building in my eyes, I slowly pulled in a breath.

"Morgan," Blake whispered, taking a step closer.

I took a step back, hitting the railing of the gazebo.

He lifted his hand and brushed a piece of my hair behind my ear. I jumped at the feel of his touch, then trembled.

"God, you're so beautiful."

With a trembling voice, I replied, "Blake, go back inside."

His eyes moved slowly over my face. When they landed on my mouth, I licked my lips before pressing them shut tight.

"I should, but I don't want to."

"What do you want to do?" I asked with a breathless voice.

Blake smiled at me, and my legs felt weak. I reached out and grabbed the railing to hold myself up.

"I want to kiss you."

Before I could voice my disapproval, his lips were pressed to mine. His tongue swept across my lower lip, urging me to let him in. I tried to fight it but quickly gave up the battle when he growled.

Our tongues moved in slow rhythms. The taste of whiskey and red wine mixed in a heady concoction. We both moaned, and I went to reach for him, but stopped myself, forcing my hands back to the rail. If I touched his body, I knew I would give him more.

When Blake withdrew his mouth from mine, he cursed softly and took a step away. The urge to reach out for him was so powerful I had to grip the rail with all my might.

"Blake? Morgan? What are you two doing down there?" Nash called out.

Not taking his eyes off me, Blake casually stepped a few feet away and called out, "Showing your sister the gazebo I designed and you built."

I sucked in a breath of air, taking in the gazebo once again, this time giving it a better look. His words from earlier rushed back. The gazebo was designed for romance. Blake had designed it. Since when did this man standing in front of me believe in romance?

"Rose is looking for you. Said something about needing to leave," my brother called out.

"I'll be right there," Blake said, still keeping his gaze locked on me. "See you later, princess."

Nothing would come out. No words, no breath. Nothing. Something froze me in place. My head spun with so many emotions, and none of them made any sense.

Blake turned and walked down the steps of the gazebo, picking his pace up to a jog.

My fingers went to my tingling lips. I closed my eyes and whispered his name, "Blake."

∽৽∾

I STARED AT the bare canvas in front of me. The image was there, begging me to paint it. My mind told me to bury it deep inside and to forget all about it. If only I could.

Picking up the brush, I made the first stroke. Calmness spread through my body as I let my brush flow freely. Painting made me happy. It eased the guilt, pain, and anger that had seemed to take up residence in my heart and soul since Mike died. Maybe it had been there even before Mike. I never could explain the emptiness I had felt, even when I thought I was the happiest I had ever been in my life. I sometimes wondered if I knew deep down that my happiness wasn't meant to be with Mike. Maybe it was being saved for someone else.

Blake.

I thought back to that first time I had met him—at a party Nash had brought me to. The way Blake had looked at me that night made me feel on fire. I didn't really think he noticed me. I figured he was simply being polite because I was his best friend's little sister, even though I was attending the same school. A part of me wanted to get to know Blake more that night, but I pushed it aside and let guilt replace it. Guilt that I had thought of another man like that when Mike was in the army.

A strange thought hit me.

Maybe Mike felt my emptiness as well.

My hand froze, and I felt a tear slip free and make a slow path down my face.

"How did I not see how unhappy we were? Why didn't you talk to me?" I whispered.

Wiping the tear, I pushed away the guilt and buried it deep down inside. It did me no good to sit here and question it now. I could only move on and pray that I could help someone like Mike. Give them the chance to see the light and not be caught in the darkness.

An hour later, I stood and stretched. I stared at the painting, knocked breathless by what I saw. I had gotten so lost that I hadn't even realized what I was painting. A blue sky with a sinking orange sun. Trees, rolling hills, and a path that led to a gazebo. A man stood with his hands resting on the rail, his back toward me as he watched the sinking fireball in the sky.

"Blake." My fingers slowly came up and pressed against my lips. The memory of him kissing me the other night made my heart race.

"Oh Morgan, what have you done?"

I had promised myself I could handle one night of passion with a man I trusted. That was all it was supposed to be. No feelings attached to the sex, no expectations from either of us. But what happened that night wasn't what either of us had expected. I knew it the moment he looked into my eyes when he first pushed inside me, bare, and every emotion so raw. Both of us tried to ignore the rush of emotions we had locked deep inside us. He'd felt it too. I knew he had, and he'd proved it by kissing me the other night in the gazebo.

I stumbled back some, hitting the door to the studio I had set up in the spare room of my bungalow. Sinking to the floor, I pulled my knees up and hugged them close to my body.

I stared at the painting as I let the realization of that night sink in. I had let myself fall for Blake. I had let him in, and now I had no idea what to do.

Nine

BLAKE

"WHAT IN THE hell is wrong with you?"

Facing Nash, I shrugged. "What do you mean what's wrong with me?"

Nash stared at me with a blank expression. "In all the years I have known you, Blake, we have never gone out for a run and you not hit on at least one woman. But lately, you haven't so much as glanced toward one. What's going on with you?"

Turning away, I focused on the path in front of me. We had stopped to fill up water bottles, and Nash was staring at me like he knew my dirty little secret. I had fallen for his sister. One night of pure heaven in the same bed with her, and she was all I could think about. Dream about. Lie awake fantasizing about. Hell, I couldn't even remember the last time I slept a full night's sleep in the last month.

"Nothing is going on with me. I've been busy with work."

"Work? So let me get this straight. You're putting work before your sex life?" He smiled wide. "Holy shit. You met someone, didn't you?"

I groaned and rolled my eyes. "I've always put work first, Nash. You know that. Plus, I'm up for that promotion, which will only bring more work. Just because you're happy with your blissful love life doesn't mean all of us have fallen into that sinkhole."

He laughed and clapped me on the back. "Dude, it's okay if someone has caught your eye. There's nothing wrong with wanting to be with one person. You're a great guy, Blake. Any woman would be lucky to be with you."

Would he be saying that if he knew it was his sister who had caught my eye? But he was right. My heart only wanted one woman. Morgan.

"It's not what you think, Nash."

"No? Then tell me what it is."

"It's nothing. It was a onetime thing with an amazing woman, but she wants nothing more out of it."

He frowned. "She wanted nothing else, or you didn't?"

I shrugged. "Both of us, I guess. It was an incredible night, and maybe that is all it was meant to be."

Filling up my water bottle, I felt his gaze on me.

"Do I know her?"

My entire body froze.

I can't do this. I cannot lie to my best friend.

Turning to face him, I nodded. "Yeah. You know her. Listen, Nash, I didn't mean for . . ."

His cell phone rang, and he pulled it off the holder he had wrapped around his arm. When he smiled, I knew it was Kaelynn.

"Hey, baby. What's going on?"

I watched as he walked over to a bench and took a seat. Looked like our run was over.

"Blake?"

Her voice made my body come to life. Memories of her whispering my name into my ear while she wrapped her legs around me, pulling me deeper inside her, hit me like a fucking Mac truck.

"Morgan?"

She ran in place, a soft smile spread over that beautiful face of hers. Her blond hair was pulled up into two pigtails.

Holy shit. God, give me the strength to not reach out and pull her in for a kiss. Please.

"Hey, fancy meeting you here," I said.

"Yeah. Are you finishing up with your run?"

I pointed to Nash. "Yeah, your brother and I hit the trails earlier. He's talking to Kaelynn now."

She smiled, seemingly unaffected by the fact that her brother was with me, or by the fact that she was in my presence. How in the hell did she not feel anything that night?

"Hey, Morgan." Nash approached his sister and gave her a kiss on the cheek. "You here alone?"

"Yes, I am," she frowned, preempting the lecture I was sure Nash was about to give her for running alone. "And before you start, I stay on this stretch of the path, so no worries."

When Morgan glanced my way, her eyes seemed to light up. "What are y'all up to?"

Nash answered. "Nothing. Getting in a run and then heading over to a site for Blake to look at the building. I'm not so sure about the design the homeowners had their architect draw up. I need another set of eyes on it."

Morgan looked at me. "Well, you've got the best standing next to you. I mean, you're good too, Nash."

I laughed. Nash had gone to school for a business degree, but he went behind his folks' backs and also gotten a degree in architecture. It had been a secret desire of his, but his father owned a construction company and only wanted his son to focus on taking that over, regardless of his own dreams. Nash had drawn up a few projects, all houses, and I had to admit, he was talented. He had even designed and built Tucker and Charlie's house.

"Well, thanks for that, Morgan. Do you want to join us for lunch? We shouldn't be long over at the Miller project. Maybe grab some Home Slice?"

My stomach growled at the mention of my favorite pizza place.

Morgan's eyes bounced from me to Nash, then back again. "Um, I'd love to join y'all, if it's okay with Blake."

Before I said anything, Nash hit me on the back. "Of course it's okay with him. Maybe you can figure out what in the hell is wrong with him lately."

Lifting her brow, Morgan tilted her head slightly as she regarded me. Then she gave me a sexy smirk. "What's wrong, Blake?"

I returned the smirk with my own sexy spin on it. "A woman."

"A woman?" Morgan asked in a drawn-out voice.

"Yes. I spent one incredible night with a woman who wanted no-strings sex. Problem is, I can't stop thinking about her."

Nash let out a roar of laughter as Morgan stared at me, shocked.

"Dude, I knew it. I haven't ever seen you this twisted up before."

I smiled at Nash's teasing. Morgan opened her mouth to say something, then quickly shut it.

"I say go for it. You need to make the next move. Doesn't he, Morgan? I mean, she probably thinks that was all you wanted. Maybe she was into you."

The corner of my mouth slowly lifted as I stared at Morgan. "What do you think, Morgan? Should I make the next move?"

Her lips pressed together, and I could feel the heat between the two of us. It was beyond me how in the hell Nash hadn't noticed what was going on.

"Yes," she finally said as she gave me a brilliant smile. "I think you should make the next move—and quickly. She might have given up hope that you were interested and moved on."

"Moved on? That would suck."

She nodded and walked backward. "Yes, it would. I'll see y'all in what, an hour?"

"Sounds good!" Nash called out as I followed him down the path. One quick look behind me showed Morgan giving one more glance my way. My heart pounded fiercely in my chest, and for the first time in a few weeks, I felt myself looking forward to something.

∽§∾

NASH TALKED NEARLY the entire lunch. He talked about the Miller project, about Kaelynn, the wedding, the baby, all the plans they had for building their house. He asked my thoughts on a few projects before turning his attention on his sister.

"Have you, Charlie, and Terri decided on showers for Kaelynn?"

Morgan smiled, and my breath caught in my throat.

"Yes! I think we'll combine the bridal shower and the baby shower. That way Kaelynn's family only has to fly down once, and it'll be easier and less stressful for Kaelynn. Her mom mentioned wanting to do a dinner up in Utah for their family and friends. I wasn't sure what you and Kaelynn would think about that."

Nash nodded and smiled. "I'm down for that; I know it would mean a lot to Kaelynn."

"Okay, I'll get with Kaelynn on that too. We were thinking late August or earlier September for the combined shower?"

Nash reached across the table and squeezed Morgan's hand. I tried not to feel jealous that he got to touch her and I couldn't.

"That's perfect." Nash's phone went off, and he glanced down at it, leaving a moment for me and Morgan to exchange looks.

"Y'all okay together if I jet out?"

"Sure, we'll be fine," Morgan said with a sweet smile. Nash stood, clapped me on the back, then leaned down and kissed his sister.

"I'll talk to you later, Morgan. Blake, can we meet for drinks soon? I've got a business proposition for you."

That piqued my interest. "Sure, just let me know when."

We said our goodbyes, and I watched as he walked out of Home Slice and past the front window. Then I focused in on Morgan.

Her eyes met mine, and we stared at each other for what seemed like the longest time.

Finally, she was the first to speak. "We shouldn't be doing this."

"Doing what? Having lunch together?"

Her cheeks turned pink. "Tell me what it is you want from me, Blake."

"Right this moment?"

She nodded.

"I want to kiss you. Pull your body close to mine and bury my face in your neck while my hands explore every inch. I want to strip you naked and make love to you."

Her mouth parted open and her tongue darted out to wet her dry lips.

"What do you want from me, Morgan? Because I can't tell if you want me or not. Every time I see you, you act like nothing happened between us. Like you didn't feel the connection we made that night."

"What?" she whispered. "I haven't . . . well . . . I mean . . ." Her gaze darted around the room before it landed back on me. "I haven't been able to stop thinking about you. About that night."

Leaning in closer to her, I softly asked, "Do you want me again?"

She nodded.

"Say it."

"I more than want you, Blake. I need you."

We were totally backsliding on our arrangement, but I didn't give two shits. I'd deal with Nash and everything that went with him finding out about me and Morgan later. Because I knew for a fact that he had to know the truth. There was no way I would sneak around behind his back. He meant too much to me, and so did Morgan.

"We need to tell Nash," I said, taking her hand in mine.

"I know, but not yet. Please. I want whatever this is between us to stay between us. No one is looking at it and judging or saying it's wrong. I need to know if there is really something here, or if maybe we both just need . . . someone."

My brows pulled in and I shook my head. "What do you mean?"

"I don't know. I'm lonely, Blake, and I have been for some time. I feel connected to you, but I need more time to understand it. I've never felt like this before. Not even with Mike. And I don't know if that was because we were so young when we started dating. This thing I feel with you is so . . ."

"Different," I finished softly.

She nodded.

It felt like a vise was on my chest, slowly closing tighter. It was in that moment I realized that Morgan Barrett had the power to complete destroy my heart and soul. That was something I had never given to a woman. Ever. The night I lost my mother, I vowed I would never love another woman and risk being hurt. But I'd handed my heart over to Morgan freely the moment I met her. If it meant holding her in my arms again and hearing her call out my name when she came with me deep inside her, it was worth it.

Her eyes met mine, and we both smiled.

"Let's go," I said, pulling her up and nearly dragging her out of the restaurant.

Ten

MORGAN

BLAKE PUSHED THE door open to the hotel suite bedroom and quickly pulled his shirt over his head before we were even fully in the room with the door shut.

I giggled, helping him get it over his head. "I can't believe you got a hotel room. We could have gone to either of our places."

"I have been waiting long enough to be inside you, Morgan. I want you now. So get undressed."

I did as he demanded. Slipping my sneakers off and pulling my T-shirt over my head. "I should probably shower. I'm all nasty from running."

"So am I."

His hands were pulling my jogging pants down. He dropped to his knees and smiled as he took in my baby-blue thong.

"Fuck, you are the sexiest thing I've ever laid eyes on."

My body heated at the compliment. I knew it wasn't true. Blake had been with other women, all of whom I was positive were more beautiful than me. I was a plain Jane. There was nothing special about me. I liked my body, though. I wasn't too skinny, and I wasn't fat. I had a good ten pounds extra on me that left my hips shapely.

"Princess, look at me."

I did as he asked, and our eyes met, stilling my breath in my chest. "You are the most beautiful woman I've ever been with."

"Blake, I'm going to sleep with you. I don't need you filling my head with silly, fake compliments."

He frowned then stood. "What?"

I shrugged. "I can't possibly the prettiest woman you've ever been with. Look at me."

Blake stared at me like I had grown two heads. Then he took my hand and pulled me into the bedroom. We stood in front of a floor-to-ceiling mirror. All I had on were my sports bra and panties.

"Look at you," he whispered, his mouth against my neck. The heat from his breath caused my entire body to shiver, leaving goosebumps trailing all over my skin.

I stared at myself in the mirror as I let myself lean back against Blake's chest.

"Do you know what I see when I look at you?"

Shaking my head, I whispered, "No."

Blake's fingers moved up the side of my body lightly before he gently rubbed his thumb over my cheek tenderly. My hand lifted instinctively to grasp his arm.

"I see a woman who is so beautiful she takes my breath away every time I look at her."

Narrowing my eyes, I replied, "Liar. You never looked at me like this before."

"Then you weren't paying very close attention."

I glanced down, and he moved his hand to run his finger along my bra line.

"I see a woman who is confident, smart, and not afraid to go after something she wants. All of that is a huge turn-on. At least it is for me."

This time I couldn't help the smile that spread over my face.

When his hands moved to lift off my sports bra, I fought the urge to reach up and hold it in place.

"That's it, princess. Look at how you beautiful you are."

When his fingers teased my nipples, I sucked in a breath and let out a low moan. Watching him touch me in the mirror was turning me on even more.

"Do you have any idea how much I've been thinking about you? Dreaming I could touch this body again. Feel your soft skin against mine. No woman has ever made me desire her like you have."

"I have?" I said, hearing the uncertainty in my voice. I hated that I was questioning myself. I never did that, but something about this moment was tearing me open, exposing my fears for Blake to see. My deepest secret felt like it was about to explode from my chest and be laid out for him to see.

I wasn't good enough. For anyone.

Blake dropped to his knees behind me. "Yes, you have."

Slipping his fingers barely inside my panties, he slowly pulled them down. Our gazes locked in the mirror, and my breathing picked up to almost a pant.

The feel of Blake's heated stare and his hands moving over my naked body was becoming too much to bear. I could feel how wet I was getting from his touch.

"I've wanted no one like I want you, Morgan. Never. The next time I tell you how beautiful you are, you will know I mean every damn word." He placed a kiss on the side of my hip, causing my entire body to shake.

"Do you want me?" he asked, his voice shaking.

I nodded and barely whispered, "I want you."

Turning away from the mirror, I looked down at Blake. My fingers raked through his hair as he closed his eyes for a moment.

Then I told him the truth. "I want you like I've never wanted any other man before."

The words were true. So true. A part of me felt the sharp pain of guilt in my chest. I had loved Mike with all my heart, but it had never been like this. The connection I felt with Blake was so new and different. It was something other than physical. With Mike, it had started out with a physical attraction. Then he left for the military and I don't think we ever learned to know each other. With Blake, it felt like an explosion of every emotion and feeling hitting me all at once.

Blake stood, and the unspoken question in his eyes mirrored my own thoughts. He was too much of a gentleman to ask it, and I was too afraid to tell him the truth.

"I'm sort of feeling like I'm floating around on a raft, lost and confused. I feel guilty for wanting you the way I do, but I also feel like this is something I've been searching for my whole life," I finally said.

His hands cupped my face, and he leaned his forehead to mine. He opened his mouth to speak, but instead he kissed me. It was one of his dizzying kisses that left me panting and needing more. The kind that made me forget everything and everyone. I was only in this moment. Only with this man.

My hands shook while I worked at getting his pants off him. Once they were removed, we both climbed onto the bed, Blake moving over me, our hands all over each other's bodies as he slowly pushed inside me. This time he didn't even ask about a condom, not that I would have told him any different from the first night we were together. I needed to feel him without a barrier between us.

His hard warmth caused me to cry out in pure pleasure when he lost control, pushing in quick and hard. He stilled, and I urged him on by wrapping my leg around him.

"I'm sorry, princess. Did I hurt you?"

Digging my nails into his shoulders, I panted, "No. Please move. Blake, I need more. Please give me more."

"Shit, Morgan, you're gonna make me come before we even get started."

I smiled as he moved to his knees. He grabbed my body, pulling me to him and did exactly what I asked for. He moved fast and hard, in and out of me in a delicious, pounding rhythm. The sounds of our bodies hitting together and his moans mixing with mine were exotic. When his fingers moved down between our bodies and touched my clit, I exploded into a mind-blowing orgasm. Clamping my hand over my mouth, I attempted to keep in my cries of pleasure.

"Morgan, I'm going to come."

"Yes!" I softly moaned, feeling him grow bigger inside me.

He lifted me higher, changing the angle he was entering me at, and another orgasm raced through my body, nearly leaving me breathless as we came together.

The only word to describe sex with Blake was bliss. And not just bliss, but pure, heavenly, take-me-to-another-world bliss.

Blake rolled to his side and pulled my body against his. Our breathing slowly settled to a normal pace, and I soon heard Blake's soft breathing. He had fallen asleep holding me.

The feel of this man's arm draped over my body felt so right. A tear slipped from my eye, but it wasn't from sadness. It was because I was finally ready to admit it: I was falling in love with Blake.

I was falling in love with Blake, and it felt so different from how I'd felt about Mike. I knew Mike loved me, but he never showed me how much he loved me. Maybe it was because he never showed me how much he desired me like Blake had.

Turning over, I stared at Blake. This was Blake Greene. All these years I'd thought I had known him. Yet I had a strange feeling he was keeping a part of himself from me. It was an odd thing to feel, but it was so strong.

My mind drifted back to the last time we were together. Smiling, I traced my fingertip over my lower lip. He had made me feel so alive. Had whispered such sweet things as he made love to me. He had even admitted in front of Nash that he was confused by a woman. Me. I had left him confused. Left him not himself. Could we really make this work? I wanted more, and I was positive he wanted more as well.

Blake stirred next to me, and I felt my body still.

"Damn woman, you got me so relaxed I fell asleep."

I smiled as he opened his eyes. I wanted desperately to ask him where he saw this going. But maybe it was for the best that I pushed my growing feelings to the side, at least for now.

A buzzing sound came from the floor.

"Shit, my phone."

Blake stood, and I watched him walk across the room naked. He was so confident with himself, and he had good reason to be. The man was perfect. How could he have just woken up and still look as handsome as ever? I was positive I looked like a mess.

Reaching into his pants pocket, he took out his phone and read the text message. He frowned, then blew out an exhale while he replied. He set his phone on the side table and then crawled onto the bed, kissing me softly on the nose. The gesture made me swoon.

"I'm going to take a shower. Care to join me?"

The way he wiggled his eyebrows made me moan softly. More sex with Blake? Yes. Please.

"Well, I do have to shower."

He smiled and then got off the bed. "How I am going to live if I don't have your body every day?"

I drew my lower lip between my teeth and bit down, wondering the answer to that same question.

"Come on, let's go shower."

"Give me one minute to just lay here. I'm still in blissful heaven."

Blake winked and headed into the bathroom.

With a long satisfied exhale, I stretched my body and then sat up. The sound of the water turned on and my insides quivered at the thought of sex with him again.

Blake's phone was sitting on the side table with the messages open to the last text he had sent.

> *Nash: Dude, are you free right now? I want to talk to you about that business proposition I have.*
>
> *Me: Free, not doing anything important. Let me finish up this project. Give me like an hour and I'll meet you at your office.*
>
> *Nash: See ya then.*

Standing, I stared down at his words. *Not doing anything important. Finish this project.*

It was irrational for me to feel so hurt. I had asked him not to say anything to Nash. Told him I needed it to be kept a secret. So why did this hurt me like a knife in the heart?

It was the word "project." Covering my mouth, I tried not to feel sick.

I grabbed my clothes and got dressed. My hands shook, and I tried not to overthink the text messages, but that evil little voice in the back of my head kept telling me Blake would never want a woman like me.

The only thing I could think of was that I needed air. I needed to breathe and think this through.

Getting control of my emotions, I took a deep breath and stepped into the bathroom.

"Blake? I need to leave."

He poked his head out of the glass shower. "What? Why?"

"I had an urgent message from a client. It's best if I head on over to my office."

"I thought you were closed today?"

With a shrug, I replied, "I'm not meeting him there, but his chart with all my notes is there. I'll need it before I call him back."

He stared at me, and I was positive he could tell I was lying. "Are you okay, princess?"

I nodded. "Yeah, sure. Um, thanks for . . ."

For what? The amazing sex? The hotel fuck? The friends-with-benefits hookup? What was this thing between us called?

" . . . for the amazing afternoon. Talk soon." Before he said anything, I headed to the door.

"Morgan! Morgan, wait!"

His voice sounded pleading, but I moved my feet faster and headed for the stairwell. Before the door shut, I could hear him behind me.

"Morgan! Stop!"

A few moments later my phone rang, and I looked to see Blake's name. I declined it and then sent him a message.

Me: I need some time to myself.

He replied instantly.

Blake: I know you saw the text. It wasn't meant like that, Morgan. Don't run from me.

Me: I need time, Blake. Please just let me be for now.

Blake: Time for what? Why are you pushing me away?

Me: I'll call you. See you soon.

No more text messages came after that. I sat down on a bench a few blocks from the hotel and covered my mouth, trying not to cry. I only wished I had someone to talk to. Someone to tell me what I was doing. Why was I freaking out? And why had I just pushed him away?

Eleven

BLAKE

THE SOUND OF my keys hitting the table seemed to echo in my empty condo. After the damn week I'd had, I needed a drink.

The intercom buzzed, and I sighed as I answered it. "This better be good."

"Hey, Blake, it's Raine. Let me up, will you?"

I frowned. *What in the hell is she doing here?*

Raine and I had been friends in college. Once we graduated though, our friendship was strictly platonic. She was a good friend and someone who had been there for me a time or two when I needed to vent about things.

My finger hovered over the button before I closed my eyes and pushed it. A minute later the elevator doors dinged, and Raine walked around the corner and smiled at me.

Giving me a wink, she said, "Don't you look good."

"I feel like shit. What do you want?"

She pouted and slid onto the bar stool at my kitchen bar.

"Can't a friend come visit another friend?"

Taking a drink of my whiskey, I replied, "It depends on why the friend felt the need to visit."

"Company. An ear to listen. One friend to help another out. Someone to—"

"All right, I get it. What happened?"

Raine shrugged. "I didn't get the promotion I was hoping for."

With a shake of my head, I let out a laugh. Raine worked at a major banking firm. She'd been up for a VP position, and it was a sure thing with her uncle being on the board.

"How in the hell did you screw that up, Raine?"

She sighed. "God, Blake. I was stupid. Really stupid. I was having a little . . . fling with one of the guys in the office."

I raised my brow. "Who?"

"His name was Ryan. Ryan Lancer. He was the VP of marketing. He was also married . . . to our boss's daughter."

My mouth fell open. "No way."

She nodded. "Yes way. He happened to leave that bit of information out when he asked me out the first time. My luck, right?"

"Hell, Raine. How were you not fired?"

Shrugging, she answered, "I have no idea. Maybe Mr. Collins thinks I'm worth hanging on to. Who knows? All I know is I needed someone to talk to."

"So you came to me?" I asked.

"Well, we have a . . . history."

"We messed around in college when we should have been studying, Raine. That doesn't make for a history."

"It does when I need you."

I lifted a brow and knew I would regret my next question.

"Need me how?"

"To pose as my boyfriend."

I laughed. Hard.

"Blake, I'm serious. My parents are throwing a charity event, and I promised them I would bring a date. Ryan said he would go with me but, well, as you can imagine, he isn't now."

With a shake of my head, I let out a sigh. "When is it?"

"It's on Wednesday night. And it's black tie. You have a tux, right?"

I shot her a smirk.

"I'll take that as a yes."

I sighed. "I do. What is the event for?"

Shrugging, she replied, "I have no clue. I'm just told when and where to show up."

"Wow, Raine. Don't let me see your true colors."

She rolled her eyes and slipped off the bar stool. "Just remember, I need you to pose as my boyfriend who may or may not be close to asking me to marry him."

"What!"

"I said may or may *not*. Now, it's Wednesday night at the Four Seasons, and dinner will be promptly served at seven thirty. We need to be there about thirty to forty minutes earlier so we can mingle. You don't have to pick me up. I'll come here, and we can go together."

"Trying your damned best to make it easy on me, aren't you?"

"I owe you, Blake. And I'll even turn a blind eye if you find a girl you want to hook up with while we're there," she replied, kissing me on the cheek before I walked her to the door.

I thought of Morgan and the way she had left earlier today. I'd acted like a jerk by not texting her back. Shit, I had no fucking clue what to do. She said she would call. She needed time. Should I push her or leave her be?

Spinning around, Raine placed her hand on my chest to stop me, then looked up at me through those long, fake eyelashes of hers. "I'm serious. I owe you."

A part of me almost asked Raine for advice, then I thought better of it. She'd ask a million questions about who the girl was and try to analyze every detail. No, thank you.

"You're right. You do owe me."

She smiled. "Thank you for helping me out. You're the only one I could think of who would do this with no strings attached."

I winced. Her choice of words hit my battle wounds. She was right though. Raine and I were friends. Nothing more.

I opened the door, and Raine rushed out as quickly as she had rushed in, calling out, "Wednesday it is!"

Shutting the door, I raked my hand through my hair and made my way back to the kitchen, pouring another shot of whiskey.

My mind drifted back to earlier, when I'd met with Nash after leaving the hotel.

"A design firm. You and me. Let's make this happen, Blake."

His words rattled around in my head. Nash wanted me to leave my firm and start a new one with him. Go in as business partners. He trusted me and wanted me to go on this new adventure with him. And where I had been hours before that meeting? Having sex with his sister.

Sighing, I took my drink and sat on my leather sofa. I knew in the long run it would make me more money. But was I really wanting to design homes when I was designing skyscrapers all over the world? The bigger question was whether I could work alongside Nash knowing I had kept a secret from him. I thought I knew where Morgan and I were going earlier today, until I fucked it up with the stupid text message she'd read. Now I had no clue what in the hell was going on. The only thing I did know was that I had to tell Nash the truth. Either way, this wasn't something I could keep from him. I was already holding on to enough secrets to last me a lifetime.

Taking out my phone, I sent Nash a text.

Me: Hey, I need to talk to you. When are you free for lunch or dinner?

He sent a text back almost instantly.

Nash: This week is insane. Can we do Thursday? Lunch?

Me: I'll pick you up at 11.

Nash: I hope this is what I think it's about. We could make this work, Blake. I know it. See ya Thursday.

I stared down at my phone before I stood. No matter how this turned out, I could lose a hell of a lot more than I wanted to admit.

Another text came through from a friend I explored caves with.

Rick: Dude, we found another tunnel that must have been washed out from the recent floods. You in for some caving?

A rush of excitement flowed through my body. Maybe this was exactly what I needed. A chance to forget everything and explore the unknown.

Me: Me. Fuck yes. Tell me when and where.

Rick: You free Wednesday?

I laughed.

Me: Make it early in the morning and I'm there. Have a function that night.

Rick: See you at six on Wednesday.

Twelve

BLAKE

"HOW DO I look?" Raine asked, spinning around in a black evening dress.

"Nice."

She frowned. "Nice? Blake, honestly, is that all you can give me?"

"Honestly? Yes, Raine, it is. I'm at a charity dinner pretending to be your boyfriend because you're too chickenshit to tell your parents you were having an affair with a married man."

Raine stared at me. "How foolish of me to think you might give me a compliment because we're friends. And what in the world happened to you? You have a huge bump on your forehead."

"I went caving this morning."

Her mouth gaped open. "You're still doing that crazy stuff? Why do you take that risk?"

Chuckling, I shook my head and looked around. "I like the thrill of it. Keeps my mind off of other things."

Caving was something my therapist had suggested after my mother had passed away and I was dealing with all the anger and guilt. It was a way for me to push myself hard. A way to forget.

"Blake?" Raine asked, snapping her fingers in front of me.

Groaning, I shook my head. "Sorry. I've got a lot on my mind."

"No kidding. What is wrong with you, anyway? You haven't been acting like your normal self. You haven't made one sexually inappropriate comment about me or any woman we've seen walking in here. Are you sick?"

"Something like that."

She paused and then looked up at me. "Holy crap, Blake Greene, have you met someone?"

"Not now, Raine."

We walked around the ballroom, her arm hooked over mine as she smiled while people greeted us.

"How are you, Mr. and Mrs. Willfore? It's so nice to see you," Raine said with a fake grin. An older couple nodded their heads, and the gentleman smiled at me. He looked familiar.

Raine grabbed onto my arm tighter as we walked farther into the room.

"I'm not letting this go. You will spill the beans about who she is," Raine said. "Okay, so my parents will ask how long we have been dating."

"Three minutes?"

In a hushed voice, Raine said, "Ha-ha. Blake, please, I *need* you to play along. My mother has been riding my ass about settling down. She has threatened to take me out of her will if I don't stop playing the field."

"Raine, you honestly can't tell your mother you are not seeing a man? Why can't we be friends who went to college together? Maybe your boyfriend, Ryan, was busy this evening. Maybe he is at home, having make-up sex with his wife."

She pinched me, and I laughed.

"If you do this for me, I will owe you. Besides, my folks know you. They've met you. It won't be uncomfortable, and it will be more believable if I'm with you."

"God, I hate playing games. This is just for tonight, right? I'm not going to have to show up for family dinners, am I?" I asked.

Raine chuckled. "No. I'll tell them we broke up. Things just weren't working out. You know, the whole 'we're better as friends than lovers' bit. And let's say we've been dating for three months. That's how long I was with Ryan. She knows I was with a guy."

I sighed. "Great. My first long-term relationship isn't even a real one," I said, glancing around the room. I glimpsed Raine's parents at the same time she did.

"There's Mom and Dad. Come on."

I nearly tripped over my own two feet when I saw who they were talking to. Panic raced through my entire body as I scanned the ballroom.

"Raine, what type of charity is this dinner for?"

With a plastered-on smile, Raine pulled me closer to her parents as she answered. "The Austin Builders Association. Daddy is the president."

"Fuck me," I whispered as she dragged me closer to the group of people straight ahead of us.

If I thought I had messed up with Morgan the other day, things were about to get even messier.

Thirteen

MORGAN

"WOW! YOU LOOK beautiful."

Glancing up, I met my Rich's gaze in the mirror. "Thank you. And thank you for coming with me to this thing. I know how much you hate them. I couldn't bear to go alone, though. I texted someone else earlier this morning, but he never texted me back."

"I will try to not let that insult me."

I smiled and gave him a playful push on the shoulder. When I had texted Blake earlier to ask if he wanted to go to the dinner with me tonight, I knew it was a big step. With my parents and Nash being there, we would be letting everyone know there was something between us. When he never responded, I had my answer. It was my fault for pushing him away. I was so angry with myself, but I was even angrier that Blake hadn't even had the decency to text me back.

Rich looked me up and down. Not in a lustful way, but more in appreciation. Rich and I had dated off and on after Mike passed away. He was my rebound guy. The guy who helped me through the tough times when all I wanted to do was hide.

He clucked his tongue and spun me around with a whistle. "I find it very hard to believe you couldn't find a date, Morgan. Look at you. You're beautiful."

I swallowed hard as I glanced down at the satin gown I had on. It hugged my body like a glove. The only other stitch of clothing I had on was a thin satin thong. I would keep that bit of information to myself.

"Thank you. Truth be told I sort of forgot about this dinner until this morning when my mother called to remind me. I didn't have time to look for a proper date."

"Proper date? You are trying to hurt my ego this evening, aren't you?"

Smiling, I reached up and kissed his cheek. "I'm not. I swear. Are you ready to go? I don't want to get there too late."

Rich held out his arm for me, and we started out the door.

"Betty doesn't mind me stealing you for the night?"

He chuckled and replied, "Nah. She's working on a new design for a client of hers."

"She's okay with us going out? I mean, with our past and all?"

"She is. She knows you and I dated, but she also knows we're friends, and I help my friends when asked. I don't think she's worried."

"Oh my gosh!" I gasped as we walked out to a limo. "What did you do?"

He shrugged. "I promised you once I would pick you up for a date in a limo, but I never followed through. Now I am."

Turning to him, I smiled. "But this isn't a real date."

"It's close enough. I know how hard this time of year is for you. I wanted to do this for you."

My eyes burned with tears. How crazy was it that my ex-boyfriend was posing as my date to a charity dinner posing when his real girlfriend was at home? Why did it feel like everything in my life was back-ass-ward?

"Maybe I shouldn't go."

"Nonsense, get into the car. Nobody there will be surprised to see us together. No one will ask questions."

Nodding, I slipped into the car. He was right. My parents knew Rich. Nash knew Rich. It wouldn't be a big deal if we showed up at the dinner together. We had been off and on for a while now. Everyone knew we were still friends. The only one I had to worry about was Kaelynn.

She had asked me about Blake yesterday, and I had managed to change the subject when I saw the cutest outfit for a baby. The one thing about Kaelynn lately was that she was like a dog seeing a squirrel when it came to baby things. It was easy to shift her focus when I needed to.

Rich made small talk as the limo drove to the hotel.

"How's work going?"

"Really well. I'm slowly building up my patients. Some days are harder than others. But I really feel like I'm making a difference."

"That's amazing, Morgan. I'm so proud of you."

I grinned. "Yeah, I'm happy it's going well enough to pay the bills. Some cases are tough, though. They don't want to talk, and I can see their hurt in their paintings. I feel helpless sometimes."

He reached for my hand. "You know if you ever need anyone to talk to, I'm here for you."

I squeezed his hand and replied, "I know. And thank you."

After a few moments of silence, he spoke again. "So what is this event for?"

"It's a charity event for a Habitat for Humanity project that the Austin Builders Association does every year. I've been pretty involved, and with Dad and Nash being on the Austin Builder's board, I have to go. Honestly, I've been going to the Austin Builder Association's balls almost every year."

He smiled. Rich had gone to a few Habitat for Humanity projects with me. "I still say you're the only woman I've ever met that can swing a hammer and use a saw."

I couldn't help but chuckle. It felt good to laugh. I hadn't really felt myself feel much of anything since Saturday when I walked out of that hotel room, leaving Blake behind.

Soon we were pulling up to the front of the Four Seasons Hotel. The limo pulled up and let us out. Rich said something to the driver before he took my arm, and we made our way through the hotel and into the grand ballroom.

"How much are the plates at this thing?" Rich asked as we walked into the ballroom.

"It's all based on donations, but some of Austin's wealthier people are invited. I've seen donations as much as five thousand a plate."

"What?"

I laughed. "Yep. The rich like to out-donate the rich."

As we walked into the ballroom, I glanced around, searching for Nash and Kaelynn or anyone I might know. I knew the family hosting the dinner. Tina and Scott Franklin and their daughter, Raine.

"I don't see Nash and Kaelynn anywhere," I said, lifting on the toes of my high heels.

"Is that your parents over there?" Rich asked, pointing to the left.

As I scanned in the direction he was pointing, my breath caught in my throat. Blake was standing next to my parents, talking to Tina and Scott with his arm around Raine. Scanning through my memory, I tried to think of Raine ever mentioning Blake.

Was Blake here with her? As her . . . date? For the love of all things, this was not happening to me again. It was like Tucker and Charlie's dinner all over again.

I tried like hell to push the jealous feeling that was creeping in away. Blake had said nothing was going on with Rose. Maybe that was the case with Raine? My head spun as I stared at his arm around Raine.

"Hey, don't you look beautiful."

The sound of Nash's voice caused me to jump. Turning, I saw him and Kaelynn.

"Hey. Hi. Sorry I'm late."

Nash reached his hand out and shook Rich's hand. "Y'all back on?"

Rich and I both laughed. "No. He has a girlfriend and offered me a pity date so I didn't have to come alone."

Nash grinned. "Rich, you remember Kaelynn?"

"Yes. We met at Morgan's birthday party."

"It's nice seeing you again, Rich. How have you been?" Kaelynn asked.

"Doing really well. I hear congratulations are in order for y'all. Morgan said you were engaged."

Nash beamed, as did Kaelynn. I was sure her pregnancy also had something to do with her glow.

"Yes, we are."

I glanced back over my shoulder to see where Blake was. He was talking to Raine's parents, his arm still around her waist. The way she ran her hand up and down his back slowly made my insides turn cold as ice.

"Well, it looks like Raine has finally found the one."

My mother's voice jerked my eyes off of Blake and to my parents, who were now standing in front of us. I hadn't even seen them walking up.

Nash glanced around my folks and laughed. "Blake and Raine? You're wrong about that, Mom. They've been friends since college."

My breathing picked up. Blake knew Raine. Friends. College.

Shrugging, my mother went on. "According to Raine, they've been dating for a few months now."

It felt like someone had dropped a brick in my stomach. "Wh-what?"

I hated that my voice sounded shaky. Kaelynn, Nash, and Rich looked at me as if that one stumbled word had opened the hole in my chest, exposing everything.

Nash frowned and looked from me to our mother. "Blake mentioned being hung up on a girl, but I highly doubt it's Raine." He looked back at me.

"Blake didn't deny he was seeing her," my mother went on. "According to Tina, they're pretty serious."

Nash rubbed his jaw. If I hadn't known better, I would swear he was angry. "I mean, I guess I can see it. They messed around—I mean, they were close in college."

"They dated in college?"

Kaelynn had asked what I wanted to ask.

"If you want to call it that," Nash said with a smirk.

My father scoffed. "The boy doesn't seem the least bit interested in her, if you ask me. He kept glancing around the room as if he were looking for someone else. If I were a betting man, I'd say he was taken with someone else and is on Raine's arm just to keep her pestering mother off her back. As a matter of fact, he asked me if you were here this evening, Morgan."

When my father's gaze met mine, I froze. I didn't dare take a breath. He couldn't know. There was absolutely no way he could know what had happened between Blake and me.

Rich must have felt me stiffen next to him. He wrapped his arm around my waist and leaned down, his mouth against my ear.

"Are you okay?"

"I need a drink," I whispered back.

My mother clapped her hands as if to say the conversation was moving on. "Let's head to the table. Dinner will be served soon."

As my mother and father walked off, Kaelynn and Rich both stepped in front of me, blocking me from walking.

"Morgan, what is going on? You were white as a ghost when your father mentioned Blake asking about you," Kaelynn asked.

"Not right now, Kaelynn. Can we talk later?"

Rich looked back at Blake. "Morgan, are you . . . with Blake?"

How had these two figured it out with just a few simple words? The bigger question was how my father had figured it out? Was Nash next?

"Not. Now." My voice was stern, and they both backed off.

"What's going on?" Nash asked.

Pushing past the three, I said, "Nothing. Nothing at all."

Blake had yet to see me, and he seemed to be playing the part of Raine's doting boyfriend well. At least, I thought he was playing a part. Maybe it was more wishful thinking on my part. First Rose. Now Raine. I honestly didn't know why I was surprised. Maybe I *was* his little project.

When he pulled out Raine's seat for her to sit, I watched them closely. Raine lifted her face for a kiss, and Blake hesitated. Then he smiled and kissed her cheek. I didn't want to let myself believe it was an act like my father thought, but I felt a sense of relief when he didn't kiss her on the lips.

Rich pulled my chair out, and I sat down. When he sat down next to me, he leaned in. "Tell me you didn't, Morgan."

Reaching for the glass of wine, I drank half of it before I answered. "I did."

He groaned next to me. "A onetime thing?"

I shook my head.

"Shit. Nash doesn't know?"

"No."

It was then that Blake looked over at our table and our gazes met. He smiled, then he slid his glance over to Rich, and his smile faded.

"Oh great. He thinks I'm your date."

"Then let him think it," I said, trying to ignore the sickness in my stomach.

"You're playing a dangerous game, Morgan."

Turning to look at him, I grinned. Chewing on my lower lip, I replied, "I know, but it was a no-strings arrangement."

"Then why do you both look miserable? And why does he look like he wants to rip my damn head off now?" he asked in a hushed voice.

I shrugged. "I was confused and told him I needed time. He either changed his mind or is angry with me."

Rich took a drink of his wine. Blake still watched us, but I tried to keep my eyes anywhere but on him. It was just my luck that my seat provided a direct sightline to his table and him.

"I'm going to go with angry. I'm a man, and I know that look. I've given guys that look. He is telling me to back the fuck off his girl."

Rolling my eyes, I looked at Rich. "Seriously? I doubt it."

"Yes, seriously. We told your entire family we were here as friends, but as far as that man is concerned, we're here together."

"You have a girlfriend!"

"He doesn't know that."

Glancing back over to Blake, I felt my chest squeeze with jealousy that Raine was sitting next to Blake. Feeling his presence so close to her. That should have been me. He should have been sitting next to me.

"Better watch out, Morgan. I think you're falling in love," Rich whispered against my ear.

I felt Kaelynn hit me on the side of my leg. Not daring to look at Blake, I turned and looked at Kaelynn. She was fuming.

"I don't know what is going on, but Nash will catch on with the way you're staring over there. You're swooning over Blake and sending Raine daggers *at the same time*."

"No, I'm not."

"Really? And Rick leaning over whispering in your ear? You're supposed to be here as friends," she hissed.

She was right. My cheeks burned with embarrassment, and I felt like a fool. Why was I trying to make Blake jealous? He didn't care if I was here on a date. He'd probably blown me off because he had already had plans to be here with Raine. Suddenly, I felt like an idiot, and not just a fool.

My stomach turned again. I couldn't do this. I needed air. I needed a moment to gather my thoughts and figure all this out.

"Excuse me, I need to go to the ladies' room."

Kaelynn went to stand, but I placed my hand on her shoulder.

"Alone. Please, Kaelynn, not now."

I stood, and Rich, my brother, and father all stood. I forced a smile. "Just going to the powder room. Excuse me."

I navigated my way through the tables, lost and confused. I stopped a waiter. "Excuse me, where is the ladies' room?"

"Out that door and down the hall. Second door on the left."

"Thank you," I replied, picking up my dress so I could walk faster. The moment I pushed open the doors to the hallway and stepped out of the ballroom, I drew in a deep breath. Quickly making my way to the restroom, I threw the door open and went right to the sink. With both hands on the cold porcelain, I took in a few deep breaths. Then I looked up at myself in the mirror.

"Who are you anymore, Morgan?" I whispered to the stranger in the mirror.

After another few moments of staring at myself, I laughed. "You asked for this. You said no strings. You ran from him. Told him you would call and didn't."

I stood taller, drew in a deep breath, and slowly let it out. "Suck it up, and get over it. For whatever reason, he didn't text you back this morning. You need to stop acting like a weak fool. Go out there, stop acting like Rich is your boyfriend, and let Blake know you are a strong, confident woman. If Raine is who he wants, then fine."

With a few deep breaths and vows I would not look at Blake for the rest of the evening, I readied myself to go back into the ballroom. I knew my last affirmation was a lie. I wouldn't be fine if Blake was really with Raine, but I would never let him see it.

Staring at myself, I laughed. I had fallen in love with Blake and then messed it up because I hadn't been upfront with him about my feelings.

I leaned in closer. "Did you really go to school for counseling? Ugh."

Pinching my cheeks to give them more color, I turned on my heels and headed out of the bathroom.

I didn't take but two steps before I felt someone grab my arm and pull me into an empty room. I went to scream, but a strong hand went over my mouth. He pushed me against the door once it closed and placed his mouth to my ear. I knew who it was by the way my body reacted to him.

Blake.

Fourteen

BLAKE

MORGAN'S EYES WIDENED in surprise as she looked up at me. My body trembled being so close to her. I tried to ignore the way this woman made me feel, but seeing her with Rich nearly had me going insane.

"Are you back with him?"

Her eyes went even wider.

"Are you sleeping with him?"

She placed her hands on my chest and pushed me away as hard as she could.

I dropped my hand from her mouth and took a step back. I rubbed the back of my neck and cursed.

Holy shit. What in the hell am I doing? I basically just kidnapped her and pulled her into a closet.

"Fuck. I'm sorry I lost control like that."

"What in the hell is wrong with you, Blake?" Morgan spat out. Anger laced her words.

I turned and paced as I glanced around the small room. It was the janitor's closet, filled with mops, brooms, and miscellaneous cleaning supplies.

"What's wrong with me? Let me see, I have a long list. Should I start at the top? You're the therapist; you tell me, Morgan."

"You're not making any sense." She opened the door, but I pushed it shut.

"From the moment I saw you, I haven't been able to catch my god-damn breath."

She swallowed hard and leaned against the door.

"I wasn't looking for anyone. My heart was a damn cold stone, and I was ready to accept that. Then you came stumbling into my world and turned everything upside down. Twice. Now all I can do is think about you. What are you doing? Who are you with? Are you lonely? Do you need me in your arms as much as I need you in mine?"

"What?" she asked, her voice barely above a whisper.

"I can't even close my eyes without seeing your smile. Lying in bed I smell that cocoa butter or whatever it is you wear, and I wish like hell I knew what it was so I could buy some."

She shook her head as her expression grew more confused.

"You said you needed time. You would call me. I've been waiting, and I can't wait anymore, Morgan."

Placing my hands on either side of her head, I leaned closer to her. Her chest rose and fell to what felt like the same rhythm of my heartbeat.

"Has he touched you since we were together?"

Her mouth fell open in surprise, then it slammed shut, and anger filled her eyes. "Has she?"

I laughed. "It's a fucking ruse, Morgan. Raine doesn't have the balls to tell her parents the guy she'd been dating was married. We're friends, that's all."

A look passed over her face. Relief maybe? Joy in knowing I wasn't really with Raine? God, how I hoped that was what I was seeing.

"I need to get back out there, Blake."

Lifting my hand to her face, I cupped it gently. "Are you with him? Has he touched you?"

My other hand landed on her hip, gently squeezing it. Her breath caught, and I could practically smell her desire for me.

"Does he touch you like I do?"

My lips gently moved over her neck, causing her to tremble.

Moving my hand down, I slowly lifted her satin dress.

"Did he tell you how seeing you in this dress instantly made him hard?"

"Blake," she gasped, grabbing on my arms.

"All I can think about is turning you around and fucking you. Showing you who this body belongs to."

She lifted her chin as she placed her hand on my chest. "It belongs to me."

My mouth quirked up into a smirk. "Fuck yes, it does. And it turns me on more than you will ever know. The thought of another man touching you makes me want to kick his ass."

Her tongue slipped between those pink lips, wetting them before I pressed my mouth to hers.

It took prodding with my tongue before she let me in. When she did, her hand moved up, and she slipped her fingers into my hair, tugging hard to deepen the kiss. It was hungry and needy at first, then it slowed and we both moaned. Morgan pulled back, panting for air.

"He's only here as a friend. He has a girlfriend who knows he is with me tonight. I tried to text you this morning and ask you to come with me tonight, but you never replied."

I placed my hand on the door and cursed. "I went caving this morning and lost my phone."

Her eyes lit up, then she saw the bump on my forehead. She reached up and touched it, causing me to wince.

"What happened?" she asked.

"When I was in high school . . . something terrible happened. I had a lot of anger to deal with, and my therapist suggested I go caving. It's been an outlet for me when I'm dealing with guilt, hurt . . . anger."

She pressed her lips together. "I'm sorry I didn't call. I acted like a stupid fool when I saw the text, and—"

I placed my finger to her lips. "It doesn't matter. Did you mean it? You wanted me to come with you tonight?"

Morgan grinned. "Yes. I don't want to keep what I feel for you a secret anymore."

With a sigh of relief, I whispered, "Thank fuck."

Her eyes met mine, and I could see she wanted me as much as I wanted her.

I pressed my mouth to hers. "I want you, Morgan. Right now."

"No. No, we can't," she panted between kisses.

"Yes, we can," I growled as I dropped to my knees. I lifted her dress and moaned when I saw the thin satin panties. Lifting her leg, I placed it over my shoulder. I slid the thin fabric to the side and kissed what was mine.

"Oh my God!" Morgan whimpered. "We . . . oh . . . yes. Wait. Stop. No, don't stop," she said between breaths.

Her fingers went to my hair, pulling my head closer to her has she rocked her hips against my tongue. I smiled as I licked and sucked her, slowly slipping a finger inside her.

"Blake, it feels so good," she softly cried out.

Lifting my gaze, I watched her play with her nipple from the outside of her dress and nearly came in my pants.

"I'm going to come. Yes!" She clamped her hand over her mouth to keep her moans from being heard outside of the closet.

Once she stopped shaking, I stood.

"Turn around. Put your hands on the door."

She did what I asked. I undid my dress pants and took out my cock. Rubbing it over her wetness, I tried to remember how to breathe. Her panties were still on and pushed to the side. As my cock slid inside her, I nearly lost it. This had to be one of the hottest experiences of my life.

"Oh Blake," she whimpered as I pushed in fast and hard.

"I can't make love to you, Morgan. I need it fast and hard."

"Yes. Please. More."

Grabbing her hips, I moved in and out of her. She angled her hips as she looked over her shoulder at me. When she bit down on her lip, I knew she was about to come again.

"Come with me, Morgan. I can't hold . . . off . . . fuck."

She closed her eyes, and I felt her tighten around me as I lost myself inside her. I wasn't sure how long I stood there, still buried inside her, both of us gasping for air as we held our hands pressed to the door.

Pulling out of her, I reached for a towel and wiped myself off, then dropped to clean her.

Her breathing was still rapid, and her body trembled.

"What are we doing, Blake? We just fucked in a damn cleaning closet while my whole family is sitting in the other room."

Standing, I looked at her, feeling like a complete asshole for taking what I wanted, not even thinking of her.

"I'm sorry, Morgan. When I'm around you, I can't think straight. When I saw him with you . . . I nearly jumped the tables to pound his face in."

A tear slipped from her eye and trailed down her cheek, making me feel like someone had punched me in the gut.

"I'm sorry. I'm sorry I made you feel that way. I feel the same way when it comes to you. I saw you with Raine, and I went crazy for a minute."

He smiled and played with a curl that had fallen out of my bun. "Blake, we need to talk to each other and be open. If we do this, it has to be exclusive. No fake dates, no ex-boyfriends posing as dates."

I kissed her neck. "I'm okay with that."

"We have something between us. I don't think either of us can argue with that. I don't know what it is, but I have feelings for you I've never experienced before. I mean, look at us. We get around each other and the next thing you know we're fucking in the janitor's closet."

"I'm sorry I lost control."

Her hand came up to my cheek. "We both wanted that. I think we both needed it."

"I missed you."

"I missed you."

I touched my forehead to hers, then jerked when the pain raced through my head. "Ouch, shit."

She raised up and kissed the bump gently.

"What do we do now? I can't let Raine down."

"I understand. Let's go back out there and finish this night up. Then we need to talk."

Nodding, I leaned down and kissed her again. The kiss deepened, and Morgan pulled away and smiled.

The door opened, and she was gone before I could say another word.

༺

I WAITED THIRTY minutes after Morgan left before I went back into the ballroom. With a grin, I sat down and looked around the table. "I'm sorry about that. A client in Japan needed to have me sign off on something before they could move forward."

Raine smiled, knowing I was lying my ass off. I had missed most of dinner. Everyone was on their desserts as I ate the roasted chicken and vegetables. I glanced over to Morgan's table twice. Both times she was talking to someone sitting across from her. Rich caught my gaze once and gave me a look that said I needed to stop staring at Morgan. He had watched me like a hawk when I stood and pretended to take a phone call, leaving through the same door Morgan had gone out of.

When the damn dinner was finally over and everyone was saying their goodbyes, I slowly guided Raine toward the exit. I watched as Morgan hugged her entire family goodbye. Kaelynn whispered something into Morgan's ear, making her nod. Then Rich placed his hand on her lower back and guided her out of the room. She must have felt me staring at her, because as they stepped out of the room, she looked back. The second our eyes met, she smiled. I returned the smile and rubbed my hand over my chest, feeling that familiar flutter that happened each time Morgan entered or left a room.

"You want to tell me what is going on with you and my sister?"

The sound of Nash's voice made everything in the room go silent. Without looking at him, I replied, "Not here. Can I meet you at Sedotto in thirty minutes?" I asked, turning to look at him.

He nodded, then smirked. "If you figure it's a safe place for whatever it is you are about to tell me, you're wrong. I'll probably want to hit you no matter where we go."

"You probably will."

Fifteen

MORGAN

MY PHONE BUZZED in my clutch purse, but I ignored it.

"Morgan, do you want to talk about it? I mean, I'm almost positive I was not the only person to notice you and Blake leaving at the same time. I will give the guy props for waiting so long to come back."

"What do you mean?"

He laughed. "Your brother leaned over and asked me what was going on with you two. He said neither of y'all could keep your eyes off each other. You both suck at this, you know?"

I looked at him, shocked. "Was it that obvious?"

"To those who love and care about you? Yes. Not to mention that when you walked back into the room, you had clearly been thoroughly kissed."

Groaning, I dropped my head back on the seat.

"To everyone else, no. Your father's comment alerted Nash, though."

"How in the world does my father know?"

He shrugged. "I have a feeling Nash knows. Or Kaelynn."

"Kaelynn!" I shouted, opening my clutch and digging my phone out. I stopped when I saw three missed calls from her.

"Oh no. Kaelynn tried to call me. Three times."

I hit play and put it on speakerphone.

"Morgan, you need to call me back. I know how your father knows. Your father saw you leaving the hotel on Saturday and then saw Blake leaving not long after. He said he didn't have to put much together when Blake asked about you this evening and you looked ready to be sick when you thought he was with Raine. Then Blake nearly passed out when he saw you. He said something about how beautiful you looked. You two really suck at this! Nash figured it out not long after. That little rendezvous the two of you pulled was not smart."

I groaned and dropped my head back against the limo seat yet again. This time I hit it a few times.

"Y'all didn't . . . Did you?"

I gave Rich a look that said he was an idiot for asking.

"Holy shit. Your parents were in the same building!"

I hit him on the chest and then dialed Kaelynn's number. I had no idea why I put it on speakerphone. Maybe I needed Rich's help with this call. Some therapist I was—I couldn't even take a phone call alone.

"Hello?"

"Why are you whispering?" I whispered back.

"I'm in the backseat of my in-laws' car."

"Oh, freaking great."

"Yeah."

"Does Nash know?"

"Yep."

"Has he talked to Blake?"

"Um, that is so sweet to invite us. Nash is heading over to Sedotto to meet up with his friend Blake, so maybe another time?"

"Shit!" Rich and I said at the same time.

"Yes, I'm sorry about that."

"Whose idea was it to meet there?"

She cleared her throat.

"Blake?"

"Yes."

"Does he have a death wish?"

"It would seem that way, yes."

"How angry is Nash?"

"Surprisingly? Not at all."

"Huh?"

"Yeah, my thoughts too."

"Being in love must make him soft," Rich said.

I hit him on the chest again. "Shut up, and tell the driver to go to Sedotto! Fast!"

Kaelynn cleared her throat and said, "Maybe that isn't such a good idea."

"Why?"

"Just trust me. I'll text you all the details. Bye."

"Wait! Kaelynn! Kaelynn!"

The line went dead.

I stared at the phone and then looked at Rich. "She hung up on me."

Rich took my hands in his. "Listen, I think she's right, Morgan. You need to let Blake and Nash talk this through."

"But what if—"

"What? Blake tells him the truth? You have to let him do this on his terms. Please trust me on this, Morgan."

My hand went to my forehead. I was getting a headache. "I don't honestly know what Nash will do. And Blake said things to me tonight that had me so confused. He told me he hasn't been able to catch his breath since he first saw me. But I also know he's keeping something from me, Rich."

"Like what?"

"I don't know. It's something that is troubling him."

Rich gave me a warm smile. "Morgan, I'm going to guess this relationship with Blake has been a whirlwind. Take a breath, and just let things happen. It's okay to not tell each other everything right at the very beginning. Blake will open up to you, if he really is keeping something in. Just give him time."

"Do you know what he told me tonight? He saw a therapist for anger issues. That the therapist told him caving would be a great escape. He still does it. He did it this morning. What if I can't help him? What if he doesn't trust me, and I can't—"

Rick put his finger to mouth. "Stop. Blake is not Mike. Get that into your head right now."

I wiped a tear away. "I know."

"Do you? Because what I'm hearing from you sounds like you're trying to save him from a problem you aren't even sure exists. Take a deep breath, and let Blake and Nash talk."

Sweat started to bead on my forehead and neck.

"Is it hot in here?" I asked, cracking the window and taking in a few deep breaths of fresh air. My body was beginning to ache, and my headache was growing worse by the second.

"Why would he ask to talk to Nash tonight?"

Laughing, Rich pulled me close to him and let my head rest on his shoulder.

"Love makes us do crazy things."

"Love?" I whispered. "That's impossible, Rich. Blake Greene is not in love with me."

"I think you're wrong. And I wasn't just talking about Blake, Morgan."

❧

I HAD BEEN home an hour, changed out of my gown, and took a hot shower. Now I was pacing my living room, waiting for Kaelynn to text me. Everything Blake had said ran over and over in my head. One minute I was swooning over his words, the next I was confused.

When my doorbell rang, I jumped. Glancing over to the TV screen Nash had set up with the security cameras, I saw it was Kaelynn.

"What in the world?" I said, rushing to the door.

"Kaelynn, you shouldn't be out this late!" I said, pulling her into the house and shutting the door. She was carrying a bag of Blue Bell ice cream. My head was still killing me, even after I had taken three aspirin.

"I told Nash I was coming to spend the night at your place."

Wringing my hands together, I asked, "Have you heard from Nash?"

"Yep. Two minutes ago. I called him to let him know I was here. He and Blake are on their way to getting drunk. Tucker sent me a text and said he'd make sure they both got home safely."

"Drunk?" I asked.

"Yep. They started after Nash punched Blake in Tucker's office."

I slapped my hand over my mouth as I gasped.

"Blake's fine. Nash only hit him twice."

I was stunned. "Twice?"

Kaelynn walked into my kitchen, pulled out two bowls, two spoons, and the ice-cream scoop. "Yeah, once in the jaw and once in the stomach. Tucker said Blake took it well, like a champ."

I dropped onto the sofa and groaned. "Dear God. All I wanted was one night of raw, hot sex with someone I trusted."

Kaelynn stopped what she was doing and stared at me. "When I told you to go out and have sex, I didn't mean with Blake!"

With a shrug, I replied, "It sort of happened. Then it happened again, and then again."

She pressed her lips together to keep from laughing.

"I always knew you had a thing for him. I suspected it was mutual. I used to always catch him stealing glances your way."

"Really?" I asked, thinking about Blake's earlier comment about not being able to breathe since the first time he saw me. I no longer thought he was referring to that night in the bar.

"Really. How was it?" she finally asked.

Reaching for a throw pillow, I pulled it to my chest and hugged it. I could feel my face heating. It felt so good to be finally be able to talk about Blake with someone.

"Amazing. Different from any other guy I've been with. Not that I've been with many. It's scary. Thrilling. Romantic. Confusing."

"I get the scary, thrilling, and romantic, but you lost me at confusing."

"How? Think how I feel."

Kaelynn handed me the bowl of ice cream and the chocolate syrup. I sighed and drenched my vanilla ice cream in the syrup.

"I'm listening."

"I think I want to eat my ice cream first."

She nodded and waited patiently.

Six bites in, I talked.

"First, let me disclose that I never once thought about cheating on Mike or leaving him."

She raised a brow.

"I know that sounds like a terrible way to start out. It's just, the first time I ever met Blake was in college. Nash took me to Tucker's birthday party. When I met Blake, there was something there. At least on my end there was. A spark. I honestly think had I not been with Mike, I probably would have flirted with him. I mean, he was so hot. Still is."

Kaelynn giggled, and I continued. "He really wasn't in my league, but the way he looked at me. I'll never forget it. My body actually tingled from his stare."

"Really?" Kaelynn asked.

I nodded. "Yeah. I felt really guilty for feeling that way. We talked for a bit, and once Blake found out I had a boyfriend, he seemed to pull back. I hadn't really thought about it until tonight, but I remember catching him staring at me that whole night. He even offered to give me a ride home. He was a gentleman, though. He never once tried to make a move."

I blew out a breath.

"I guess I should just start with how this whole thing began recently."

She spooned ice cream into her mouth and said, "Go on."

Setting the ice cream on the table, I leaned back and pulled my knees to my chest. "I was at a bar, Butch's Place, drinking like I always do on the anniversary of Mike's death. It's not a good coping mechanism; I know that. Butch is Mike's father. I told you that, right?"

Kaelynn nodded.

"Anyway, Butch was really there for me when Mike died. The only thing Mike would talk about was some mission he was on that went wrong. A few guys died, and Mike blamed himself. He wasn't the same after he came home. He spent a lot of time at his father's bar and even more time near the end back in North Carolina, at the base where he was stationed. I knew he was having a hard time adjusting to civilian life, and he enjoyed being around his former army buddies."

I shrugged and stared down at the floor. "Anyway, Blake evidently likes this bar too. It's sort of his safe place as well, but I don't know why. He hasn't told me. He happened to be there the night I was there. I'm honestly shocked we hadn't run into each other there before. According to Butch, Blake's been coming there since he was twenty-one. Never on the same day, but always during that one week. The same week Mike killed himself."

Kaelynn listened quietly as I told her the whole story. My proposition of no-strings sex at the café the morning after Blake brought me home. Me going back to the bar a couple weeks later and Blake finding me. The club Blake took me to, the first time up in his condo, the morning I ran into Blake out running, the hotel, me running, and earlier, in the janitor closet. I spilled everything while she sat there, stunned, staring at me with her mouth nearly on the ground.

"You guys had sex in the janitor's closet tonight?" she asked.

"That's it? That is the first thing you're going to say after everything I told you?"

"Well . . . I mean . . . I'll be honest with you, Morgan, I'm shocked by all of it. Especially the little orgasm in the club."

I smiled. "It was not little. Trust me."

She scrunched up her nose and kept talking. "I mean, I get you wanting some meaningless fun, and we even talked about it . . . but Blake? Why in the world would you ask Blake?"

I swallowed hard and wiped at the corners of my eyes, where I felt the tears building. "He was someone I knew and could trust. And let's be honest, I've been attracted to him for a while now. When he moved back to Austin and he would come around, it was hard to ignore the way my body reacted to him."

Kaelynn giggled. "Please. I knew you both had a thing for each other, and I would honestly be shocked if Nash didn't suspect it as well."

I blew out a breath.

"Okay, so get back to you and Blake and why y'all couldn't keep it to one night only."

With a drawn-out exhale, I replied, "I don't know. When we're together, I can't describe my feelings, Kaelynn. It's explosive on so many levels. Even the first time I came—like a whore in the club, all grinding on him—I felt a connection to him I can't explain."

Kaelynn shook her head. "You're not a whore. If Nash and I were in a sexy night club tucked in a corner, I'd do the same thing."

I chewed on my lip, knowing she was telling me the truth. She motioned for me to go on.

"I've never felt these types of feelings before. Not even with Mike, and I know with all my heart I loved Mike. It's just, there was always something between us. A wall he had put up that kept me from really getting in, or maybe it was me who put up the wall. Maybe we were just comfortable with each other. Even though he asked me to marry him, I couldn't seem to make him happy, and I'm not 100 percent sure I was truly happy. It was almost like he felt obligated to propose and I felt obligated to say yes because we'd had been together since high school. Maybe I didn't love him enough to see he was in pain. That he was hurting."

Kaelynn grabbed my hands and squeezed them. "Don't you dare do that. Don't you dare blame his death on you."

I'd never told Kaelynn about Mike's confession in his suicide note. I'd only ever told two people besides the police. Those two people were Butch and Nash.

"I don't, but I can't help feeling lost. Blake makes me feel treasured. He says things that a man who truly cares about a woman would say. Mike never made me feel this way." I clutched my hand to my heart. "I feel something completely different with Blake."

My chin trembled as I looked into Kaelynn's eyes. "And . . . and I can't stop myself from thinking that being with Blake has been the most amazing moments of my life. Kaelynn, the way he makes me feel, the way he worships my body and tells me I'm so beautiful. The connection we feel when we make love. I see it in his eyes—I know he feels it too. Then when I really think about it, I'm so angry at Mike for not doing that! For not making me feel like I was completely his. I can't help but want Blake, and I tried so hard that first night to not want him. I tried so hard to ignore the way my heart feels when he smiles at me. Or the way my body aches for him each time I think of him or I'm near him or he touches me. I feel myself falling in love with him, and I can't stop it. I don't think I could stop it even if I wanted to, and I don't want to."

"Morgan, I'm pretty positive Blake feels the same way. I wish you could see the way he looks at you."

I smiled and wiped away a tear. "That's all I've ever wanted. For a man to look at me the way Nash looks at you. The way Tucker and Jim look at Charlie and Terri."

Kaelynn reached up and kissed me on the forehead, then she frowned. "Morgan, you're burning up."

Sixteen

BLAKE

I OPENED AND closed my mouth while rubbing my jaw.

"Did you have to hit me so hard?" I asked, rubbing the soreness away and letting out a cough. I had finally just gotten my breath back from the sucker punch Nash landed on my stomach.

"You slept with my sister."

Tucker leaned against his desk, arms folded across his chest and a smirk on his face.

"You appear to be enjoying this," I spat out.

"Oh, I am. Don't you worry, I am."

Nash shook his hand and groaned. "Damn, your jaw is like granite, you asshole."

Turning to him, I frowned. "I'm so sorry to have hurt your hand when you punched me."

He shrugged. "It's okay."

I rolled my eyes and let out a deep exhale. "I'm sorry I didn't tell you. It's just . . . I didn't know how to tell you, and it all happened so damn fast. The way this whole thing started still has me in a tailspin."

My gaze lifted to Tucker, and he nodded. I needed to tell Nash everything.

Nash sighed and said, "Then the best place to start is at the beginning."

I rubbed the back of my neck and exhaled. "First, I need to go back to college."

"College?" Nash asked, a confused expression on his face.

"When I told you I was leaving after graduating because of the night my mother died, it wasn't exactly the full truth."

"Okay." Nash looked at Tucker then back to me.

"After my mother passed away, I was filled with so much anger and grief, and I vowed I would never let myself fall in love. I couldn't stand the thought of my heart being ripped from my chest again. Then you brought Morgan to Tucker's birthday party to introduce her to us."

Nash leaned back in his chair. "You didn't."

"No, no. I would never do that. But the moment I met her . . . I don't know how to explain it. It felt like she stole the air from the room. I was instantly attracted to her. Then we started talking, and for a quick minute, man, I thought she was attracted to me. Then she told me about Mike. I took her home, dropped her off, and then couldn't stop thinking about her. Whenever she came around, I wanted her even more. Fuck, I even started making plans to get her to fall for me and leave Mike."

"What?" Nash said, leaning forward. "Jesus, Blake."

I nodded. "I know. Then a week before graduation, I met Mike and saw Morgan with him. She looked happy. The way she smiled at him . . . it wasn't how she smiled at me. I knew then that I needed to leave. I wouldn't be able to see her with him every day."

"Dude, why didn't you tell me?"

With a small shrug, I replied, "I thought it was a fucking infatuation. She was the first woman who ever made me want to share something real. I figured if I left town and hooked up with a few random women in another city, I'd be able to forget about Morgan."

Nash smiled. "Dude, you think I didn't notice the way you looked at her when you came back to town? You think any of us didn't notice?"

I stared at him and then Tucker, who nodded in agreement.

"You knew?"

"Not really, but I suspected you liked my sister. I just figured you thought she was cute, and that was it. I knew the day I saw the two of you together at Town Lake when we were running."

I ran my fingers through my hair. "Well, shit."

"Why don't you skip to how the two of you hooked up."

Swallowing hard, I leaned back in the chair. "I saw Morgan at a bar. She was pretty drunk."

Morgan had never shared with Nash how she went to Butch's Place each year on the anniversary of Mike's death, so I left that part out.

"When I saw her, I knew I couldn't leave her there, so I made sure she got home. I brought her into her house, and that was it. Besides leaving her a note and some Advil for in the morning, I left. I didn't touch her, and nothing happened, I swear to you. I won't lie and tell you I wasn't tempted to kiss her when she asked me to, but I'm not that kind of guy. You know that."

Nash nodded. "I know that, and I believe you."

"She called me the next day because I had her key. I picked her up, and we went out for breakfast. I'm not going to sugarcoat it, I thought about her the entire night after I had dropped her off. Then seeing her the next morning and all, it made it all those feelings from college resurface. I was determined to ignore it though, but then she . . . well . . . she, ah . . . um . . ."

Nash shot me a dirty look. "For fuck's sake, dude, spit it out."

"Well, forgive me, Nash, but this isn't something I think a brother would want to hear."

His brows pulled in tight. "I can take it."

My eyes darted over to Tucker, who shrugged. Then I focused back on Nash. "Fine. She said she wanted one night of no-strings-attached sex. A night to have fun with someone she trusted and was attracted to. After the night was over, then we would walk away in the morning and return to being friends."

Nash's mouth dropped and his eyes widened in shock. "Morgan said that?"

I rubbed the back of my neck. "Yeah, and I'm telling you, I turned her down immediately. I mean, at first I thought she was fucking with me, and I might have been playing around with her until I realized she was being serious."

"Okay, then what happened?"

"I told her no. I mean, deep down I wanted to scream yes."

Nash made a fist.

"But I told her no. She got upset and told me to forget she'd ever brought it up. A few minutes later, she got up and said she was going to the restroom. But instead she walked out the front door and jumped into an Uber. Two weeks later, we ran into each other again. Same bar. She was upset and spewing bullshit about me not being attracted to her. She stormed out of the bar, and I went after her. Long story short, we ended up at my place."

Nash groaned and looked away from me.

There were parts of the story I was keeping to myself. It wasn't anyone's business what Morgan and I did together. All Nash needed to know was how she had changed me.

"I've never in my life experienced a connection with a woman like I have with Morgan. Hell, I felt something for her the first day I met her. She makes me feel things I honestly didn't think were possible. The woman can drive me to my knees. Or drive me insane. I do and say things with her I would never dream of doing. She makes me confused, and sometimes I can't even concentrate. I say the stupidest shit. It's fucked up, dude! Your sister is fucking me up in the head."

The corner of Nash's mouth rose slightly in what looked like a smile. "Do you care about her, Blake?"

"Yes. I feel it in here," I pounded my fist on my chest. "The air around me gets warmer, my heart races faster, and I feel like I need her close by to breathe. Hell, she only has to smile at me, and my knees feel weak."

Tucker and Nash exchanged a look before Tucker cleared his throat and spoke.

"Dude, I hate to tell you this, but you're in love."

I swallowed hard. My heart already knew it. I'd known it since the moment I slid into her the first time we made love. "It's too soon. Right?"

Nash stood. "I know the real you, dude. I know you've played around, but I also know you have the biggest heart of anyone I know. There isn't anything you wouldn't do for your friends. So I will trust you with my sister. I don't know how this will turn out, but I only ask for one thing."

I stood. "I'll do anything, Nash."

"Don't hurt her."

His eyes filled with something I hadn't ever seen before. It wasn't anger. Or concern. It was trust.

"I won't hurt her. I swear to God, Nash, I would rather die than hurt her."

With a nod, he shook my hand.

"Now that I know you two won't kill each other, I need to check upfront. If you leave, lock up."

Nash and I nodded as we both watched Tucker leave his office. When the door shut, Nash faced me. A serious look on his face.

"I need to tell you something, and I didn't want to say it in front of Tucker."

"Okay."

Nash pulled in a deep breath then exhaled. "Mike told Morgan he cheated on her in his suicide note. What she doesn't know is that he has a son with the woman he cheated on her with."

My entire body swayed as he stepped back and looked into my eyes. For once in my life, I didn't have a damn thing to say.

Nash hit me on the shoulder. "You're not asking me, but I'm giving you some advice. I'm headed over to Morgan's house in the morning to pick up Kaelynn. If I were you, I'd be right behind me."

I nodded.

Nash smiled, and a part of me felt guilty as hell. He was letting me off too easy. I needed to be punished more, suffer more. But that wasn't the way Nash Barrett rolled. Placing his hand on my shoulder, he gave it a squeeze and said, "Now, let's go get drunk."

Before we could even walk out into the bar, Nash's phone rang.

"Hey, how's girls' night?"

His smiled dropped, and he looked at me. "We're on our way."

My heart felt like it went to my throat as I waited for him to hang up.

"What's wrong?" I asked as he hung up.

"Kaelynn said Morgan is running a fever. She checked it a few minutes ago and it was a hundred. Then Morgan suddenly got super tired. She just checked it again; it's a hundred and three."

Remembering that Nash had told us once Morgan hated hospitals, I said, "I'll call my father and have him meet us there," I said.

If anything happened to Morgan, I wasn't sure what I would do.

Seventeen

MORGAN

THE NEXT MORNING, I moaned as I rolled over and attempted to get up. My body felt heavy and ached all over. I was freezing, but I was drenched in sweat.

"Don't move."

I froze at the sound of his voice. Then I opened my eyes and saw Blake.

"Am I dreaming?" I asked, feeling like my head was lost in a cloud somewhere in the sky. I had to be dreaming. Last I remembered I was on the sofa with Kaelynn, eating ice cream.

"Kaelynn called last night and said you started to feel bad and you had a fever that was going up. Naturally Nash raced over here to check on you. Then he made Kaelynn leave, but not before he had her drink some vitamin-B immunity drink. My father and I stuck around to take care of you."

"Take care of me? Your father?" I asked, trying to swallow. My hand came up to my throat, and I rubbed it. "My throat hurts."

"You also have a fever."

I shot up in bed, then gasped as the entire room spun.

"Hey, hey, don't do that. Lie back down, princess."

"Kaelynn!"

"She'll be fine."

"But if I have a fever?"

"My dad checked her out and told her what to do if she started to feel bad. Your fever climbed all night. Do you not remember any of that?"

I looked up at him, trying to make my memory work.

"I don't remember anything. Your father was here?"

He smiled. "Yeah, he was. Sucks you don't remember meeting him for the first time."

Closing my eyes, I let out another groan. "I didn't say anything to him, did I?"

He laughed. "No. I don't think I've ever seen anyone come down with the flu as fast as you did."

My phone buzzed on the side table, and I reached for it.

Oh my gosh . . . My entire body ached.

"It's Rich."

I wasn't positive, but I was pretty sure I heard a growl come from Blake.

> *Rich: I think I'm getting the flu. I hope you got the flu shot.*

My eyes hurt like hell, but I managed to text him back.

> *Me: I'm in bed, feeling like crap.*

He texted back instantly.

> *Rich: Dammit! You got me sick!*

I dropped the phone to the bed and closed my eyes.

"My head hurts. My everything hurts."

Blake took my temperature.

"Your fever is at a hundred and three. Let's get you into a bath to try to bring it down."

We stared at one another for a few moments. "I don't think I can move. I feel like death."

I was positive I looked like it too.

He pushed a strand piece of hair back, then used the back of his cool hand to feel my forehead, then ran it slowly down my cheek.

"That feels like heaven."

"I hate that you're not feeling good, princess."

There was no doubt he meant every word he said.

"I'm so tired."

Blake stood. "I'll run the bath."

The next thing I remembered was feeling someone lift me and carry me through my bedroom. At least, I thought I was in my bedroom. Cool water hit my body, instantly making the heat go away. Then I felt a cool washcloth on my forehead. Over my neck and chest. Water gently pouring down my body.

"Morgan, baby, can you look at me?"

I opened my eyes and scanned the room. Instead of turning on the overhead light, he'd lit candles. If I hadn't felt so bad, I would say it looked romantic.

"I didn't want the harsh light to hurt your headache, so I used candles."

Staring into his deep brown eyes, I tried to say something, but I didn't have the energy to talk. Instead, I relaxed in the water for a few minutes and let him run a cool washcloth over my body until I started to tremble.

"Are you cold, princess?" Blake asked.

I nodded.

"Let's get you back to bed then," he said. Reaching down to help me out of the tub, he wrapped me in a towel. The cold air had me shivering even more, and I had to sit down. Blake helped me to the floor, and I closed my eyes. Next thing I knew, I felt a warm blanket being wrapped around my body. Then the feeling of being rocked had me opening my eyes.

"Blake," I whispered as he carried me in his arms.

"I've got you, princess. I've got you."

When I felt my head hit the pillow, I let out a sigh.

"Don't leave me, Blake."

Tingles raced down my spine, and they had nothing to do with the flu. It was Blake's touch. His lips pressing against my forehead.

"I swear I'll never leave you."

Smiling, I felt myself drift off to sleep. My dreams were filled with sunsets and long walks. Blake making love to me on what felt like a cloud floating in the sky. It felt like my dreams went on for days. Then I heard a baby crying. I walked from room to room down a long hallway, opening door after door. The pull of that baby drew me closer and closer. I had to find her. She had the answers I was looking for. The answers I needed. When I got to the last door, Blake stood in front of me.

"Don't. Let it go, Morgan. Please let it go."

I smiled and shook my head. "Let what go? Blake, there is a baby crying. She needs me!"

Throwing the door open, I rushed into the room and stopped at the sight before me. My entire body shook, and I covered my mouth to hold back my cries.

Jerking up, I let out a scream. Strong hands were around me in an instant, pulling me to a hard, warm body.

"Shh, it's okay. I'm here. I'm here, Morgan."

My hand came up to Blake's chest. The feel of his cool skin and the sound of his voice soothed me at once. I squeezed my eyes shut again before the onslaught of tears hit me full force.

"I've got you, Morgan. I'm here."

I was acutely aware of the fact that being in Blake's arms and hearing his voice calmed me.

"Bad dream?" he asked, his lips pressing a kiss to my brow.

"Yes."

"Do you want to talk about it?"

His question lingered in my mind for a moment or two. *Did I want to talk about it?* For someone who made a living attempting to get people to express their feelings, I sucked at following my own advice.

"Maybe you want to paint?" he asked, causing me to pull back and look at him.

"Paint?"

Blake shrugged. "If you can't talk about it, maybe you should paint it."

I smiled, flexing my fingers through the small bit of dark hair on his broad chest. How could this man know me so well already? It was like he had a window into my heart and soul. It should scare me, but it made my insides melt with happiness.

"Maybe. Later. My head is pounding."

The back of his hand went to my forehead. "Let me go grab water and more medicine and check your temperature."

It was then I noticed I was naked.

"I'm not wearing anything."

His brows waggled a few times, and he winked. "I didn't bother with dressing you after your last bath. It was easier getting you in and out to help control your fever."

"My last bath? You gave me more than one?"

Blake nodded. "Doctor's orders."

"Doctor?" I asked.

"My dad, remember?"

He pushed a thermometer into my mouth and smiled.

I wanted to ask him more about his father, but he gave me a stern look.

Once it beeped, he pulled it out and looked at it. Then he smiled.

"Are you feeling any better? Your temperature finally broke."

The tenderness in his actions made my heart swell, and another rush of tingles swept down my spine.

"I guess. I can't believe how fast that hit me. What day is it?"

"It's about two o'clock Saturday morning. Friday night. However you want to look at it."

I gasped. "I lost two days! My clients."

"Have all been called. You told me your password Thursday, and I got on to your laptop and calendar. I called everyone and told them you had the flu. I'm just glad you had no one scheduled Thursday morning."

When I attempted to move, my entire body ached. "Ugh, I feel like crap."

He kissed me again before sliding off the bed and adjusting the sheet back over me. "Well, you don't look like it. Even sick, you're stunning. Let me go get some soup heated up for you. Be right back, princess."

I couldn't ignore the way my heart raced, and it had nothing to do with the flu.

Eighteen

BLAKE

AS I WALKED out of Morgan's bedroom, I took a deep breath.

Her fever had broken. Thank God.

The last few days had scared the living shit out of me a few times, even though everyone kept telling me not to worry. It was only the flu. Since when did the flu knock you out for hours and make you incoherent? I had even called my father to come over again when Morgan's fever got too high. I'd never been so happy in my life to have a doctor for a parent.

I pulled up Nash's number. I knew it was late, but he had made me promise him I'd call when she woke up and her fever had broken.

"Hello? Blake?" His voice sounded tired and scared.

"She's awake and talking. Her fever has broken."

"Thank fuck. How is she feeling?"

"Seems okay. Weak and maybe a little achy. She's in the restroom now."

"Make sure she gets lots of liquids, and maybe some of that soup I brought by earlier. Do you want me to head over so you can go home?"

"No. I'd rather stay here and I'll make sure she gets some fluids into her. You don't want to risk getting sick and taking something to Kaelynn."

He was silent on the other line for a few moments.

"Nash, I've got this."

"I know you do. It's just weird. I mean, it's my sister, and you're all . . ."

I narrowed my eyes at the soup I was heating in the pan. "I'm what?"

"Acting all . . . boyfriend-like."

Laughing, I shook my head. "Is that your problem? That I'm being attentive to your sister?"

"It's not a problem at all. It's just . . . weird."

"Well, if that's all, I need to make sure she's okay. She's up and moving around."

"Call me if she needs anything."

"I will. Night, Nash."

I hung up, placed my phone on the island, and made my way to Morgan.

"Do you want to be in the living room for a bit? A change of scenery?"

She stared at me, a confused look on her beautiful face.

"Um . . ."

"I've already got the couch set up for you."

Smiling, she nodded. I walked up to her and reached down, lifting her into my arms. I figured she would complain, but the trip to the bathroom must have zapped all the energy out of her.

After I placed her on the sofa, I pulled the blanket off the back and draped it over her. Morgan glanced up at me, and I was so happy to finally see color in her face. Reaching down, I ran my fingertips gently over her cheek. When she inhaled a quick breath, I felt my chest flutter.

I needed to stop before I did something stupid like kiss her. I grabbed her water from the coffee table and handed it to her with some medicine. "Here, take some Tylenol and drink water, princess."

Morgan did as I asked, then giggled when her stomach growled.

I smiled, and she pulled the blanket up to her chin. "I guess I'm hungry."

"How about some soup? Nash dropped some off earlier this morning. Well, yesterday morning."

Before I left, she reached for my hand, drawing me to a stop. "Wait. I was sort of hoping we could talk first."

"Now? Why don't we wait until you're feeling better?" I asked, both scared shitless and excited. What did she want to talk about?

She shook my head. "No. I want to talk now. Please, Blake. The last time I even remember speaking to you was in the closet."

Sitting back down, I took her hand in mine and kissed the back. With a smirk, I said, "That was fun."

We both smiled at one another. I could tell just the effort to smile took something out of her.

"What happened with you and Nash? Did you tell him about us?"

"Yes. I told him almost everything," I answered with a wink. "Some things are for you and me only."

Her already pink cheeks darkened.

"How did he take it?"

"He hit me. Twice."

Morgan winced. "I'm so sorry."

"Don't be. I would have done the same if I were in his shoes."

She searched my face, almost as if she were trying to figure out if she was dreaming.

"He asked me how I felt about you, and I told him."

This time those blue eyes of her sparkled. "What did you tell him?"

"That I care deeply about you. More than I've ever cared for any other woman. I can't say I'm in love, but it sure as hell feels like it. Maybe I am, but my mind is trying to tell me I couldn't possibly fall in love that quickly."

A brilliant smile broke out over her stunningly beautiful face.

"It's sort of soon to be throwing that word around, I guess."

I nodded. "That's why I don't want to say it . . . not yet. Not until I know we're both ready."

It was Morgan's turn to nod in agreement. "What do we do from here?"

There was no way I could stop the smile on face. "Well, I was hoping we would date exclusively, like you said."

"I want that too."

"There is no doubt in my mind I want to be with you, Morgan. These last few days when you've been so sick, it's been killing me. I felt so damn hopeless, I still do. I wish it had been me who got the flu."

"I'm sorry."

I closed my eyes briefly, then looked at her.

"Don't blame yourself for getting the flu. You do that too much."

"Do what?"

"Blame yourself for things. I hated seeing you sick, but being here for you the last couple of days has been amazing. Watching you sleep, giving you baths. Holding you in bed while you snuggled against my body. I never in my life thought I would love all those things."

She grinned. "I wish I could remember it all. It's foggy. I think a few times I woke up and thought I was dreaming. Nobody besides my family has ever cared for me like that. Thank you."

I needed to stand up and move away from her before my greedy ass decided it wanted something from her. Like a kiss. Or to touch her body everywhere. I stood and kissed her on the forehead. "Rest on the couch while I get the soup. I think you'll feel better with food in you. You haven't eaten a thing in two days."

"Maybe I'll finally lose that ten extra pounds."

I gave her a stern look, and she shrugged. She grabbed the pillow and was soon lying down with her eyes closed.

I had turned off the stove, but the soup was still hot. The perfect temperature for her to eat it. I filled a bowl for Morgan and one for me, then I headed back into the living room.

"Here ya go, princess."

Slowly sitting up, she watched as I put a TV tray in front of her and then placed the soup and some crackers on it.

"Chicken noodle soup straight from your mom's kitchen."

She sighed, picked up a cracker, and ate the whole thing in two bites.

"Are you eating anything?" Morgan asked, looking up at me with the sweetest expression. I knew I was falling in love with this woman, but my heart needed to slow things down. There was something between us, a secret I knew I needed to share with her and a truth she needed to know. Until we had that taken care of, I wasn't sure we could truly move on with our future.

"Yep, let me set up another tray and then I'll go get my soup."

After getting my tray set up and grabbing my bowl, I settled on the love seat across from Morgan. When I glanced up, she was staring at me.

"What's wrong?" I asked.

I realized she was attempting to keep her tears at bay.

"Why are you doing this?"

I frowned. "Doing what?"

"Taking care of me? Eating soup with me in the middle of the night."

"I already told you. I want to, Morgan."

She couldn't keep her chin from trembling, and it nearly broke me in two.

"Why?" she asked, my voice sounding so weak I hardly recognized it.

"Why?" I repeated.

"Yes, why are you doing this?"

I swallowed hard and sat back. My brown eyes locked with her blue. "Why is it so hard for you to believe I want to be here? To care for you?"

A tear slipped down her cheek, and she shrugged. "I honestly don't know. I've never . . ."

Her voice broke off, and she covered her mouth. Moving the tray out of the way, I sat next to her, pulling her into my arms. I hated seeing her upset.

"You never what?" I asked in a soft voice.

She nuzzled her face against my chest and attempted to settle herself.

"Mike and I dated when we were in high school. He was my first for everything. The first boy I kissed. First boyfriend. First man I had sex with. Everything with him seemed to be my first. When he left for the army, things seemed fine with us. When he would come home on leave, everything was good. Even being with him, nothing felt off."

I tried not to let my jealousy show. It was stupid of me to be jealous of a man who was no longer here. Someone who was in Morgan's life years ago. But I was, and that was something I couldn't ignore. I had never been bothered hearing another woman talk about an ex. Not one. But with Morgan, just thinking about another man touching her made me want to kill someone.

"Then things weren't okay. Every time he came back, he was different. He treated me fine, but not like he used to. His touch didn't feel the same. His kisses felt empty. I kept telling myself it was me, I wasn't doing enough to welcome him home. Or maybe I was just used to him being gone. That guilt tore me apart. So I tried harder. I gave more, but I still felt empty. God, that played havoc with my mind. Then, he wanted to do things differently in the bedroom. He wanted to tie me up once, and at first I thought it would be thrilling, but he seemed so far away. Like he was with me, but he wasn't with me. I hated it and told him I never wanted to do it again."

My eyes closed as I tried to push the sick feeling away. "Did he hurt you?"

Her fingers moved softly over my chest in a rhythmic motion. "No, never."

After taking a deep breath, she slowly let it out. "I know he loved me, but looking back, I don't think he was in love with me. Maybe I felt the same way. I loved him, but I wasn't in love with him. I hate myself for not seeing it then. I hate that he made me think less of myself, but at the same time, I hate myself for not giving him more. Maybe it was my fault."

I pulled back and titled her chin up to make her look at me. "Your fault he took his own life?"

She nodded. "That, and . . . and . . ."

Damn it all to hell. I would never speak ill of the dead, but in this moment, I hated Mike for making this beautiful, strong woman doubt herself.

"And?" I softly asked.

"For cheating on me. He confessed in his suicide note he had been having an affair. I don't know who with, and I wanted to believe it was a lie at first. That it was just a way for him to make me hate him for cheating rather than for taking his own life. But I knew he had secrets. Right before he was discharged, a mission went wrong, and one of his closest friends was killed along with a few other guys. It tore Mike apart. Lance Merchant was his name. He'd been married, but not for very long. Just two years, I think."

I didn't want her to feel my body stiffen as my mind went back to Wednesday night and Nash telling me about the woman Mike had cheated on Morgan with. The woman who had gotten pregnant and given birth to Mike's child. Her name was Lynn Merchant.

Fucking hell. What did you do, Mike?

I looked down at Morgan. She had no idea. Nash had never told her he had hired ma PI to find out the truth about Mike's affair. And it was Nash and Butch who had decided to keep the truth from Morgan. Something I was now stuck in the middle of.

"Mike tried to be there for Lance's wife."

I swallowed hard.

"When he asked me to marry him, it wasn't the fairy-tale proposal I had always dreamed of, but he had seemed so happy. Like maybe what had been bothering him had somehow slipped away. It felt like the old Mike was back. It didn't last long though. He grew distant and . . ."

Her voice broke off into a sob, and I was about to ask her if she wanted to talk about this another day, but I didn't. I had a feeling this was the first time Morgan had talked about Mike at all.

I held her tighter as she drew in a shaky breath.

"I told him maybe we should split up for a while. Take a step back and look at our relationship."

My breath stilled in my chest.

"Mike asked me to not leave him. He said things were okay and that he would go to counseling. I believed him. He said he needed to go out of town for a few days. Be around his old army buddies and get closure. I told him I thought it would be a good idea."

I glanced down at Morgan as she stared off into space. It was clear a memory was hitting her.

"I really thought things would be different when he got back. We would be different. He would be like he was before."

"Was he?" I asked.

She pulled in a deep breath. "No, not really. He had something on his mind, and I asked him to go to a counselor with me. We needed to figure out what was wrong. I didn't want to give up on our relationship. He told me he would go. Two days later, he killed himself, and I've been trying to wrap my head around what I missed. What I did wrong."

Goddammit. She needed to know the truth.

"You did nothing wrong, Morgan. Nothing."

Then she did a one-eighty and changed the subject. "Do you know what's my favorite time of year?"

My eyes closed as I asked, "What's that?"

"Christmas."

Smiling, I kissed the top of her head and reached for her soup bowl. She took it and positioned herself next to me so she could eat.

"Why Christmas?"

After taking a few spoonfuls, she answered. "It's filled with so many beautiful memories. Fun times with me and Nash, going skiing and taking long road trips. When I look at a Christmas tree, it's like all those happy memories come rushing back, and I get to forget every bad one from the last six years."

"There must be some good memories since Mike passed away."

She smiled. "There have been." When she turned and looked at me, our eyes met. "You've been one of them. You seemed to have sparked something back up in me, and I have to tell you, Blake, it scares me as much as it excites me."

"Me too."

Eating more soup, she gestured for me to go back to my own bowl. We ate in silence until she finished, laid down, and drifted off to sleep.

I picked up the bowls and made my way into the kitchen. Picking up my phone, I sent Nash a text. I didn't give two shits it was early in the morning.

Me: *You have to tell Morgan the truth. If you don't, I will.*

I set my phone down, jabbed my fingers through my hair, and cursed. I was in new territory with all of this, and I had no clue what in the hell I was doing. The only thing I knew for sure was there was no way I would lie to Morgan and no way I would fuck this up with her. Once Morgan found out the truth about Mike, I would tell her about that night and pray to God it didn't change her opinion of me.

Nineteen

MORGAN

I WOKE TO my body pressed against someone. For the first time in a few days, my head wasn't pounding. I didn't feel feverish, and the fog lifted.

The sound of a soft sigh from behind me had me smiling.

Blake.

He was still here, still watching over me. I moved slowly as I somehow managed to get out of his embrace. I was dressed in the T-shirt and panties I had put on sometime Saturday afternoon.

Tiptoeing into the bathroom, I quietly shut the door and gave myself a good look in the mirror.

"Dear God." I looked like death had been knocking on my door.

My hair was a mess. I had black circles under my eyes, though I had no idea how; I was positive I had slept more the last three days than I had in the last few months.

I brushed my teeth, stripped out of my clothes, and got into the shower. The warm water felt good as I closed my eyes and let it run over my head.

"How are you feeling?"

An instant rush of tingles raced over my body at the sound of Blake's voice.

"Much better, thanks to you."

He chuckled as he opened the glass shower door and stepped in. I let my eyes roam over his perfect body. I blushed when I realized he was doing the same. I didn't think I could ever get used to the way this man looked at me. The dark passion in his eyes made my body tremble.

"I did nothing but watch over you."

"And feed me. Bathe me. Make sure my fever didn't get too high."

He winked then motioned for me to turn around. "Let me wash your hair."

I felt my breath quickening, and I was hypersensitive to Blake's every touch. The feel of his fingers working the shampoo into my scalp nearly had me melting to the floor.

"Lean your head back some, baby."

Good Lord. His pet names alone were enough to make me push my ass back and beg him to take me. My lady bits throbbed.

He pulled me back into the water and rinsed the shampoo from my hair. Then he worked the conditioner in as my body built up more and more. I was positive if he touched my nipples right now I would have an orgasm.

Then he ran his fingers through my hair while letting the water slowly wash away the conditioner.

"Blake," I whispered, needing to hear him say something. Anything.

He turned me around and stared into my eyes with the most glorious look on his face. It was almost like he had just designed the world's tallest skyscraper, and I was his prize.

When he touched my body, I jumped. His hands moved easily over my skin, the result of the body soap he had lathered on. He dropped down, cleaning down one leg and then back up the other. I willed him to touch me, but he didn't. He simply placed his hands on my stomach and started slowly working his way up. He took each breast in his hands and rubbed his thumb against each nipple. I gasped, and he smiled devilishly at me.

"Blake."

My voice was more commanding this time. I was tired of this. I needed more.

"Not yet, princess. You're still weak, and I will not make love to you while you're sick."

"I'm not sick anymore. I mean, I feel so much better." My hand reached down to stroke his long, hard shaft.

Blake groaned and closed his eyes. I pumped faster, making his body jerk in response. He squeezed my nipples, and I moaned with pleasure.

His eyes opened, and then he bit into his lower lip.

Jesus, Mary, and Joseph.

My legs went limp, and he grabbed me.

"Shit, see. This is too much. I knew it!"

I frantically shook my head. "No. No, it's not. You bit your lip!"

He pulled his head back and stared at me. "Oh no. You've got another fever. You're not making any sense."

Laughing, I shook my head.

"No, you bit your lip a second ago, and it was the sexiest thing I've ever seen."

He drew in his brows. "I did?"

"Yes, it made me weak in the knees."

Leaning down, he brushed his lips over mine. "Please let me feed you something, then I promise I'll make love to you."

I smiled. As much as I wanted him this moment, I couldn't deny the fact that I was starving and food sounded better than sex.

"Fine. But only because I'm so hungry."

His dimpled smile almost made me rethink my decision. He opened the shower door and stepped out, taking my hand in his to help me out. Then he wrapped a towel around himself and then me. Lifting me, I carried me to the bedroom. I buried my face into his neck and let out the most contented sigh of my life.

"Morgan, you are so precious."

Tears stung at the back of my eyes and all I could do was whisper his name.

"Blake."

He set me down, gently dried me off, and then dressed me in a T-shirt and sweatpants. It was the sweetest thing any man had ever done for me, though I didn't miss that he neglected to put a bra or panties on me.

"Pinch me," I said when he brushed my hair and then put it in the worst-looking ponytail I'd ever seen.

"Pinch you? Why would I do that?" he asked with a laugh.

"Because I have to be dreaming. No man stays with a woman for days, taking care of her while she has the flu, then bathes her and dresses her, all while dropping sweet kisses on her forehead or the tip of her nose."

Blake stared at me and then shrugged. "I guess I'm different then."

My heart swelled in my chest. "Yes, you are," I said softly, lifting onto my tippy toes and kissing him.

He took my hand in his and led me out to the living room.

"Sit while I make you something to eat."

I did as he asked, watching him walk into the kitchen and smiling as I took in his fabulous ass. Desire bloomed in my lower stomach, and I chewed on my lip to keep from cat calling him.

With a sigh, I spied my work laptop and reached for it. Positioning it on the throw pillow, I pulled up my schedule. Blake had somehow managed to reschedule everyone. I scanned the schedule for tomorrow. Three, and all of them in the morning.

I was about to say something when I looked up and gasped. Closing my laptop, I tossed it onto the sofa and made my way over to the corner of my living room. The white lights blinked off and on, pulling me closer. A slight sob slipped from between my lips as I reached out and touched one of the handmade hearts that dangled from the tree.

"It's not much of a Christmas tree, but it was the best I could do while you were sleeping. I found your tree, but not the ornaments, so I cut some out of the colored paper in your office."

I spun around and looked at Blake standing there. My throat felt thick and heavy, and my body instantly warmed with a feeling I had never experienced.

Was this what true love was? Real love? When someone loved you so much they would put up a Christmas tree in the spring and decorate it with handmade ornaments?

"You did this? For me?"

He nodded. "Yes."

"Blake," I whispered as I crossed the short distance between us. He caught me as I launched myself into his arms, laughing right before our mouths crashed into a passionate kiss.

"I want you," I murmured against his mouth. "Now."

"But you're . . ."

"Fine. I'm fine. Blake, please make love to me. Right here. Right now. Please."

"You said you were hungry," he said, looking straight into my eyes with a concerned expression.

"The only thing I want right now is you inside me."

Twenty

BLAKE

MORGAN PLACED HER hands on my chest, a look on her face I had never seen. My heart slammed against my chest as she reached down and pulled my T-shirt over my head. She tossed it to the side and smiled before placing a kiss on my chest.

Fucking hell. What is it about this woman?

She had the power to bring me to my knees. There wasn't anything I wouldn't do for her.

When her hands went to my jeans, I grabbed them.

"Let me, please."

I closed my eyes and dropped her hands, letting her unbutton my pants and push them down. I held my breath as she took me in her hand and slowly stroked my cock.

My breathing increased, and I somehow managed to get her name off my lips.

"Morgan, baby, I—"

Then she took me in her mouth, and my entire body jerked.

"Oh fuck. That feels so good."

She moaned, and it vibrated through my dick and shot through my entire body, hitting every single nerve ending.

When I couldn't take it anymore, I reached down and lifted her up, kicking my jeans off and away from me.

The way she looked at me told me she liked having control, and hell if I didn't like her having it.

I lifted her T-shirt and pulled it off. She didn't wait for me to remove her sweats; she did it herself. Then she laid back on the floor, right next to the Christmas tree I had put up for her.

Lowering my body over hers, I took one of her nipples into my mouth while my one hand went between her legs. She was so wet and ready it nearly made me dizzy pushing my finger into her.

"Yes. Blake, yes."

"God, you drive me wild, Morgan. I can't control myself around you. I want you so much. There isn't anything I would deny you, Morgan."

The words were out of my mouth before I could take them back. Hell, I didn't want to take them back. I needed her to know how much I cared for her.

If I were honest with myself, I would admit I was falling head over heels in love with her.

Her leg hooked over mine.

"I need you inside me."

Moving over her body, I positioned myself and slowly pushed in. Then she went rigid.

"Wait."

That one word had my entire body freezing.

"Wait. Blake, wait. My birth control. I haven't taken my pills."

"I've been giving them to you. That first night you were so out of it and I called my dad, he saw your pills and told me to make sure you took them. I had no idea what they were. He had to explain."

Her face went a shade of red I'd never seen.

"Your father saw my birth control pills and told you that?"

He laughed. "He's a doctor, Morgan. I'll bet he was probably happy to see them."

She groaned. "How embarrassing."

Pushing deeper into her, I kissed along her neck. "I want you to know

I had to hear a lecture about how important it was I wore condoms. We're playing with fire, Morgan. Not using them."

Her fingers moved over my back lightly. "I love feeling you bare inside me. I love when you come inside me, but if you want to pull out, you can."

I closed my eyes and moved painfully slow. In. Out. God, it took everything I had not to lose control.

My lips brushed over hers. "I want to come inside you. Always. You're mine, Morgan. No one else can have what is mine."

Her eyes sparkled. "I don't want anyone else. Ever."

"Good," I whispered, kissing her softly. With one hand, I cupped the side of her face, my thumb stroking softly over her beautiful face. Then I let go of all my fears and worries. I told her how I felt.

"I love you, Morgan."

Her chin trembled for the briefest of moments. When a tear made a path down the side of her face, I brushed it away with the pad of my thumb.

It felt like an eternity before she finally said something.

"I love you too."

Smiling, I crashed my mouth to hers and made the sweetest of love to her. We came together in the most beautiful experience I had ever had with a woman in my entire life.

Morgan Barrett was it for me. The only woman I would ever love for the rest of my life.

And I was never letting her go.

∽✤∾

THE BUZZ ON my desk made me jump. With a quick glance down, I saw it was Nash.

"Hello?"

"Are you free now? I'm downstairs in the hotel lobby."

I stood. "I'm on my way down. Meet you in the Starbucks."

"Okay."

The line went dead as I grabbed my keys and headed out of my office. Grace, my assistant, looked up at me.

"Leaving for lunch?" she asked.

"No. Yes. No. I'll be back in thirty minutes. I'm meeting someone downstairs."

She nodded. I was behind with a project my boss wanted since I had taken Thursday and Friday off to be with Morgan. This morning I'd arrived to find him sitting in my office at my desk.

Asshole.

It still pissed me off he had let himself in. I would have been off today if Morgan hadn't insisted she was well enough to go to work this morning. And she'd proven it at three in the morning, crawling on top of me and riding me until I came so fucking hard I saw stars.

"No one is to go into my office."

Her cheeks blushed. It was Grace who had let Mr. Phillips in this morning.

Once I was in the elevator, I pulled up my text messages from Morgan. The last one said she had one more patient. A new patient. I knew she would most likely not be finished until after lunch, but I sent her a text anyway.

> Me: *I can't stop thinking about you. About last night. About the last few days. Will you come over to my place and stay the night?*

I pushed one hand through my hair as I used the other one to shove my phone into my pocket.

I needed to see her. Feel her against my body. It was driving me insane. All of it. The way I felt about her. The need to protect her, figure out how to make both of us let go of the past and focus on the future. On us. The hardest thing right now was trying to figure out a way to tell her about the baby and the night my mother died.

"Shit." I mumbled as the elevator doors opened. I walked out and across the lobby to the Starbucks. Nash was sitting at a table, staring out over Congress Avenue. He wasn't people watching. He was lost in thought.

"Hey," I said, slipping into a chair.

He turned, and gave me a smile that didn't reach his eyes. Sliding the coffee to me, he let out a breath.

"You've got to explain this, Nash, because I cannot wrap my head around why you didn't tell Morgan about the baby."

His face went pale, and he looked down at the table.

"I told her I loved her last night."

Nash's head jerked up, and he pulled his brows in tight. "Why would you do that?"

I let out a harsh laugh. "Because I do love her."

"You love her? You know after a few weeks? Hell, two months ago you were chasing skirts, and now you say you love my sister."

Anger pulsed through my veins. "You don't fucking know what I was doing two months ago. Or four months or, hell, four years ago. I already told you, I think I fell in love with her the first time I met her."

He stared at me before exhaling. I could tell he wanted to say something else, but he didn't. I could only imagine the guilt he, himself, was dealing with by withholding the truth about Mike's baby.

"I'm sorry. It's just—she's my sister, and I care about her."

"And I care about her too. That's why I can't keep this from her, Nash. I vowed to her we wouldn't keep things from each other. I need you to give me a damn good reason you didn't tell her."

Nash turned and looked out the window. He shook his head and closed his eyes. What he said next caught me totally by surprise.

Twenty-One

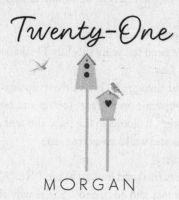

MORGAN

LISA PRICE, A new patient of mine, sat in front of a canvas and moved her brush with ease. She wasn't the best of painters, but she was trying. As she painted, I sat off to the side, working on the painting of Blake in the gazebo. Most of the patients took a few sessions before they opened up to me. Hell, before they even uttered one word, but Lisa soon set her brush down and stared out the large picture window. I had a bird feeder outside the studio window, and the patients seemed to be calmed by the birds and their singing.

Following her gaze, I smiled at the blue jay sitting on the very top of the feeder. He swooped down and got a piece of corn that was on the ground. I loved birds, and I might have been slightly obsessed with feeders, but my patients enjoyed watching them, too, and many ended up painting the birds. It was a win-win for me.

Picking up where I left off on the painting, I waited patiently while I worked. Then out of the blue, Lisa started to talk.

"I loved being his wife."

Stopping what I was doing, I quietly set my brush down. When she'd made the initial appointment, she had told me she hadn't served in the military, but that her husband had served. She had gotten my name from a friend whose husband was a current patient of mine. She opted not to give me the name of the referral, and I had thought that was strange, but I let it go.

"How long have you been married?"

"It would have been ten years this July. He died six years ago."

"I'm so sorry, Lisa."

She smiled and shrugged. "I have these dreams he's standing over my bed with this big smile on his face. I sit up and ask if he's come back, and before he answers, he looks to the right and sees another man in my bed. Then he turns and walks away from me."

"Did you remarry?"

This time she turned and looked at me. "No. When he died, it was hard on me. I was lost and confused." She slowly shook her head and wiped a tear away. "I was so lonely. His army buddies would come and check up on me. I don't think I could have made it through without them. We had been trying to have a baby."

I gave her a soft smile and nodded to keep her talking. She had trailed off and stared out the window.

"Shortly after my husband died, something happened between me and his best friend. Something sexual. One night after everyone had left. Neither of us wanted to stop it, so we didn't."

Oh dear.

"Were you both having the affair before he passed away?"

She shook her head. "No."

"And you feel guilty that you moved on? That's a normal emotion to experience, Lisa."

She wiped a tear away and sighed. "I feel tormented for a few different reasons. One of them was sleeping with my husband's best friend. Another was knowing that best friend wasn't single."

"Was he married?"

"No," she softly said. "When it first happened, we decided it could never happen again. He was tormented by his own demons. He felt responsible for my husband's death. Then with what happened between us, he felt so guilty he ended up asking his girlfriend to marry him. I know he loved her. I know he did, but he was so lost. With me he said he found he could be . . . himself."

I had picked up my pad of paper and made notes. "And did it happen again between the two of you?"

"Yes. We tried so hard to stop. You have to know."

Smiling, I tilted my head. "Lisa, I'm not here to judge you."

Her chin trembled as she went on. *This poor girl.* I was hoping she wasn't still carrying on the affair with this man. For the sake of all parties involved.

"It was like we both felt closer to my husband when we were to-gether, as crazy as that sounds. He didn't live in the same town as me, so he didn't come to visit often. When he did, we enjoyed each other's company. Sometimes it led to sex, and sometimes it just led to hours of talking. Then I got pregnant."

My eyes jerked up to meet hers. Her expression concerned me, but I couldn't put my finger on the reason.

"He came to visit me after he got out of the army. Told me he had to end things with me. He owed it to his fiancée to give her a hundred percent of himself. They had dated since high school."

A strange rush of dread raced across my body, and I felt myself holding my breath as I waited for her to continue.

"When I told him about the baby, I was ready for him to freak out. But he didn't. He told me he was confused. He loved me, but he loved her. I told him I couldn't be his mistress. I needed a father for our baby. I gave him an ultimatum. I . . . I forced him to pick. Me and the baby or her."

She covered her mouth and cried.

"It's okay, take your time. If you need to take a break, we can." I wasn't sure which of us needed the break more.

With a shake of her head, she pulled in a deep breath. "No, I need to do this. He sat down on the sofa and cried. It was the first time I had ever seen this man cry, and I caused it. It nearly destroyed me. He already suffered so much, having nightmares about a mission gone wrong, about watching my husband die. And I'd only added to his misery."

My pencil stopped writing, and I stared at the notes in my lap. My heart beat faster. Harder.

"Then he stopped crying and stood, like he was fine. He smiled and told me he would take care of everything. I thought he was okay. I dared to believe maybe we could be happy together—that he had picked me over her. I felt guilty for feeling that way, but I knew I gave him something she couldn't. I filled a space in his soul, and I was making him a father. He loved her, but he wasn't in love with her."

I did not understand why I asked the next question, but I heard it coming out of my mouth and couldn't stop it.

"Did you get pregnant on purpose to force his hand?"

"No. He visited two months before, and things got a little . . . different in the bedroom. It was more passionate. We hadn't had sex the last few times he'd visited, and we both were hungry for each other. We didn't use protection, and we stayed in bed together for hours making up for lost time."

I stared at her. The truth pushed at the back of my mind, but I refused to let it in.

"Truth is, he filled the spot Lance had left."

The room instantly felt cold as that name settled between us.

Lance. Mike's best friend from the army.

Her gaze met mine. "I didn't know he would do it. He left and said he would fix everything. I thought he meant he would tell her the truth, then he would come back. I found out three days later he'd killed himself."

I gasped and stood, taking a few steps back and covering my mouth with my hand.

"I didn't know he would kill himself, Morgan. I thought he would tell you the truth. Mike told me he would tell you the truth."

With every ounce of energy I had, I willed for the room not to go black. I forced air into my lungs, and I closed my eyes.

Mike. How could you do this?

Twenty-Two

BLAKE

"I DIDN'T TELL her because Mike asked me not to."

I dropped back in my chair, stunned into silence. "What? You fucking knew before he died? You knew and didn't tell Morgan?"

Nash rubbed his hand over his face. "No! Just give me a second, will you? Let me explain."

Motioning with my hand, I said, "Please do. I'm really interested in the excuse you and Butch came up with."

With a sigh, Nash looked up at me. "After Mike killed himself, you can imagine how upset Morgan was. She blamed herself for not being able to see how bad things were with him. She blamed herself for not being good enough for him, for not loving him enough. Morgan was beside herself."

"I know all of this. She's told me."

Nash pulled his brows in tight, then relaxed his face. "She talks to you about Mike?"

"She has some, yes."

He reached for the back of his neck and rubbed it. "Morgan told me what was in the note. Mike told her he couldn't live with the guilt any-more. Naturally Morgan thought he meant about Lance. But when she kept reading and found out he had cheated on her, she thought he was saying it to make her angry at him. Take the sting away of him killing himself. Butch and I agreed to look into it. It didn't take us long to find out through Mike's credit cards that he'd been going up to Fort Bragg fairly often. You wouldn't really think twice about it because he always told Morgan he was going to visit his army brothers. Well, Lance's wife still lived in North Carolina. He was visiting his army brothers, and they would go visit Lance's wife, Lynn. But Mike would go back and stay a few extra days with her."

"How do you know this?"

"Butch asked one of the guys about Mike's last trip. Butch thought Mike had stayed a week, but the buddy said Mike never stayed more than a couple days with the guys. He hinted that he was with Lynn the rest of the time, and we knew his plane tickets were always for weeklong trips. That meant he was staying with Lynn. After the funeral, when everything calmed down, I went through my mail, and there was a letter addressed to me from Mike. He had mailed it the day he died. He confessed to everything: his affair, the baby. He said he'd come back to Texas to break things off with Morgan but couldn't do it. He said the guilt of letting his best friend die, sleeping with Lynn, and hurting Morgan was eating him alive, and he couldn't take it anymore. He asked me to not tell Morgan about the baby. He begged me. Said it would devastate her if she knew the full truth of his deception. I took the letter to Butch, and we decided to honor his wish."

"Jesus Christ," I said, scrubbing my hands down my face. "You've seen how his death had affected her. You didn't think to tell her? So she'd know it wasn't her fault?"

"I didn't know what to do, Blake! No matter what I did, my sister would be hurt even more. I thought I was doing the right thing."

"Nash, you kept this from her. You kept the truth from her."

His eyes filled with tears. "And there is not a goddamn day that goes by when I don't feel guilty about that, Blake. At the time I thought I was doing the right thing."

"Some of the worst things that have happened in life happened because people thought they were doing the right thing."

Nash looked away.

"Tell her the truth. Before she and I can move forward, she needs closure. She needs the truth."

It was then I saw Morgan. She rushed into the building and ran right into someone, knocking everything out of the guy's hands.

"Morgan?" I asked, standing up and rushing out of Starbucks.

Nash was right beside me. We got to her at the same time.

"Morgan, what's wrong?" Nash asked, grabbing his sister by the arms.

She turned and looked at me.

"What's wrong?" I asked, my heart beating so damn hard in my chest I thought it might beat right out and land on the ground at my feet.

"He had a baby. He . . . he had a baby."

Nash jerked his head and looked at me. "You told her?"

Morgan's face went even more pale, if that was possible.

"What? You knew?" she asked Nash, then turned to me. "Blake . . . you knew?"

"Wait, Morgan. Just calm down, and let's get out of here."

She glanced back and forth between me and Nash. When the single tear slipped free, I wanted to kill someone.

"Can we go to your place, Blake?" she softly asked. "The three of us."

I wrapped my arm around her waist. "Yes."

Taking out my phone, I called Grace. "I've got a family emergency and am leaving for the day. I'll check in later."

Hanging up, I pushed my phone into my pocket and led Morgan to a taxi.

The three of us slid in, and Morgan stared out the window during the short drive to my condo. Nash and I exchanged looks with each other. He looked sick to his stomach.

No matter how this went down, no one would come out a winner.

৵৽৵

I HANDED MORGAN a cup of tea, and she pulled her legs up under her and took a drink.

Nash stood at the large window looking out over Austin.

"How long have you known?" Morgan asked me.

"Not long. Nash told me Wednesday night."

The pained look on her face nearly killed me.

Her gaze looked past my shoulder to Nash. "And you? How long have you kept this from me?"

Nash slowly turned and made his way over to the chair across from Morgan.

"Not long after the funeral."

Morgan closed her eyes and slowly shook her head.

"Wh-what?"

"Mike sent me a letter the day he died. I didn't see it until after the funeral, and when I read it, it shocked the shit out of me. He admitted to having an affair with Lance's wife, Lynn. I guess it had been going on for almost a year."

"What did it say? The letter." Morgan asked.

Nash looked at me, and I nodded. He needed to tell her the truth. All of it.

"He said he couldn't live with the guilt of Lance's death and the affair. And that a piece of him loved you enough that he couldn't break your heart by leaving you for Lynn."

Morgan pressed her lips together, forcing herself not cry.

My brave, beautiful Morgan. I wanted to pull her into my arms and hold her. She dropped her hand to mine and intertwined our fingers. I gently squeezed her hand, letting her know I was there for her.

"Why didn't you tell me, Nash?"

His voice cracked as he answered. "I . . . I didn't know what to do, Morgan. He begged me not to tell you. He didn't want you to know what he had done. I showed Butch the letter, and he agreed. We couldn't bear the thought of hurting you again."

Morgan looked away from her brother. It was obvious she was struggling with her emotions.

"I understand why you didn't tell me," she whispered before focusing back on him. "But I really wish you would have told me. I've been blaming myself for his death, not knowing why he was so unhappy. Nash, the guilt nearly drove me mad."

He came up and dropped to the floor at his sister's feet. Taking her other hand in his, he said, "I'm so sorry, Morgan. I knew in my gut you needed to know. I didn't know what to do."

Morgan ran her fingers through her brother's hair while his body shook from his tears.

"Shh . . . it's okay, Nash. It's okay."

"It's not okay. I'm so sorry, Morgan."

Leaning over, she let my hand go and kissed the top of his head. Morgan made her brother look up at her.

"I understand why you did it. *I do*. Mike should never have put that burden on you."

Her thumbs wiped away her brother's tears.

My God. This woman was incredible. Here her entire world had turned upside down, and she was comforting her brother.

"I love you, Morgan. More than the air I breathe, I never wanted to hurt you."

She smiled. "I know, Nash. I know."

Twenty-Three

MORGAN

I STOOD AT the window, my arms wrapped around my body as I watched the day get swallowed up by darkness.

"Morgan, do you want something to eat?"

Blake's voice warmed me. I glanced over my shoulder and gave him a smile as I replied, "Sure. I'm starving."

The events of the day swirled in my head, and I tried to make sense of it all.

Mike's lover, the mother of his child, had lied to make an appointment. The way she had told me the truth was cruel, but in my heart I knew it was the only way she thought she could do it.

Then finding out Nash knew . . . I had been so angry with him, and I was even more angry that he had pulled Blake into the mess.

"I ordered us a pizza and can make us a salad. I haven't really been home since last Wednesday, but I think the lettuce is still good."

I walked over to him. He opened his arms and wrapped them around me, holding me close to him.

"Pizza is fine; no salad. Did you order a large?"

He chuckled, and the sound vibrated through my body.

"Yes, I did."

We stood there in silence for a few moments before Blake pushed me back and looked down into my eyes.

"Tell me what I need to do to make this better for you. Tell me, and I'll do anything."

My heart swelled in my chest. This man truly loved me. The way he looked at me, touched me, made love to me. Blake was what I had been longing for. The missing piece I had been searching for in all the wrong places. The one person to heal my wounded soul.

I reached for his hands and guided him over to his sofa. I sat, pulling him down next to me.

"I love you, and I love that you want to make this better. But I realized something today, just this very moment, to be honest with you."

"What's that?" he asked, kissing the back of my hand. The gesture nearly made me melt on the spot.

"You are the only man in my life who has ever truly known me."

His brows pulled in slightly.

"I know it seems crazy because we've only been together for such a short period, but when you look at me, I can't even explain how content I feel. The first time we were together, I knew."

Smiling, I looked down at our intertwined hands before I met his eyes.

"Blake, I don't need saving. I don't need a prince on a white steed to swoop in and protect me. I need someone to take my hand and be there with me as I figure things out. I need someone who wants to run away with me from time to time just to be alone together. I need you."

He let go one of my hand and brought it to my face. I leaned into the touch and let out a slow, soft breath.

"Then I'm here for you. I will go with you to the ends of the earth, Morgan."

Slowly leaning back onto the sofa, I pulled him to me and let myself go. I let everything go. The past. The guilt. The confusion. The only thing I held onto was my future. I wasn't certain what that future would be, but I knew would be as amazing as this moment was, because I had

Blake in my life.

⁓⁂⁓

ROLLING OVER, I ran my finger along Blake's jawline. He played like he was about to bite it, and I jumped and let out a giggle.

Blake and Nash had asked me how I found out about Mike's baby, but I had I needed to process the event before I retold it. Now, at three in the morning, after Blake had made love to me again, I was ready.

"She made an appointment under a false name. Then she told me her story. Her husband was in the army. He died, and his best friend came to her shortly after. One thing led to another, and an affair began. She told me everything. How he wrestled with cheating on his girlfriend. How after the first time they were together, he told her he felt so guilty that he went back home and asked me to marry him. I had no idea she was talking about Mike in the beginning. It was only after she told her husband's name and then it all came together. No, that's not true."

Blake drew his brows in as he kept his gaze locked on me.

"I was beginning to piece it together as she told her story. She gave him an ultimatum."

Blake pulled me into his arms. "What sort of ultimatum?"

"The week before Mike killed himself, he found out Lynn was pregnant with his child. She told him he had to pick. Her and the baby, or me."

Kissing me on the forehead, Blake whispered, "I'm so sorry."

"Do you know what bothers me the most? He gave up the chance for his child to know his father because he couldn't tell me the truth. I can't help but wonder why he would do that. Why he thought I was such a weak person he couldn't leave me. He didn't know me at all. All those years together, and neither one of us truly knew each other."

His arms tightened around me more.

"Maybe that wasn't it at all. Maybe he truly couldn't pick. He loved you both."

Lifting my head, I stared into his eyes and smiled. "But you know that's not true. The letter he wrote to Nash said he meant to pick Lynn."

"But he couldn't. There was so much more going on in his head,

Morgan. Things that neither you nor Lynn saw. I think demons tormented his soul, and he didn't know how to control them. It was no one's fault—not even Mike's."

I stared at him, letting his words settle into my mind.

"You're right. I tell my patients that all the time."

He winked. "It would be good of you to remember this, for future arguments and such. The part about me being right."

Laughing, I snuggled closer to him, letting my face press against his chest. The sound of his heartbeat eased the tension in my body, and I relaxed even more.

"What happened with Lynn after you figured it out?"

"I asked her why she felt like she had to tell me the truth and why she felt like she had to deceive me to do it. She said she couldn't stop the nightmares. So I sat back down, looked her in the eye, and told her she needed to let go of the guilt or she could never move on. That Lance would have wanted her to move on. I didn't have to say anything to her regarding Mike. I've just now figured it out myself. I think she'll be okay, though. At least, I hope she will be. Then when she left, I freaked out and came looking for you. You know the rest."

Blake rolled us over and hovered over my body, using his fingers to sweep away my loose hair. Then he kissed the tip of my nose, forehead, jaw, neck, and each side of my mouth, finally placing the sweetest of kisses onto my lips.

"You are the most incredible woman I have ever known."

I felt his hardening erection against my body and smiled.

"Ready so soon?" I teased.

"For you, I'm always ready."

"Good, because what I really want right now is you. And no sweet lovemaking. I want more."

His brow lifted. "You want to be fucked?"

"Thoroughly."

Blake's fingers found their way between my legs, pushing deep inside me. He growled at how ready I was for him. I raised up slightly, and he pushed fast and hard into me, causing me to cry out from both the slight burn and the extreme pleasure.

Reaching over my head and holding onto the headboard, I lifted my hips, silently begging him to take me.

"This will be fast and hard, princess," he grunted as he pulled out and pushed back into me.

"Yes. Please. Harder."

"Damn it. I'm not going to last long. Baby, I need you to come."

He moved back onto his knees, lifting my hips and finding the angle I needed. I reached my hand between us, finding that tight bundle of nerves that ached for relief.

It only took a few motions with my fingers and I came. Bursts of light exploded behind my closed eyes, and I called out Blake's name as he pushed in, letting himself go while he buried his face in my neck.

The sex might have been fast and hard this time, but I could feel how much this man loved me, and that feeling set me free.

Twenty-Four

BLAKE

THE MOVIE HAD ended, but I let the credits roll as long as I could, relishing the feeling of Morgan lying nestled against my side. It had been a month since Lynn told Morgan the truth about Mike, and things had been going amazingly. We split our time between my house and Morgan's, at mine one week and hers the next.

"Have you decided whether to join Nash in the partnership?" Morgan asked, pulling me from my thoughts.

"Yes. I was going to talk to you about it."

Morgan sat up faced me, crisscrossing her legs and tilting her head. Her sweet smile made my heartbeat pick up slightly in my chest.

"Me? Why?"

"Well, it's your decision too. If I break off and start a new partnership with Nash, I won't be making as much money as I make now. At least not for a while. I have my trust fund, though, which gives me a decent allowance every month. I've been putting it away until now, and I've stockpiled a decent savings and a pretty good stock portfolio."

She laughed. "Blake, I don't care about how much money you have. I'm perfectly content with my little house and simple life. You should know that by now."

I leaned over and kissed her on the mouth. "I know that. But I'm walking away from a six-figure job."

"So? You and Nash could do amazing things together. Nash has expanded the construction company so much. It isn't just homes anymore. You could still design your skyscrapers."

"I know that. We'll find a few good clients, and things will pick up. Not to mention my stress level will drop dramatically."

Morgan took my hand in hers. "No matter what you do, I'll support your decision."

With a wide grin, I pulled her to me. Morgan straddled my lap and looked down into my eyes.

"I'll tell Nash it's a yes."

She squealed and pressed her lips to mine.

"I'll keep some of my trust-fund allowance for monthly expenses for a while, rather than investing the whole forty thousand."

Morgan's smile dropped. "Wait, forty thousand a month?" Her eyes moved back and forth as she did the mental math. "You get almost half a million a year from your trust fund?"

I smirked. "Did I never tell you how my granddaddy made his money?"

"No. You didn't."

"Oil. My father learned a lot from his father-in-law, so invested in oil too. Between them, they made more money than they knew what to do with. Dad really doesn't even have to practice medicine anymore. He does it because it's truly his passion."

She looked up at me like what I had told her made no difference in the world.

"Morgan, you're not even batting an eye. I don't even have to work if I don't want to."

With a small shrug, she replied, "I knew your family had money, but that makes no difference to me, Blake. I love you for you. Not your pocketbook."

"I could design you your dream home and pay cash for it. That means nothing to you?"

"No," she said with a chuckle. "The only home I dream of is one with us and maybe a kid or two. A dog, two cats, and lots and lots of bird feeders."

My eyes went to the living room window, where Morgan had hung three feeders. She loved her birds, and someday I would buy her enough land so she could have as many feeders up as she wanted.

"I think I can make that happen. But you know we can't stay in my place after we get married?"

Her eyes widened in shock. "Married?"

"Yeah. It's too small. Who wants to raise kids in the middle of Austin?" I looked around her cute little house. "Then there's your place. It's not big enough to have kids and animals. We'll need more room."

When I looked back at her, she was staring in disbelief. "You've thought about this? About . . . marrying me?"

"I have. I told you, I love you and I want to spend the rest of my life with you, princess."

Her mouth opened, then snapped shut. Then opened, then shut again. She was about to say something when the doorbell rang.

"Wait, I . . . we . . . wait."

I was confused as I watched her walk to the door. Didn't all women dream about getting married and having kids?

Morgan looked out the peephole and then gasped.

"What in the world?" she said, throwing the door open.

I stood and saw a large guy standing in the doorway. His hair was cut into a military buzz, and the fucker was built like a brick house.

"Jarod? What are you doing here?"

He reached down and picked her up, swinging her around before placing her back down. A part of me wanted to knock the shit out of him for touching her, but the other part was curious as hell about who the guy was. There was no way he was a patient.

Jarod looked past Morgan and smiled bigger when he saw me.

"You must be Blake."

I frowned. *Who is this guy, and how in the hell does he know who I am?*

As Morgan motioned for Jarod to come in, I made my way toward them and extended my hand.

"Jarod, this is my boyfriend, Blake Greene."

His grip wasn't too tight, but he was no pussy either.

"It's a pleasure to finally meet you."

I glanced down at Morgan and raised a brow. "Finally?"

"Jarod was in the army with Mike. They were both in special forces. We've kept in touch since Mike's passing, and when I wrote him last, I told him about you."

Nodding, I said, "Special forces. I would think you were away a lot."

"Yes, sir. More often than I cared for toward the end. I'm officially out of the army now, though. I had an interview with a job here in Austin, and I thought I would surprise Morgan."

Morgan wrapped her arm around my waist, and that made me feel like the king of the world. Jarod didn't even bat an eye at it.

"When did you get here?" she asked.

"Last night. I met up with some friends and hit a few clubs, had more fun than I wanted, and found myself with a pretty little thing in my hotel bed this morning."

Morgan and I laughed.

"Listen, I know I dropped in unannounced. I wanted to surprise you. Let me take you guys out to dinner. It's on me."

"No, let us take you out," I said. "What are you in the mood for?"

"Salt Lick," Jarod and Morgan said at the same time.

"Jarod loves Salt Lick."

He nodded in agreement. "If I get the job here, I'm moving next door to the joint."

"That would be awesome if you moved here. Let me grab my purse and a jacket. Be right back."

Morgan rushed into her bedroom, leaving me alone with Jarod. He gave me a polite smile.

"I'm glad she's finally found happiness. You've got a gem there."

"Thank you, she makes me even happier. And trust me, I know how lucky I am."

Jarod shoved his hands in his pocket and glanced around the house.

"Looks like a cute place. Do you guys live together?"

"Sort of. Sometimes we stay at my place, sometimes here. I have a place downtown."

That caught his attention. "Really? I'm looking at some places down there, I mean, it's pricey, but I've stumbled across a few foreclosures. If I get this head of security job, I want to be close to downtown. It'll be convenient, and I'd love to be close to the music scene, but man, it's expensive."

I agreed with a simple nod of my head.

"I'm ready! Let's go."

We spent the rest of the evening eating barbecue, drinking beer, and hearing Jarod tell tales of his time in the army. He didn't really mention Mike very much at all, which I thought was strange, considering they'd been good enough friends for Jarod to stay in contact with Morgan after all these years.

Unless he is interested in Morgan as more than a friend.

I watched him closely. The way he touched her now and then. I hadn't noticed it before, but now I couldn't *not* notice it. He had squeezed her hand several times, too. Suddenly I got a weird feeling about the guy.

"So, Jarod, how is that you and Morgan stayed in touch all these years?"

They both turned to look at me. Jarod shrugged. "Through Mike, really. He and I were damn good friends. Tore me apart when he died. After Butch called and told me and I had to break to everyone . . ."

He broke off, his voice going silent.

Shit. Maybe he didn't talk about Mike because it was too hard.

You're a dick, Greene. Way to go.

"It was hard. Mike was a good guy. He had his share of faults, but we all do. We had a pact, the guys in our unit. If anything happened to any of us, we would watch out for his girl and his family. Keep in touch. I've failed Morgan a few times and gone radio silent, but I always kept her in my thoughts and prayers."

Morgan reached across the table and took his hand. He smiled, but he didn't seem bothered when she pulled her hand away.

"Well, I'm glad you made it through safely. Thank you for your service," I said.

A wide grin erupted over his face. "Thanks, dude. I like you. I was worried I wouldn't, for obvious reasons, but you're good people."

Morgan leaned into me. When I looked down at her, she stretched up to brush her lips over mine. I wanted to deepen the kiss to show everyone this woman was mine, but I settled for the chaste peck.

When I looked back at Jarod, he was looking away, deep in thought.

My gut still told me something was off. For now, I would keep my eye on this guy, especially if he did get that job.

Twenty-Five

MORGAN

THE FIRST DAY of May was always my favorite. It meant the end of spring and the beginning of summer. The thought of spending more time with Blake doing fun things like camping, taking trips to the beach, and hiking some of my favorite state parks made me feel giddy inside.

After cleaning up the art room, I made my way into my office. I entered all my patient notes into their files, backed up my computer, and got ready to leave. Blake would be working late tonight, so I was picking up takeout and heading back to his place.

As I opened the door of my office, I let out a small scream.

"Jesus! Jarod, you scared me to death."

The smile on his face told me had good news. He'd been here for a week now, negotiating the logistics of his new job.

"I signed the contract!"

"That's wonderful!" I exclaimed as he picked me up and spun me around. That had always been something he did, ever since the first moment Mike had introduced us. Mike said it was just his thing.

"We need to celebrate. Are you and Blake free?"

I chewed on my lip. "Blake has to work late tonight. He's put in his notice to leave the company he's with so he and my brother can start their own architectural firm. I guess they're trying to get as much out of him as they can before he leaves."

"That sucks. Would he mind if we got something to eat and grabbed a beer?"

With a small shrug, I replied, "I don't think so. I'll send him a text and let him know. Anywhere you'd like to go?"

"How about Pinthouse? I heard they have great beers on tap."

"Sounds good. I'll follow you over there."

Before I started up my car, I sent Blake a text.

> Me: Hey! Jarod stopped by my office to invite us out for pizza and beer to celebrate him accepting the job. If you get off in time, we'll be at the Pinthouse on South Lamar.

I stared at my phone, waiting for Blake to message me back, but he didn't. He must've been in a meeting.

An hour later I was laughing so hard I could hardly breathe.

"Oh hell. I forgot how crazy Mike was." Jarod said, taking another long drink of his beer. "Let me get you another one."

I was feeling the effects of my one beer. "No, I'm good."

"Come on, I know you're not a lightweight, Morgan. And we're celebrating. Besides, if you drink too much, Blake can give you a ride home."

I chewed on my lip as I pulled out my phone. Nothing from Blake. It was so odd he hadn't text me back.

"One more, and that's it."

He winked at me and slid off the bench. I watched as he made his way up to the bar. It didn't take him long to flirt with a girl standing there. I rolled my eyes and chuckled. Some things would never change.

After another hour and one more beer, it felt like I'd had six. There was no way I could drive home.

"I will have to Uber, these beers were pretty big," I said, feeling the buzz big time. I wasn't drunk, but I was not driving.

"Nah, I'll give you a ride. Still haven't heard from Blake?" he asked, a worried look etched on his face.

"No. So strange."

Jarod got up and took my arm.

"I think I'm just going to call Nash," I said. "He and Kaelynn can come, and Nash can take my car home. No, wait, I'm supposed to go to Blake's tonight. Or was it my house?"

Laughing, Jarod took out his keys. "Listen, I'll take you home. When Blake gets there he can ride back with me and get your car."

"You're okay to drive?"

He nodded. "I only had the one beer."

Now that I thought back on it, he had nursed that one beer.

"I drank too much. I feel stupid."

"Nah, come on. You probably needed a good night out."

Jarod spent the drive home talking about his new job. He was excited about it, and I was happy for him. I hoped he could settle down and adjust to the private sector with no issues.

Unlocking my front door, I walked in.

"No alarm to shut off?" Jarod asked.

"No. I have one, but I never use it."

I dropped my purse to the floor and headed to the sofa. My head was pounding, and my body felt heavy. I always felt like this when I drank beer, which was why I hardly ever did.

"Jesus, I feel like I had a lot more than I did."

He laughed and sat down across from me on the love seat. "Those IPAs are good and strong."

Grinning, I dropped my head back against the sofa and looked back at him, my face turning serious.

"Are you doing okay? Settling in and all?"

He nodded. "Yeah. It's different, and I'm sure it will take getting used to. The missing adrenaline is the hardest part."

"No nightmares or anything?"

"No, I'm okay, Morgan. I promise you."

I pressed my lips together. "It's just, I know what y'all went through and Mike never wanted to talk about it and . . ."

He stood and came to sit next to me. We faced each other, and I took care to slip back some away from him. I don't think he had realized how close he had sat down next to me. When he reached for my hair and rubbed it between his fingers, I wasn't even sure he was aware he was doing it.

"I'm not Mike, Morgan. If I need help, I'll reach out. I had a therapist in the army. He helped me a lot."

"You did?"

"Yeah, honey. I did. Please don't worry about me."

The sound of the lock clicking caused us both to look toward the front door. Jarod dropped his hand away right as the door opened and Blake walked in. He stopped and looked at both of us, his brows pulled in tight with a questioning look.

"Hey, I tried calling you."

I reached into my purse for my phone. I had a missed call from him. Shit. I had somehow turned my ringer off.

"Crap. The ringer was off. I must have accidentally done that."

Blake made his way over to us. I stood and allowed him to pull me into an embrace. When his lips met mine, I melted.

"I missed you," I whispered.

"I missed you too. Where is your car?"

Jarod stood. "She drank a little too much, so I offered to drive her home and wait for you. I figured I could just take you back to get her car."

Blake smiled, but I couldn't help notice the look in his eyes. It was not happy at all. He looked . . . angry.

"Nah, that's okay. I've been gone all day, the last thing I want to do is leave again. We can get it tomorrow."

"Will it be okay there all night?" I asked.

"Yeah. It'll be fine," Blake said, glancing down and giving me a wink. "How much did you have to drink?"

I laughed. "Two beers. But they must've been stronger than I'm used to. I for sure felt buzzed. I said I would Uber home, but Jarod insisted."

Blake held out his hand to Jarod. "Thanks for making sure she got home okay. My phone had died somewhere around four, and I didn't get back to my office to charge it until closer to seven."

Glancing at the clock, I saw it was nine.

"You worked later than I thought you would."

He rolled his eyes. "I'm so ready to get this shit wrapped up and get out of there. Bryce even demanded I come in to work tomorrow."

I frowned. "But we were going to Pedernales Falls tomorrow." I'd been looking forward to the first hiking adventure of the season.

Blake started to reply, but Jarod cut him off. "The state park? I'll go with you. I wouldn't mind seeing some of the trails around here."

Blake pulled me closer to him, a clear sign he didn't like that suggestion one bit.

"You're more than welcome to join us. I won't be going to the office on a Saturday. I wouldn't give up a weekend with Morgan."

I placed my hand on his chest, smiling up at him. This relationship of ours was still in the early stages, but it felt like we had been together forever. My insides warmed just being near him, and the hint of jealousy in his voice made my lady parts tingle. He had nothing to be jealous of. Jarod truly was only a friend—there had never been romantic feelings between us.

"It's a great date place, if you've met anyone," Blake added.

Jarod smiled. "That's a great idea. I have met someone in the building I'm renting out of. Maybe I'll ask her out. She might feel better knowing it's a double-date sort of thing."

Blake's tension seemed to slip away some.

"Let me get on out of here so you guys can start your weekend. Thanks for the company tonight, Morgan."

Blake stepped aside and followed Jarod to the front door.

I lifted my hand in a wave. "Call me if you want to go tomorrow. We could meet at the park around nine."

He lifted a hand and replied, "Sounds good. Night, Blake."

"Thanks again for seeing her home."

I couldn't help notice how sharp Blake's voice sounded. Once the door shut, he turned back. He reached for his tie and undid it, pulling it out from around his neck and casting it to the floor. Then he pulled his shirt out of his dress pants.

My breathing increased, and I followed his lead, undressing while I walked backward toward my bedroom. By the time we reached the room, we were both naked, I was in his arms, and Blake was sliding into me, taking me to a euphoria only he could summon.

Twenty-Six

BLAKE

"FOR FUCK'S SAKE, is this really their first date?" I asked, staring at Jarod and his date, Renee.

"I think they've talked a few times, but he said last night he would ask her out, so I'm guessing yes," Morgan replied.

We both stared at the couple. They were sitting on a rock, heavily petting each other while kissing.

"I mean, there are kids around, and I'm worried he'll fuck her right on that rock."

Morgan laughed and hit me lightly on the stomach. Then she pulled me by the hand to lead me down a path.

"Come on. Let them fend for themselves. I want to enjoy this beautiful day, not watch them make out."

We walked down the path hand in hand. I loved being with this woman so much that I couldn't understand how in the hell I had survived before her.

"I bet you're ready to be done and out of the firm. They're working you to death."

With a sigh, I nodded. "Yeah. Wednesday is the last day. I gave them plenty of notice, and I've finished up or passed along all of my projects. Now the asshole is just being a dick."

"That's a shame. You've done so much for his company."

"It doesn't matter. I'm excited about working with Nash. I think the two of us are doing to do great things together."

She smiled. "I don't think it; I know it."

"I told Nash I wanted to take a little time off before I hit the ground running with him. I was hoping maybe we could spend time together. I know you still have to work, but at least I can have dinner ready and waiting for you when you come home."

Morgan's eyes lit up and she let out a soft giggle. "I like the sound of that."

I cupped her face and kissed her gently. Her arms wrapped around my neck as her body pressed against mine.

God, she drove me mad with desire. Mad with love.

"Y'all ready to head on out?"

The sound of Jarod's voice caused us to slowly pull away, but not before I looked deep into those beautiful eyes and said, "I love you."

Her teeth dug into her lower lip while she smiled sweetly. "I love you too."

We turned around, and the way Jarod looked at me was startling. His eyes were dark, and I couldn't tell if it was anger or jealousy I saw. Maybe it was hard to see Morgan with another man besides Mike.

"Y'all want to join us for dinner, or are you in a hurry to get back?" Morgan asked.

Renee shrugged. "I'm good with dinner."

Jarod agreed, and we met them at Z'Tejas, where Morgan and Jarod soon got lost in stories of times they spent together when Mike was still alive. I didn't mind; I was glad she could surround herself in good memories, but it left Renee and me sitting there awkwardly with our drinks. We tried to strike up a conversation or two on the side, but couldn't find much common ground. When an hour and a half had passed with only Jarod and Morgan talking, I had pretty much had enough of being left out of the conversation, and so had Renee.

She cleared her throat loudly to get Morgan's and Jarod's attention.

"Maybe you two would like to continue this evening alone while Blake and I head on out?"

My eyes widened in shock at her directness, but I had to give the woman props. She would not sit there any longer and be ignored.

Morgan reached for my hand. Her cheeks were red with embarrassment.

"I'm so sorry. It was rude of us to keep going on and on and leave y'all out."

Renee said nothing as she dropped money onto the table and then looked at us. "It was a great day. I'm going to be heading on home."

Jarod looked confused as hell. Either the guy had dated very little since getting out of the army, or he really wasn't interested enough in Renee to go after her. Finally he realized the girl was walking off, and he got up.

"Don't worry, we got the check," I said, glad he would finally be gone. I tried hard to like the guy, but there was something about him that sat wrong with me.

"Thanks," he said then turned to Morgan. "I'll call you tomorrow."

And like that, Jarod was gone.

I sighed and ran my fingers through my hair. I was glad that was finally over.

"Blake, I'm so sorry. I guess I got caught up in the memories."

Taking a drink of my beer, I nodded. "Well, Jarod was making sure you did."

She frowned. "What do you mean?"

"Morgan, the guy was purposely talking about Mike, bringing up stories about your past with him. He knew Renee and I would be left out. He liked having your undivided attention."

Sitting back, her eyes narrowed. "What? You have that so wrong, Blake."

I pulled out my wallet and threw some money down onto the table, slid my chair back, then stood.

"Really? Then why did Renee get so fed up she walked out?"

Morgan opened her mouth to say something, then shut it quickly.

"I'm tired. Let's head home."

I held my hand out to help her up, but Morgan grabbed her purse and pushed past me. She walked straight toward the front door. I guess she didn't like to be proved wrong.

"Looks like we're having a fight."

The drive back to her house was silent. Morgan slammed the car door and rushed to her front door. Once she opened it, she didn't even bother to see if I was following her before she shut it behind her. I opened the door and stopped in the doorway.

"I'm going to head on home."

She paused then spun around. "What? Why?"

I stared at her in disbelief. "I figured you didn't want me here tonight."

"Why would you think that?" she asked, her arms folded over her chest.

"Let's see. For one, you're not talking to me. Two, you shut the door on me. Three, you're heading to your bedroom. Looks like you've had your fill of laughing and reminiscing with Jarod tonight."

Her eyes went wide and her mouth formed an O. Then she laughed.

"Oh my God. You're jealous of Jarod."

"Jealous? No, I'm pissed off."

She arched her brow. "Pissed off?"

"Fuck yes. You spent the last hour and a half giving your undivided attention to another person, so yeah, Morgan, I'm pissed. Hell, the guy's own date got up and walked out. The two of you were so wrapped up in each other you didn't even realize Renee and I were bored out of god-damn minds."

She swallowed hard. "He's a friend, and I value his friendship."

I stared at her in disbelief. "You value his friendship over me? You value it over being rude to two people who were also sitting at that table?"

"Blake! You cannot be serious right now. Jarod was there for me during a time when I needed someone, and we share some tough memories. If that is something that bothers you, then I don't know what to tell you."

"What bothers me is that I sat next to you and you ignored the fact that I was even there. And it's clear the guy is interested in you as more than a friend."

Morgan let out a roar of laughter. "Okay, yeah, right. If he's so interested in me, then why has he never made a move?"

I shrugged. "He was in the army. He was never around. You don't think it's odd he happened to have a job interview in Austin?"

Morgan shook her head. "He was all over Renee today. Blake, I can't believe you don't trust me."

"I trust you. I don't trust him."

"Then I don't know what to say, because Jarod is a part of my life, and I will not cut him out because you got your feelings hurt when you weren't a part of our conversation."

Anger raced through my veins. I took a deep breath and then took a step back. "I'm sorry you feel that way, Morgan, but I can't help wonder how you would feel if the roles were reversed. If Renee and I had talked and kept you and Jarod out of the conversation, would you be pissed at me?"

She swallowed hard and said nothing.

Turning, I headed to the door. I waited for her to call my name, tell me to wait. I wanted her to at least see how it looked from my side.

But she didn't.

I threw open the door and headed to my car. When I got in, I looked back at the door, hoping to see Morgan there. She wasn't there, and the door was shut.

My mind swirled with every stupid emotion I could have. She defended him. Took his side. I had no damn clue how to deal with that. I knew I had probably overreacted, but she had to see what they did tonight was downright rude.

Twenty-Seven

MORGAN

WITH MY PAINTBRUSH in my hand, I stared at the blank canvas. I had been like this all morning, simply staring at a blank page, trying to will myself to paint something. Anything. I hadn't heard from Blake since he walked out the door last night, and it was killing me, especially since I had texted him this morning to please call me. We needed to talk. He was so angry last night, and I couldn't blame him. A part of me was ashamed I hadn't gone after him. What I had done last night was downright rude, and the more I thought about it the angrier I was with myself. Especially for defending the action.

The sound of the doorbell made me jump and rush to the front door. I didn't even bother to check who it was.

Throwing it open, I said, "Blake!"

But Jarod stood there, and a disappointed look crossed his face before he replaced it with a look of relief.

"Hey, it worried me when you weren't answering."

"What?" I asked.

"I've tried calling you all morning."

A sick feeling hit my stomach, and I rushed to the kitchen where my phone was plugged in.

"Shit!" I said when I noticed the ringer was on but turned down to where I hadn't heard it go off. When I opened the phone, I saw I had a missed text from Blake along with two missed calls from Jarod. Opening the text message, I held my breath.

> Blake: *I agree we need to talk. I don't like how we left things. Do you want me to come over or meet?*

"Shit. Shit. Shit."

The text was from almost three hours ago.

I pulled up his name and hit *call*. My breath felt like it was stalled in my throat. After a few rings, it went to voicemail.

"Damn it."

I left a message for Blake telling him that I hadn't heard my phone going off and asking him to come over.

"I've got takeout," Jarod announced.

I looked at him, not sure if I should ask him to leave.

He set the containers of food on the counter. "Blake told me you liked McAlisters."

"He did? When would he have told you that?"

Jarod shrugged. "I don't remember."

I sent Blake a text.

> Me: *Didn't hear my phone. I'm sorry. I'm home if you still want to come over and talk.*

"Here, I brought soup and sandwiches. Why don't we set up the table and eat? I brought extra in case Blake was here."

I chewed on my lip. I needed to talk to Blake, and the reason I needed to speak to him was currently standing in my kitchen. Was Blake right about Jarod? Or just jealous?

"Jarod, I'm not really hungry, and now is not the best time."

"Nonsense," he said, continuing to set up the food. Before I knew it, it was all on the small table out on my patio. "Grab something to drink for us, would you?"

Agitation built as I watched him continue to set up the food.

"Blake and I had a fight, and truth be told it was about you."

He glanced up. "Me?"

I nodded. Walking outside, I sat.

"Why me?"

"He thinks you have a thing for me."

Jarod stared at me, a little too long at first. I moved in my seat, feeling very nervous. Then Jarod sat down and sighed. He ran his hand over his unshaven jaw and stared out in the backyard.

"Since Mike died, I've been keeping something from you."

I frowned. "Keeping something from me?"

"Yeah. Morgan, it was me who pushed Mike to Lynn after Lance died."

"What do you mean you pushed Mike to Lynn?"

"Fuck, I don't know how to tell you this."

My stomach felt ill. "Just tell me, Jarod."

He looked me right in the eyes and let the words spill out so fast I could hardly process anything.

"Mike had been cheating on you as long as I'd known him. From what he had told us, he cheated before he even joined the army."

My hand came up to my throat, and I whispered, "What?"

"He told us a bunch of crazy shit. How he took your virginity and felt like he owed it to you to stay with you."

The instant ache in my chest nearly had me letting out a sob.

"You knew Mike and Lynn were having an affair after Lance died."

He nodded. "When Nash and Butch called to tell me about Mike's death, they asked me if I knew about him seeing anyone. I didn't come out and say I did, but I mentioned Lynn."

My body trembled. I wasn't sure if I should be angry or sad.

"Did you know she ended up getting pregnant and giving Mike an ultimatum? Her and the baby or me."

He shook his head. "I didn't know she was pregnant. Mike didn't tell me that. He came to me a few days before he went back home. Told me things had changed with Lynn and that he had to tell you the truth. When you didn't mention it in your letters, I figured he hadn't said anything to you."

"Mike confessed to an affair in the suicide note he left. That was all."

"I'm so sorry, Morgan. I asked him if he was okay. We talked about how he was feeling confused about it all. He said he felt guilty for lying to you, but if I had thought for one moment he was going to do what he did . . ."

I stood and turned away from Jarod. My arms wrapped around my shaking body.

"You knew, and all these years you said nothing. Why?"

"I'm your friend. I care about you. What difference would it have made?"

Jerking back around, I gaped at him. "What difference would it have made? I thought it was my fault. I couldn't figure out why I couldn't make him happy. For all these years I've been blaming myself because a bunch of selfish goddamn men couldn't tell me the truth!"

Blake appeared in the door. "What's going on?"

Jarod let out a heavy breath and turned around. Blake's eyes narrowed when he looked at me. "Are you upset? What did he do to you?"

"He did nothing . . . well . . . not really."

"What in the hell does that mean?" Blake demanded, taking a step closer to Jarod.

"He's been confessing," I spat out.

Blake raised an eyebrow. "About what?"

Another long sigh escaped Jarod. "I told Morgan the truth about Mike."

"The truth," I bit out. "You exposed the lies, you mean? Turns out Mike wasn't only cheating on me with Lynn, but several women, even before he joined the army."

Jarod took a step closer. "Morgan, I didn't mean to upset you."

I trembled from head to toe. "What in the world would you think would happen, Jarod? Why did you push Mike to Lynn?"

"You deserved better than him."

My eyes widened in disbelief. "What are you saying?"

"I'm saying I care about you, Morgan. I always have."

I slowly shook my head before I whispered, "I think you should leave now."

"That's a good idea," Blake agreed.

With a nod, Jarod started for the door. "I'm so sorry, Morgan. I never meant to hurt you."

I turned and faced the back window. Birds flew across my backyard, looking for spots to land on the feeders. The sight calmed my soul, but not much. I needed to get out of here. Away from all of this. I needed to think.

Once I heard the door shut, I felt Blake's presence behind me.

"Are you okay?" he asked softly.

"No. I'm not. I want to scream and shout. I want to punch someone. I want to know why Mike did the things he did and then left me to live in a world of guilt and regret for so many years. Why couldn't he have been man enough to just tell me the whole truth? Not just a sliver of it."

He placed his hands on my shoulders but remained silent. I closed my eyes, enjoying his touch on my body. I loved that he didn't feel like he had to say something; he was here for me. Letting me know if I needed him, he wasn't far.

I leaned my body back against his, letting a long exhale.

"I feel like the last few minutes have been a terrible dream. It only just occurred to me I was in love with a man I knew nothing about. He lived in a different world, and I was clueless about all of it."

Blake wrapped his arms around me and held me close.

I watched as a blue jay landed on a branch. It looked beautiful sitting in the tree.

"Everyone is keeping things from me. My own brother! Jarod. Butch. Please tell me you're not keeping something from me too."

Twenty-Eight

BLAKE

A SINKING FEELING moved through me. So much had been kept from Morgan. So many lies told, truths withheld. She deserved so much better than this. She had said she wanted to leave the past in the past, and a part of me wanted that as well, but I knew deep in that if I didn't tell her about my own past, I was no better than Mike and Jarod.

I swallowed hard. Now was not the time for that conversation, though. I had no idea how she would react when I told her about that night. I did know today was not the day to tell her.

"Do you want to go for a drive?" I asked.

She turned and faced me with a sweet smile. "Yes. I would love to go for a drive."

Morgan was silent the first few minutes we were in the car.

"Penny for your thoughts."

She looked my way as I waited at a red light.

"It's hard to think I didn't notice the signs about Mike's whole other life. I thought we had this perfect little relationship. Dated in high school, college. He was my military guy who went off to serve his country while I waited dutifully until he returned. I feel so stupid."

"You're not stupid, Morgan. He lied to you."

She chewed on her lip and looked straight ahead. "Do you still explore caves?"

With a grin, I replied, "I haven't since the day of that dinner, but I love being in them."

"It's not dangerous?"

"Sure, it can be. There is something about it though that gives me a rush. Discovering places that maybe no other person has been to yet is thrilling. In a cave, I have to pay attention. I can think about what I'm doing and let everything else in the outside world go. I think that's why my therapist suggested it. Why, you want to try it sometime?"

She laughed. "No. But I've never been in a cave."

"What? Never? Not even when you were little? On a field trip?"

"Nope. Our class was supposed to go to one once, and I was so afraid I pretended I had a sore throat and stomachache. My mom let me stay home, but I think she knew all along I was afraid."

"What about now? Would you go with me?"

I felt her heated stare. "I believe I would go anywhere with you, Blake Greene."

My chest fluttered, and I reached over for her hand, giving it a gentle squeeze. "Let me take you then. I know a guy who works at Longhorn Caverns. We might get a private tour."

"No unexplored parts, though, right?"

"Promise," I agreed with a slight chuckle.

"Did it help, exploring the caves?" she asked.

I shrugged. "Yeah, for a little bit."

Morgan wasn't about to press me, but I knew I needed to give her something. "It was after my mother died. I'd like to tell you about that someday, but not today."

She squeezed my hand. "When you're ready, I'm here for you."

Trying to swallow the lump in my throat, I managed to speak. "Thank you, princess."

✸

AN HOUR AND a half later, I pulled into the parking lot of Longhorn Caverns. This state park had been like a second home when I was younger and really into cave exploration.

"It's so beautiful out here. No wonder Nash and Kaelynn want to be in the hill country with Tucker and Charlie," Morgan said.

Taking her hand in mine, I led us to the main building. Once we stepped inside, I glanced around. There were a handful of people in the building, most likely waiting for the next tour to start. When I spotted Rick, I let out an internal sigh of relief. It would have been just my luck he was off today.

"Blake, dude," he said when he saw us, "you should have told me you were coming. I could have arranged a wild cave tour." Then he focused in on Morgan. "Who do we have here?"

I wrapped my arm around Morgan and grinned like a damn fool. "Rick, this is my girlfriend, Morgan Barrett."

"Hey, Morgan, it's a real pleasure meeting you," Rick said, casting a sideways glance in my direction and winking. "I see someone finally caught your eye. You're a lucky bastard," Rick said.

With a glance down to Morgan, I watched her cheeks slightly blush. "You don't have to tell me how lucky I am," I said.

She met my gaze and melted into my side.

I turned back to Rick. "Morgan has never been down in any cave. I was hoping maybe you might pull a string or two and get us on a tour."

"I'll do you one better. How about a private tour, just the three of us?"

"Oh, I don't want you to go to any trouble."

Rick laughed and waved off Morgan's comment. "Because you're here with Blake, it is no trouble at all. Give me a second to let them know I'm taking y'all down."

Once Rick had walked away, Morgan pulled back and gave me a look that asked what I was up to.

"Okay, why is it that everywhere we go people bend over backward for you? Are you part owner here as well?"

Laughing, I shook my head. "No. The state of Texas owns this one. I do, however, give them a nice little donation every year."

The corner of her mouth rose, and she shook her head. "In all the years I've known you, Blake, I never imagined you to have such a big heart."

I faked an expression of hurt. "Ouch. I knew everyone thought I was a player, but cold-hearted wasn't what I was going for."

"I'm glad you're both wearing sneakers. Ready?" Rick asked when he returned, looking between me and Morgan. She grabbed my hand and held on to it tightly.

"Blake, I'm not so sure about this."

I stopped and turned her so we made eye contact. Cupping her face in my hands, I asked, "Do you trust that I would never put you in any danger?"

Her teeth dug into her lower lip, causing my dick to jump slightly in my pants.

"Of course I do."

Hearing her say that made my chest warm with even more love for her, if that was possible.

"Do you believe me when I say I would walk through hell if it meant keeping you safe?"

"Yes," she answered softly.

"You will enjoy this. I promise, baby."

Reaching up on her toes, she kissed me on the lips. "I trust you."

Hearing those three words meant more than anything. After everything she had learned about Mike over the last few months, I knew having her trust wasn't something I would ever take for granted.

"Come on, let's go explore."

Twenty-Nine

MORGAN

THE STEPS LEADING down to the cave entrance felt like they went on forever. My hands were sweating I was so nervous. At the entrance, Rick turned to face us.

"Ready?"

I nodded. Blake placed his hand on my back and I instantly felt more at ease.

"It's narrow as we walk down into the cave, but then it will open again." Blake said.

"Okay."

Goodness, why in the world is my voice shaking?

As we walked deeper into the cave, I couldn't believe how beautiful it was.

Rick's voice pulled my gaze from the walls of the cave.

"Longhorn Cavern is a rare form of cavern. You'll notice there aren't a lot stalactites." He paused and looked at me. "I guess you've never seen a stalactite before."

I shook my head, and that was all it took. Soon Rick was pointing out stalactites, a bat, hidden caves, a lipstick wall women used to kiss back in the 1920s when they were down here dancing and having parties.

"They had parties down here?" I asked, twirling around in a giant chamber.

"Yes. It was a speakeasy for several years. They still have weddings and events down here. Over there is what's left of the original wooden dance floor."

"That is amazing. I bet it's beautiful down here when they have it set up for a wedding," I said, letting my gaze roam every inch of the cave. The sound of trickling water was so peaceful. Everywhere I looked I saw something even more breathtaking than the last place I looked. "It's breathtaking," I whispered. "Utterly stunning."

Blake took my hand in his. "I told you."

"I've been missing out."

He grinned. "Ready to go explore a wild cave? Maybe an underwater one?"

I scrunched my nose. "Underwater cave? Have you done that?"

He nodded, and I felt my stomach drop. I would never tell him to stop doing things he loved, but the thought of something happening to him made me feel nauseous and for a moment, and the idea of losing him made me dizzy.

"Hey, you okay?"

I nodded.

"Then why did your face go pale?"

"It's silly. Never mind. Let's enjoy our time down here. I'm in awe with this place."

I started to walk toward Rick, but Blake held me back. His eyes met mine, and my entire body tingled. The way this man looked at me was like nothing I had ever experienced before. He could communicate so much to me with one simple look.

"Talk to me, Morgan."

Swallowing hard, I averted my eyes. "It scared me for a minute, thinking about you doing something dangerous. Something that might take you away from me."

Blake's strong hands cupped my face. He lifted my chin so our gazes meet.

"I wish I could promise you that nothing will ever happen to me, but life doesn't work that way. I can promise you I will never knowingly put myself in a dangerous situation."

"There is no way I would ever ask you to stop doing the things you love to do. Never."

He smiled and my stomach fluttered. I wanted him to take me back home this instant and make love to me.

"I know you wouldn't, and I love you even more because you said that. My life is different now. I have different priorities. Making you my wife someday, having kids, designing and building your dream home. Those are the things I want in my life. Okay, and maybe talking you into exploring one wild cave before you're too pregnant to do it."

It felt as if the entire cave was moving under my feet. This was the second time Blake had mentioned marriage and kids. Tears pricked at the back of my eyes—tears of pure happiness.

"I can't believe you think about those things."

Kissing my forehead, he softly replied, "Every single day."

"Oh Blake, I love you."

He drew me into his arms and held me.

"Come on, you two lovebirds. There's another tour that is about to catch up with us."

The rest of the cave tour was fascinating. Rick was the perfect guide, and I loved hearing him and Blake talk about other caves they had explored. As we climbed the stairs back above ground, I missed the peacefulness of the cave. I had snapped a few photos on my phone, and I couldn't wait to get back and put it onto a canvas.

"Did you enjoy the cave, Morgan?" Rick asked.

"I did. I have no idea why I've been so afraid all these years."

"The unknown, probably. You're not the first to be worried. I've had people ask me what happens if we have a flash flood or an earthquake or any of that kind of thing when we're in the cave."

"Um, I hadn't thought of those until you mentioned them."

Blake and Rick laughed.

"Great, Rick. I'll never get her back down in a cave now."

"Nonsense. I'm thinking that main chamber room would make a

beautiful backdrop for a painting session."

Blake tilted his head and gave me an inquisitive look. "You mean like with a patient?"

"Well, I hadn't thought of that. I was thinking more just for me and a few friends who like to paint, but that might work. As long as they didn't have any issues with being confined."

I turned to Rick. "I'm an art therapist. My practice is geared toward veterans, and I specialize in post-traumatic stress syndrome."

"Really? What exactly is art therapy?" Rick asked.

"Not everyone wants to sit in a chair and tell someone their problems, so we use art to help them open up. It's mostly painting, but I have patients who like to work with clay too. It might take them five or six sessions before they are ready to talk, and then they do a lot of expressing through their art. You wouldn't believe what I can get from someone by seeing something they drew."

"Morgan, I think this is a great idea. I have a small group of caving guys who like to come once a month—all veterans. I know for a fact one or two of them are dealing with issues on their own. One thing about my job is I have to read people. I see how certain things cause them to react. A loud noise if a rock happens to fall. A tight area where we have to crawl. Sometimes I think they do it to prove to themselves they really aren't afraid. What would you think about offering a session here?"

"Here?" I asked, unsure if he meant down in the cave or somewhere up here in the park.

"Yes. Maybe once a month."

"Down in the caves?"

"Sure, and maybe up here too. In the spring and fall it's perfect weather, and look at this backdrop!"

He spread his arms wide and did a circle. I followed his gaze.

"You know, that's a great idea. I try my best to keep my office not feeling like a typical therapist's office, and doing something like this might make for a great experience."

I faced Blake. He was grinning from ear to ear.

"What do you think? Do you think anyone would be interested in it?"

"It's a great idea," Blake answered.

Turning back to Rick, I held out my hand. "Rick, if you can get a program like that approved, count me in."

∼≈≈∽

THE ENTIRE DRIVE back to my house, I talked nonstop about Rick's idea. Blake listened patiently and interjected when I gave him a chance to speak. I loved being able to take something so close to Blake's heart and make it mesh with what I did.

Once we walked into my house, Blake had me pushed against the door, his mouth over mine.

"I want you," he whispered between kisses.

My insides shook. "Then take me."

We spent the rest of the day and night in bed. Only getting up once around ten to give our bodies food. I never once thought of Mike or Jarod or the lies I had thought were truths.

Thirty

MORGAN

CHARLIE, TERRI, AND I stood back and looked at Kaelynn. She was dressed in a beautiful white gown that showed off her adorable little baby bump.

"I can't believe you're getting married!" I said, jumping and clapping my hands.

"Neither can I!"

"So, do you have a present for Nash for your wedding night?" Terri asked as she adjusted Kaelynn's veil.

"I do," she replied.

"Well, what is it? Don't make us try to guess. That is just so mean," Charlie said, rocking a sleeping Charlotte in her arms.

"I can't say what it is. I need to tell Nash first."

Gasping, I grabbed her hands. "You know the sex of the baby!"

Terri and Charlie looked at me and then back to Kaelynn.

She laughed. "I told y'all, we aren't going to tell anyone until the baby is born."

"No one does that anymore, Kaelynn. You're killing us with the whole 'I don't want to find out' thing."

Kaelynn shrugged. "It's what Nash and I want. I'm sorry if that doesn't make you guys happy."

I rolled my eyes. "Whatever. I want to know what you're going to give him tonight."

She blushed.

"Oh hell, it's something sexual," Charlie said.

"Never mind, I no longer want to know what it is," I said, holding up both hands and taking a few steps away.

Everyone in the room laughed before a knock on the door had us all turning to look at it. When it opened, I smiled at the sight of my mother and father.

"We wanted to come in first before your folks did, Kaelynn. My goodness, look at how beautiful you are," my mother said as she kissed Kaelynn on the cheeks.

Kaelynn turned to Charlie, Lynn, and me and asked if she could have a few minutes alone with my folks.

"Do not make her cry. We'll have to do her makeup all over again," I said, giving my mother a warning look.

My parents only spent a few minutes with Kaelynn before her mother went in and then her father. By then, Charlie had given Charlotte to the nanny while we all lined up to get ready to walk down the aisle.

Nash and Kaelynn had picked a small wedding venue out in Johnson City that overlooked the Texas Hill Country. The Lighthouse Hill Ranch had multiple places to stay on their ranch, two of them tall towers that looked out over the stunning countryside. It was planned that when it was time for Kaelynn and Nash to kiss, the sun would set in the background, offering a stunning backdrop to the beginning of their married life.

After the wedding, the party moved inside, where we ate, laughed, cried, and danced. Even baby Charlotte had the time of her life.

"It's time for the bouquet toss!" Charlie announced while Terri gathered up all the single women. When she reached for my hand and pulled me up to the front, I couldn't help but laugh. Somehow I figured Kaelynn would attempt to throw it to me on purpose. I wasn't about to lie to myself and say I wouldn't do my best to catch the damn thing.

"Ready?" Kaelynn asked, a huge smile on her face and her hand resting on her belly. My heart felt overjoyed as I watched my best friend with my brother standing next to her. I was so happy to see them filled with so much love and joy.

"One! Two! Three!"

The bouquet seemed to come right my way, but instead, it sailed right over my head. I turned to see who had caught it, only to find Blake behind me with no one else around. He was down on one knee with his hand extended, holding a blue velvet box with the most beautiful diamond ring I had ever seen. My hands went to my mouth, and I cried.

"Morgan Marie Barrett, would you do me the honor of saying yes to becoming my wife?"

My hands dropped to the side, and I reached down, cupping his face with my hands.

"Yes! Nothing would make me happier!"

Blake stood and wrapped me in his arms, lifting me off the floor while he kissed me. The room erupted into cheers all around us.

When he drew his mouth away, I shook my head.

"You little sneak. I had no idea!"

He smiled so big and bright my heart nearly burst from pure happiness.

"That was the plan, princess."

"I love you so much," I said softly, resting my forehead against his.

He held me tighter. "I love you more."

Blake gently set me down and took my hand. He slipped the beautiful oval diamond onto my finger, and I stared down at it. It was set in a white gold band with smaller diamonds running on each side.

"It's beautiful," I whispered.

We were soon engulfed with family and friends hugging and congratulating us. Nash and Kaelynn were last. When my best friend smiled and wrapped her arms around me in a hug, I started to cry.

"You knew?"

She let out a sob of her own. "I did. Blake asked us a week ago if it would be okay to propose to you at the wedding. I'm so happy for you two! You deserve this, Morgan."

Squeezing her tighter, I said, "So do you, Kaelynn."

When we stepped apart, we both dabbed our tears away. Then she looked at me with a serious face and asked in a low voice, "You're not pregnant, are you?"

"What?" I nearly choked out. "No!"

"Not that it would be a bad thing. I mean, I'm over the moon. It's just, sometimes I really wish Nash and I had been able to have a bit more time together, just us. I don't regret anything for a single moment, though. I'm so happy."

"I know you are," I said, kissing her on the cheek. "Are you excited about the honeymoon? I mean, Paris! So romantic."

She blushed and looked past me. Someone or something must have caught her eye.

"What's wrong?" I asked, turning to glance over my shoulder.

"Nothing. I thought I saw someone I didn't know. They must have been in the wrong location."

I didn't see anyone out of place. "Maybe. So come on, tell me what you got Nash for a wedding gift."

She chuckled. "Why is it so important for you guys to know what I got him?"

With a small shrug, I replied, "I made a bet with Terri and Charlie I could get you to tell me. I've got fifty bucks riding on it."

Snarling, Kaelynn shook her head before turning and walking away.

"Seriously? You'd let your best friend down like that?"

"What's going on?" Blake asked.

"Nothing. I was trying to get Kaelynn to tell me what she got Nash for a wedding gift."

"You don't know?" he asked, looking a bit shocked.

"No! She didn't tell me."

Then he looked away.

"Oh my gosh. You know! Blake Greene! You know!"

"I have no idea what you're talking about."

"I'll do anything you want me to do in the bedroom tonight *if* you tell me."

His brow rose. "Anything?"

Leaning in closer, I whispered in a seductive voice, *"Anything."*

"It's a whiskey flask."

My mouth fell open. "That's it? A whiskey flask?"

He nodded. "Yep."

I tilted my head and stared at him. "Wait a minute. You are the only person who knows the sex of the baby."

"And you're saying this because . . . ?"

Pointing to him, I gasped. "Oh my gosh! She knows the sex of the baby!"

Blake pulled me to him and covered my mouth with a kiss.

"Morgan, you're going to ruin her surprise for Nash."

"I'm the aunt! I should get to know."

"Not before Nash and Kaelynn know. It means a lot to her."

I drew back some. "She doesn't know?"

"No. I had it engraved on the flask. Kaelynn hasn't seen it. When I gave it to her it was wrapped already. It was my idea for her to give him that with the baby's sex on it. That way they are both surprised on their wedding night, and it is something they can keep to themselves and tell when they want to tell."

My body felt like I was walking on a cloud as I melted into him. "Lord help me, that was the sweetest thing I think you've ever said."

Blake laughed. "You're easy to please. I sort of figured it would have been my proposal that had you all hot and bothered."

"Oh, trust me, I was already waiting to leave to have sex with you in your car. Now I don't think I'll make it to the car."

A sexy smirk grew across his face. "I can do you one better. I bet we can find a closet."

⁓⁂⁓

ROUNDING THE CORNER, I made my way out of the ladies' room, and I was headed back to the reception when someone stepped in front of me. I froze.

"Jarod?"

He looked upset.

"Don't do this, Morgan."

I swallowed hard. "Don't do what? What are you doing here? How did you know I would be here?"

"It's my job."

My eyes widened in shock. "Your job? Are you doing security at the building?"

He let out a gruff laugh. "Damn, you always were so naïve, Morgan. My job is to look out for you. To take care of you. I knew the first moment I laid my eyes on you that was what I needed to do."

I stood up tall and lifted my chin. "I don't need anyone taking care of me, and if I do need someone, I have Blake."

He shook his head and laughed, but it sounded more like an evil laugh. "Blake? You can't be serious. I've been waiting all this time to make you mine, and all you had to do was be a little patient. You couldn't wait for me."

Taking a step back, I looked past Jarod. Surely Blake would notice it was taking me longer than normal to come back.

"I was never going to be yours, Jarod. We're friends."

"No, Morgan. Don't you see what I did for you? Mike was using you. He didn't love you like I did."

My heart started to race. Blake had been right. Oh, dear God. Blake had been right.

"Jarod, you don't love me."

"I do. The only thing that kept me going all those years were your letters."

"And in those letters did I ever once lead you to believe I was in love with you?"

He paused.

"No, I never did. Jarod, I know how hard it is to adjust to life outside of the army, and I'm someone who you can connect with. Someone who was in your life when you served and someone is a part of your life now that you're out. That doesn't mean we're meant to be together."

He pulled his brows in tight. "I pushed Mike to Lynn though. I started to make a way for us. Then you started dating that Rich guy, but I knew what you were doing. You were trying to forget. Now I'm here. You can learn to love me like I love you, Morgan. Don't you feel it? My love for you?"

Jarod took a step forward, causing me to take a few away. My chest rose and fell as my breathing rate increased. I needed to get Jarod to go back to the reception with me.

"Come away with me now, before you make the biggest mistake of your life."

My eyes met his.

"Jarod, if you truly, deeply cared about me within your heart and soul, you wouldn't ask me to do that."

"Why wouldn't I?"

I tried to keep my voice void of any hint I was scared. "Because you would see that Blake is the man I am in love with. You would be happy that I've finally found someone who makes me feel whole."

It was then I saw Blake. He was standing a few feet behind Jarod.

"Why can't you love me like that?" Jarod asked, his voice cracking.

"It doesn't work that way. We can't force ourselves to love someone when our hearts belong to someone else."

Jarod took a few steps back and dropped his head into his hands. I held up my hand to keep Blake back.

"My God. My God, what am I doing?" Jarod asked as he leaned against the wall and slowly dropped to the floor. "I feel like I'm losing my mind."

My heart broke, and I walked over to Jarod.

"Jarod, have you talked to anyone since you left the army?"

He shook his head.

"You told me once that you had a therapist in the army."

"Yeah, we were forced to talk to him after each mission."

"Did you feel better after talking to him?" I asked.

He looked up at me. "Sometimes."

"Will you do me a favor, as a friend?"

"I'll do anything for you, Morgan."

"Will you go and talk to a friend of mine? He's a therapist, and his office is in Dripping Springs. That's not far from where we are now. If I call him, will you go with him?"

"I'm not going to some psych ward!" Jarod cried out.

"I'm not asking you to. I'm asking you to go and talk to a friend of mine, that's all."

Running his fingers through is hair, Jarod started to cry. Blake walked over and bent down.

"Jarod?"

Dropping his hands, Jarod looked at Blake. "Do you love her? Do you swear on your life you will love her until the day you die?"

Blake nodded. "Yes. To everything."

Jarod swung his gaze back to me. "Fine. I'll talk to him."

I let out the breath I hadn't even realized I had been holding in. Standing, I pulled out my phone and called Larry Morris. He was one of my professors at the University of Texas. It was a small miracle that I had remembered he lived only thirty minutes away. If anyone could help Jarod deal with his mental issues, it was Larry.

Blake and I sat outside with Jarod until Larry pulled up. After talking with Jarod a few minutes alone, Larry informed he felt like Jarod was okay enough to follow him back to his office in Dripping Springs.

"Larry, please take care of him. He's a friend, and I hate seeing him hurt like this."

Taking my hands in his, he smiled. "I promise, if I can't help him, I'll find him someone who can."

"Thank you," I said, giving Larry a quick hug.

As we watched Larry and Jarod walk off together, I leaned into Blake. "I'm so sorry I didn't trust your instinct on Jarod."

Turning me to face him, Blake slowly shook his head. "It's not your fault. Do you understand that, Morgan? You didn't know, and now that you do, you've gotten him the help he needs."

I wiped a tear away. "I know. I just needed to tell you I was sorry I didn't listen to you."

Blake leaned down and kissed me. "Are you okay? Do you want to go back in?"

Pulling in a deep long breath, I smiled. "Yes. I'm okay. For a few minutes, I was scared, but I knew Jarod would never hurt me. He's in good hands, and I don't want to miss out on any more of Nash and Kaelynn's big night. Let's go back in."

I wrapped my arm around Blake's waist, and we walked back in, putting this bit of drama behind us.

An hour later I stood with Charlie and Terri on either side of me as we watched Kaelynn and Nash drive off.

"You're next, Morgan," Charlie said, wrapping her arm around me and pulling me to her.

I was positive I hadn't stopped smiling since Blake had asked me to marry him. Blake never did find a closet, but I wasn't so sure I would have been able to sneak away and have sex during my best friend and brother's wedding reception, anyway.

"Did you ever find out what she was giving him? She was so secretive about it!" Terri said.

Shaking my head, I replied, "She never told me."

Technically it wasn't a lie. Kaelynn didn't tell me, and I still didn't know the sex of the baby.

"Damn, it has to be something good if she's keeping it so hush-hush," Terri said.

"Well, I guess I can focus on you and Blake then. Any idea what you want to do for a wedding?" Charlie asked as we headed back into the building.

"Honestly, I haven't thought about it," I said as we stepped back into the large ballroom. I immediately saw Blake talking to Jim, Terri's husband.

"There's Jim. Let me go see if he's about ready to head on out. I'm exhausted," Terri said.

"Night, Terri!" Charlie and I said as we took turns hugging her.

"Night, ladies. Let's plan a dinner really soon. This time at our place. Jim has a new smoker he is itching to use."

"Sounds good," Charlie said.

We watched as Terri made her way over to Jim and Blake. The fact that this little group from college had all remained friends was refreshing. I hadn't really been a part of their group since I was younger, but I had hung out with them on more than one occasion. Even after Blake left for New York City, they all had stayed in touch.

Charlie nudged me and said, "Blake is a totally different person now that he's with you."

Turning my focus to her, I smiled. "I have a feeling Blake was always this way. He just tried to make everyone think he was something else. Some kind of defense mechanism."

She looked back over to him thoughtfully. "He always came across as a player, ever since I first met him. He certainly had a way of making women fall at his feet. Flirted with me like nobody's business, but I think he did it because he knew Tucker liked me."

I cringed inside just thinking of the women Blake had been with, even though he had told me it wasn't that many. That was in the past though, and it had nothing to do with our future.

Charlie went on as she stared at Blake. "When we were in college he used to volunteer at the battered women's shelter. Did he ever mention that?"

"No, he hasn't," I said with a shake of my head.

Charlie frowned. "He doesn't know I know. I saw him there once when I dropped off some things my sorority had collected for them. I asked the lady in charge how long he had been volunteering there, and she said for at least four years."

"What year of college were y'all in?" I asked, turning my gaze toward Blake. He was still deep in a conversation with Jim.

"Junior year."

"Do you think it has something to do with his mother? He doesn't talk a lot about his past."

I decided to keep the conversation Blake had shared with me, about talking about his mother, to myself.

Charlie looked at me. "Yeah, Blake never was one to really talk about his family. I've met his dad and of course his brother, Dustin."

I nodded. I'd had dinner with them a few times, and both were so kind. But I couldn't help but let my mind wander. "I wonder if that was when he started going to the shelter?"

My mind started spinning with every possible thought. I needed to slow down and not look at this too much. The last thing I ever wanted to do was put my therapist hat on with Blake.

As I watched Blake laugh at something Terri had said, I wrapped my arms around myself to ward off a sudden chill.

"I asked Tucker and Nash about it that day, and they both looked at each other and then changed the subject. I honestly didn't think to press it. When I think back on it though, something passed between them."

"What do you mean?" I asked.

She shrugged. "I don't know, maybe I'm not remembering it the right way, but it was almost like they didn't want me asking questions, and that was why they changed the subject. It's funny, I honestly never thought about it again until just now."

When Blake turned and looked at me, I smiled. He returned the gesture, and my lower stomach tightened with that familiar need for him.

"I'm sure whatever reason Blake had for going, it was something close to his heart."

Charlie bumped my shoulder and said, "I agree. There isn't anything Blake wouldn't do for his friends. I know that much. I think he was lost for a really long time until you came into his life."

"I've been in his life for a while now." I chuckled.

"He's headed this way. I'm going to guess he wants to celebrate the engagement."

I grinned like a silly school girl. "I sure hope so!"

Charlie laughed and gave me a quick hug. "Go have fun! I know Tucker and I plan on it—that is, if Charlotte is a good girl and sleeps all night."

Charlie, Tucker, Terri, and Jim had rented out one of the houses on the ranch for a few days. Blake and I had thought about it but decided we would rather be in our own place. Now I wished we hadn't been so silly.

Blake walked up behind me, and my whole body shivered when he leaned over me and placed his mouth next to my ear. "You ready to leave?"

I nodded. "See you later, Charlie."

Wiggling her fingers at me, she called out, "Bye, kids! Have fun!"

Blake put his arm around me as we headed toward the exit.

"You don't want to say goodbye to everyone?" I asked.

"Nope, I want to get you under me as quickly as possible."

"Well, we have a long drive home."

He looked down at me and smiled. "I booked us a room in the Arc de Texas next door."

My mouth gaped open. "When?"

"After I asked Nash and Kaelynn if it would be okay to ask you to marry me. Luckily, they still had a room open."

"Wow. You've managed to surprise me twice today!"

He winked at me and said, "The day isn't over yet, princess."

Thirty-One

BLAKE

MORGAN WAS PRACTICALLY shaking with excitement when I opened the door to the room I had booked us.

"Blake, this is stunning!"

I smiled as I set down the small suitcase I had packed for us and hidden in my trunk.

"It is, isn't it? It's the Louis XIV suite. I've got us booked for just tonight, but I sort of wish I had booked it for longer. It would be nice just to stay in that bed for the next few nights, admiring that view."

Morgan made her way over to the windows. "Look at the stars. It's breathtaking."

"I packed your swimsuit. We have access to the swimming pool on the roof, and I had the manager stock the kitchen with a few items. I wasn't sure how hungry you would be after the reception."

She turned and faced me, and a single tear made a slow trail down her cheek. My breath caught in my throat, and I rushed across the room to her.

"What's wrong? Why are you crying?" I knew the drama with Jarod would most likely catch up with her. The moment I had seen him in the hallway with her, I'd wanted to beat the shit out of him. But when Morgan gave me the look that said to stay back, I knew I had to let her handle it. And she did handle it, like the amazing woman she was.

"I don't know why I'm surprised you did this. You are the most thoughtful man I've ever known, and the way you love me . . . sometimes, I feel like this is a dream, and I'm praying I won't ever wake up."

I let out a breath and took her face in my hands, relieved that her tears had nothing to do with earlier.

"This isn't a dream, Morgan, and I love you more than I could have ever imagined I would love someone. Every time we're together, I can't stand the thought of leaving you, even for a few hours. All I want to do is show you how much you mean to me."

"Blake," she whispered as she closed her eyes. When she reopened them, I saw that spark that said she loved me as much as I loved her. I didn't doubt for one second that she loved me, but I had been waiting for this very moment. The moment she realized I wasn't going to hurt her like Mike had. I would never hurt her. I needed to always tell her the truth, and that would start with telling her about the night my mother died.

"From the moment you walked up to me that second night in Butch's bar, I knew with all my heart that I would fall head over heels in love with you. I think I knew it that morning I read your note after you brought me home. No one has ever made me feel so loved before, and I hope you know I love you just as much. You are my life. My happiness. The reason I walk around with this smile on my face all the time."

I let out a soft laugh. Morgan raised up and kissed me softly on the lips. When I wrapped my arms around her, we deepened the kiss. Her fingers pushed into my hair where she tugged lightly, causing me to let out a soft moan.

"Marry me, princess."

She giggled and pulled back to look up at me. "I already said yes."

"Right away. Tomorrow. Tonight. Hell, if I thought we could do it this moment I would."

Her eyes widened in shock. "What?"

"I want to make you my wife. Make you mine."

"Blake, I am yours. Forever. That doesn't change whether we're married or not."

Placing my hand on the side of her face, I took in a deep breath, closed my eyes, and slowly exhaled.

"Blake, do you want to tell me what is going on your head? Why all of a sudden is it so important to marry me?"

I took a step back then dragged my hand over my face. "Shit. I'm sorry. I guess I'm worried that if you knew you'd change your mind."

Her eyes widened some. "If I knew what?"

Shit. I hadn't meant to say that. I walked back into the living room and sat down on a sofa. I tried to push away that old familiar sickness that crept up every time I thought about that night.

Morgan sat down on the wooden sofa table and took my hands in hers.

"Sometimes I think back to when only I knew you as Nash's friend. You were so different."

"That was before you."

She smiled. "Charlie said that exact thing earlier this evening."

"I played a part, mostly."

With a nod, she added, "As a way to put up a wall?"

Our eyes met.

"I'm not going to try and get you to tell me what it is you're keeping in, but I know there's something. I went to Butch's place once a year for one reason: to drink away the guilt I felt about Mike killing himself. You go there for a reason, too, don't you?"

I felt my heart hammering in my chest while beads of sweat appeared on my forehead.

"Blake, if this is something you're not ready to talk about, we don't have to."

Shaking my head, I looked away and out into the darkness.

"It was on a night like tonight, unusually warm. I remember hearing my mother on the phone with my father. He was on a business trip. She was telling him about someone she had seen. This guy had frightened her, and she kept asking my dad what she should do. Next thing I knew my father was coming home early, and she told me to call my brother, Dustin, and tell him he needed to get home right away. I had no idea why she was panicking, but at the age of seventeen, I thought she was overreacting."

"Who was the guy?" Morgan asked.

I swallowed hard. "I didn't find out until later, but it was her first husband. Dustin and I never knew our mother had been married before our father."

Morgan pinched her brows in confusion.

I pulled in a deep breath then slowly exhaled. "Let me start at the very beginning. My mother was in an abusive relationship with her first husband for two years. According to my father, the beatings didn't start right away. Not until a few months after they were married. They got worse as time went on. He had beat her so badly one night she ended up in the hospital, where she lost the baby she was carrying. That's where she met my father. He was an intern working that night in the emergency room. He stayed with her the entire night and even after his shift ended."

"That was so sweet of him," Morgan said softly.

"Yeah. When it came time for her to be discharged, she had nowhere to go. The bastard husband of hers was waiting outside the hospital for her. My father took her out another exit and right to the police station, where she filed a restraining order. Then they went to her family's lawyer, where they petitioned to have the marriage annulled. My grandfather eventually paid off the bastard to make him go away and leave my mother alone. Since she needed a place to stay, Dad convinced her to stay with him. My mother had been in medical school before she married, and Dad talked her into going back and finishing. She chose her specialty because of the baby she lost." I looked at Morgan. "She was an OB/GYN. At least, that was what Dad had told Dustin and me."

"When did they realize they were in love?"

I smiled. "Dad says it was the moment he saw her. Something in him changed, and he knew he needed to be with her the rest of his life. To protect her so she would never have to face something like that again. Mom always said she fell in love with him the first night he cooked her dinner. I guess he was exhausted from working all night in the ER, then helping Mom with all of that stuff that day. He even took her to Target so she could buy some things like clothes and toiletries since she only had the clothes she went to the ER in."

"It's so tragically beautiful."

"Yeah, I guess it was. Anyway, Dustin and I never knew any of this. Mom had decided that her past was just that. Her past. Then that day, when she saw the guy she had been married to, she panicked. I begged her to tell me what was wrong. If only she had told me, I would have been able to protect her. She didn't want Dustin and me knowing. Something about being embarrassed she had gotten into such a toxic relationship."

I jerked my fingers through my hair, thinking back to it all. I could have protected her. "If only she had fucking told me."

Morgan reached for my hands and squeezed them. "Do you want to stop talking?"

I out a gruff laugh. "Why stop? I've already put a damper on the night."

She shook her head. "No, you haven't. If you want to keep going, I'm here to listen. If you want to stop, I'm here for you."

Morgan's words left me momentarily speechless. She was the most amazing woman I had ever met, besides my own mother. After my mother died, I had vowed never to let another woman into my heart. But when I saw Morgan, I knew I didn't want anyone else.

"I need to tell you, Morgan. I don't want to hold anything back from you. I don't want anything between us."

"Blake, something like this is not ever going to come between us. This is not a dirty secret you've been hiding that will change the way I feel about you."

"You don't know the whole story, Morgan."

She swallowed when she heard the darkness in my voice.

"Then tell me."

I looked at our hands clasped together.

"Dustin was pissed he had to come home, and I was mad that I had to cancel a date with the girl I had been seeing. Both of us were pretty upset with our mom. Neither of us had any idea why she was acting the way she was. I went to bed early that night, and Dustin snuck out to go to the party. After he was gone, I heard glass breaking, and I bolted out of bed. Then I heard my mother screaming."

When I glanced up, Morgan was fighting back tears.

"I ran to my parents' bedroom, and I saw a man over my mother.

He was punching her while trying to rape her."

"Blake," Morgan whispered.

"I pulled him off of her and started hitting him as hard as I could. My mother was screaming for me to stop, telling me to run, to get away. I just kept fighting him. He was bigger than me—a built son of a bitch. I couldn't get the image of him hitting her out of my head, and I just kept hitting him. He managed to get a good punch in, knocking me back enough to get up and grab my mother again. I stood up, ready to go after him again, but he pulled a knife out and stabbed my mother right in front of me."

Morgan lost her battle, and tears silently fell down her cheeks.

"Then he started to walk away. I ran over to my mom and put my hand over her wound and reached into my father's night stand. I pulled out his pistol and I . . . I . . ,"

"Shh, stop. Blake don't say anything else."

Dropping my head, I let the tears fall. I knew I had to tell her, for my own sanity.

"I yelled for him to stop, and he turned. When he saw the gun, he told me I didn't have the guts to do it. My mother reached up and grabbed my shirt. She said two words to me: do it."

Morgan got up and sat next me. Wrapping her arms around me, I leaned into her. "I shot him, and I didn't think twice about doing it. That's when Dustin walked in and saw what was happening. He rushed over to help me with our mother while he called 911. By the time the ambulance got there, she was gone. She died in our arms."

"Oh Blake, I'm so sorry."

"The last thing she said to me before she took her last breath was *thank you*. She thanked me for killing him, Morgan. She fucking thanked me for killing him."

Thirty-Two

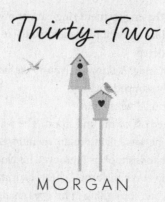

MORGAN

MY MIND HAD barely wrapped around Blake's words when he dropped his head into my lap and cried like I had never seen anyone cry. If I had to guess, this was most likely the only time he's ever allowed himself to properly grieve over the loss of his mother and the knowledge he had taken another's life.

Running my fingers through his hair, I didn't say a word as he lay on me and expelled years of built-up emotions. Had he ever told anyone? Surely he had. He said he was seeing a therapist. Did Nash and Tucker know? Was that why they'd changed the subject when Charlie had brought it up? God, I prayed he had told them. To keep something like this a secret was beyond awful.

I closed my eyes and tried to imagine what that night must have been like for him. Opening them again, I took in a shaking breath. I didn't even want to imagine it.

The air felt as if it had been ripped from my lungs as I remembered his words from earlier. How in the world would he think this would change the way I felt for him? He did it for his mother, who had been brutally beaten and murdered in front him.

My own head dropped as I let my tears fall again. I'd let myself cry now while Blake did, then I vowed to be there for him, in whatever way he needed me to be.

The sparkle of the engagement ring caught my eye, and I stared at it. I'd noticed when Blake gave it to me it looked like an antique ring. My heart raced as I pondered.

Is this his mother's ring? Is this what brought the memory on this evening?

Blake had finally stopped shaking.

"Let me hold you," I whispered.

He slowly pushed off of me and stood. The way he was staring out the window told me he was still lost in the memory of that night. I slowly undressed him. My hands shook as I removed his clothing piece by piece. I traced my fingertips over his broad chest, causing him to inhale. He looked down at me, and something in his eyes changed. He was coming back to me.

"Turn around," he softly said.

I did as he asked. His hands trembled as he unzipped my gown, letting it pool at my feet.

Soft lips touched my shoulder, causing my own breathing to quicken. His hands went to my arms, where he gently rubbed his thumbs over my sensitive skin. I dropped my head back against him and let him do what he needed to do. If it meant I would only hold him tonight, I would gladly do it.

"I want to make love to you, Morgan. Get lost in you and think only about us."

His hands moved to the front of my body, where he caressed me gently. Then he made his way to my breasts while he placed soft kisses on my shoulder and neck.

"Blake."

It was the only thing I could manage to say. This man had a way of making everything else in the world disappear.

I gasped when he pinched one of my nipples as his other hand made its way to my aching core.

"Never in my life did I ever dream someone could make me as happy as you make me."

His whispered words brought tears to my eyes. It was time both of us learned to bury the past and focus on the future.

Our future.

"I love you," I breathed, not able to think coherently enough to find any other words to express my emotions. I was so head over heels in love with my best friend. My lover. Future husband. The man who would be the father of my children.

Turning, I pulled his mouth to mine and kissed him. I poured everything I could into that kiss. I needed him to know how much he meant to me.

"I need you, Morgan."

Lifting me into his arms, he carried me to the massive king size bed and gently laid me down. I moved up to the pillows and watched as his eyes roamed every part of my body.

"You're so beautiful. I don't deserve you."

My hands cupped his face, and our eyes met. "We deserve each other. I'm nothing without you, Blake."

"I'm nothing without you," he replied with a smile tipping at the corners of his mouth.

"Then don't say that ever again. You are who I want to be with the rest of my life. I've never loved anyone like I love you, and with each passing day that love only grows."

Blake stared into my eyes for the longest time before he spoke. "The first time I ever saw you, at Tucker's birthday party, I couldn't keep my eyes off of you. I think I fell in love with you that very moment."

A tear slipped from my eye, and I touched the side of his face. "I didn't think you ever noticed me."

He laughed. "Notice you? I noticed you, princess."

His mouth crashed to mine. I opened myself to him and moaned when I felt him slowly entering me.

Blake pushed in and pulled back, resting his forehead on mine. "Don't ever leave me, Morgan. I don't think I could survive without you."

A rush of warmth filled my entire body from head to toe. I wrapped my arms around Blake and lifted my hips, prompting him to move.

"I'm not going anywhere. I promise you."

We made slow, passionate love. Blake rolled me over so I was in control. I soon trembled from my orgasm. When he gently moved back over me, I swear I thought I had gone to heaven. He was gentle. Slow. Whispering words into my ear. The night couldn't have been any more perfect.

When his body trembled, I knew he was close.

"Come with me again, princess. God, come with me."

Tingles erupted as I felt my orgasm build with his pleas. He moved his hips, and I fell gloriously into a euphoria I never wanted to leave.

◦ঞ৵◦

WHEN I AWOKE to the feel of the bed moving and a soft kiss to my forehead, I peeked one eye open.

"Good morning, princess. I want to show you something."

Smiling, I sat up and yawned. "What time is it?"

"It's six fifteen."

I groaned as Blake pulled me from the bed.

"Lift up your arms."

I did as he asked, and he slipped one of his T-shirts over my head.

When I looked past him out the window, I gasped.

"The sunrise!"

Blake chuckled. "See why I woke you up? I was sitting out here on the patio, and I had to share it with you. It's our first day as an engaged couple."

I swooned inside at how romantic that notion was.

The field in front of us was still covered in wild flowers, casting the most beautiful yellows, blues, reds, and pinks. It was a pathway that led to an orange horizon topped with clouds the color of dark purple and orange.

"I've never seen such a colorful sunrise in my life," I said while Blake wrapped his arms around me and rested his chin on my head.

"I don't think I have either. Tucker and Charlie moved out to the hill country for all the right reasons."

With a giggle, I added, "And that's why Nash and Kaelynn are following in their footsteps."

We stood there, watching and listening to the sounds of birds and wildlife waking up with the sun. It was one of the most peaceful moments of my life. I was in the arms of the man I loved, surrounded by God's beauty.

The sun slowly peeked up over the hills, and night became day.

"It's so peaceful. Even before the sun started coming up, I felt so calm sitting out here. Relaxed like never before."

I lifted my head and looked back at him. "Are you sure that isn't from the two times we made love last night?"

He winked and flashed me a grin that made my knees weak. "I have no doubt that had something to do with it. Just hearing everything, though—the creek running down below, the animals waking up, the wind blowing through the trees—makes me want to stay here longer instead of leaving today."

"I don't have any patients booked next week. We can stay here as long as you want."

Blake's gaze met mine. "We'd be hiding."

"What's wrong with hiding every once in a while?"

"Do you remember once you told me you didn't need me to come in and save you? Just being there with you was what you wanted and needed."

I nodded.

"That's how I feel. A small part of me wants to run again like I ran to New York—run and not ever come back. The bigger part of me wants to start building our life together. I want to design a house with you. I want to start thinking about when we want to have kids. Where we want to live. I don't want to be in a condo in downtown Austin. I want space for your birds and our kids."

Turning in his arms, I watched him as he looked out over the landscape.

"I want to build you birdhouses and bird feeders. I want to get a horse."

"A horse?" I asked with a lighthearted laugh.

He shrugged and looked down at me. "We could have anything we wanted."

My arms wrapped around his neck, causing him to look at me.

"The only thing I want in this world is you. *You*, Blake Greene, make me happier than I have ever been in my life."

He leaned down and picked me up into his arms.

"Let's go take a shower."

My lower stomach pooled with heat. Showers with Blake meant orgasms for me.

Thirty-Three

BLAKE

"I DON'T LIKE the kitchen."

Nash and I exchanged a quick look before I focused back on our client.

"Okay, what don't you like about it this time?"

If she noticed the rough edge in my voice, she ignored it.

"It's all wrong. I mean, how am I supposed to entertain people in a kitchen that small? You need to remove the island."

Mrs. Delany's husband moaned and scrubbed his hand over his face.

"If they remove the island, where are people supposed to sit or put their drinks down? Or their food, for that matter, since they will be in a damned kitchen!"

Nash interjected. "Mrs. Delany, you have the outdoor kitchen as well as the large breakfast area to the side of this kitchen, if you would like for your guests to be close to you while you cook."

Mr. Delany let out a roar of laughter while his wife shot him a dirty look.

"My wife cook? Please. She's never cooked a day in her life. That's why we have to pay for two cooks."

Two cooks? Holy shit. Did they have one each?

This couple had more money than sense. When they came to Venture Architecture, they'd claimed they wanted to build a smaller house now that they were empty nesters. Mrs. Delany's idea of downsizing meant going from twelve-thousand square feet to eight-thousand square feet, and even that was almost too drastic for her liking. Mr. Delany, on the other hand, wanted it to be no bigger than five thousand square feet. We were currently at sixty-five hundred, and she was not happy.

"Why don't you take a day or two to really look over the new plans? What you have to remember is that a majority of the time it will only be the two of you in the house."

Mrs. Delany sighed. "I don't need to look over the plans anymore. It's fine. Just build it."

I turned to Nash and tried like hell not to smile. Barrett Construction was the lucky winner of that bid.

Clearing his throat, Nash forced a smile. "We're not set to break ground until July tenth."

"You can't move that up? You own the company!" Mrs. Delany shrilled.

"No, ma'am. Like I've said before, we have other projects that we're working on, and that is when the foundation crew will be available."

She rolled her eyes and stomped off toward her BMW convertible. Slamming the door, she started the car and peeled out.

The three of us stood there, staring at the retreating sports car.

"How long do think it will be before she notices I'm not with her?" Mr. Delany asked.

Nash and I looked at each other, then back at the car.

"Do you need a ride anywhere, Mr. Delany?" I asked.

He threw his arms up in the air as he yelled, "Don't come back!"

Nash had to turn and walk toward his truck to hide his laughter. I stood next to Mr. Delany and silently tried to figure out why in the world he stayed married to a woman he clearly no longer liked.

"You sure you want to get married, Blake?"

"Yes, sir."

"Pains in the asses, all of them."

I cleared my throat and motioned for him to follow me over to my truck.

"How about that ride?"

"Nah. I'm going to let her get a good bit away before I call her and let her know she left me behind. She'll be back. After all, I'm the guy who has all the money to build this"—he gestured toward the surveyed spot of land—"bullshit of a house."

This time I lost the battle and chuckled.

Nash walked back over and reached his hand out to Mr. Delany. "Sir, it was good seeing you again. Once we get your written approval on the plans, I'll file them with the city. If you'll excuse me, I need to get going. I'm leaving for Utah later this afternoon."

"Utah? What's taking you there?" The older man asked.

"My wife's from there. We are going up for a wedding reception and baby shower."

Mr. Delany smiled. "Well you have a safe trip, and don't worry. I'll get her to sign off on the plans, and it will be in your inbox within twenty-four hours."

Right as he finished speaking, the white BMW pulled up. Mr. Delany turned to me and winked. "She probably tried to stop at a store and realized I wasn't there to pay."

Nash and I both smiled and bid him goodbye. Once they had pulled away, I let out a whistle.

"I think we should go back to building skyscrapers. Fuck this residential shit."

Laughing, Nash hit my back.

"Hey, don't forget I need you to drive me and Kaelynn to the airport. Morgan said she was booked with patients all day."

"Yeah, no worries. What time do you need me to pick you up?"

"Two."

We shook hands and headed to our vehicles. "I'll see you at two."

∽≈∾

KAELYNN WAS PRACTICALLY floating on cloud nine when I picked up her and Nash.

"One suitcase is all y'all have?" I asked, putting into the back of my new truck. As much as I loved my Audi, it wasn't it wasn't exactly a family car. The truck was also better for business, since I was driving more and more to building sites.

"Yep. We travel light," Nash said, winking at Kaelynn.

"So what made you decide to do a shower in Utah? I thought you were going to do it in September here in town?"

"Oh, well, um . . . we're doing that one too. Morgan and my sister Millie are planning this one. I really miss my mom. I think I'm feeling a bit homesick."

Smiling, I watched as Nash held Kaelynn's hand while she climbed into the backseat of the truck.

"Hey, you mind if I drive?" Nash asked, slapping me on the arm and jogging around the front of my truck.

"My truck? My *new* truck? You want to drive my new truck?"

"Yeah! It's not that new anymore, anyway. You've had it a few weeks." He jumped into the driver's seat and buckled up.

"That's still new, Nash."

He looked over at me and grinned.

"Okay, looks like he's driving," I mumbled to myself as I climbed into the passenger seat.

The second Nash pulled away from his driveway, he launched into work talk. Then he turned and went in the opposite direction of the airport.

"Dude, the airport is the other way."

"I have to make a pit stop first."

Staring at him, I laughed. "A pit stop? Where?"

The next thing I knew, Kaelynn was attempting to put a blindfold over my eyes.

"It's a surprise, so you have to cooperate! Please don't take this off, or we'll be forced to tie your hands together."

"What in the fuck?" I said as Nash and Kaelynn both laughed.

"You want to tell me what is going on, dude? I mean if you and your wife are into kinky shit, I am telling you right now, I'm not the guy for the job."

Nash's blow to my stomach caused me to exhale and then cough.

"Asshole. There is no fucking way I would ever let another man touch my wife. And she's pregnant, for shit's sake."

"Hey, you're the one who blindfolded me!" I shouted.

"It's okay, Blake. I promise it will all be worth it. Now, you might as well close your eyes and take a nap. We've got a long drive."

"A long drive? What in the hell is going on, y'all? Oh, come on. If Morgan is throwing me a surprise birthday party, I'm going to kill her."

Nash hit me again.

"Dude! Stop hitting me. I can't see it coming, and it fucking hurts!"

"If my sister wants to throw you a surprise party, you will be surprised. You will like it, and you will tell her how freaking amazing she is for doing it."

I dropped my head back against the seat. "I hate parties."

"It's okay, Blake. It's not a surprise birthday party. Besides, Morgan is at work."

"I'm calling her!" I said, reaching into my pocket and pulling out my phone. "Hey, Siri, call Morgan's work."

Morgan had a landline at her office, so if she was there, she would answer.

"This is Morgan Barrett."

I smiled. I couldn't wait until the day she said Morgan Greene.

"Hey, princess. What are you doing?"

"Hey! Grabbing a quick bite to eat before my next patient comes in. I'm exhausted already. My last patient spent the entire two hours critiquing my paintings. I was ready to pull my hair out."

"Sounds like fun."

"What are you doing? Shouldn't you be picking up Nash and Kaelynn?"

"I did. Nash is driving, and Kaelynn has blindfolded me."

Morgan laughed, but when I didn't join in, she stopped. "Wait. What do you mean?"

"You're not behind this?"

"Me? Why in the world would I have Kaelynn blindfold you?"

"Surprise birthday party?"

There was silence on the other line. "I knew it! You are throwing me a surprise party. Morgan, I hate parties."

"Um . . . when is your birthday? I thought it was in October."

My mouth fell open. "You don't even know when my birthday is? We are engaged! How do you not know when my birthday is?"

"Well, yes. I mean. Oh wait! It's next week! June seventh!"

Sighing, I replied, "June fourteenth. It's in two weeks."

"Oh shit. I'm so sorry, Blake. I'm committing it to memory right now. Listen, I've got to go; my next patient is here. But I hope y'all have fun with whatever it is you're doing! Just don't let them miss their flight! I love you!"

"Wait! Morgan!"

The line went dead.

"Told you it wasn't a surprise birthday party."

"How could my own fiancé not know when my birthday is?"

"Don't feel so bad, Blake. I didn't know it either." Kaelynn said, patting me on the arm.

"Dude, this is going to be epic. Trust me."

"Trust you? You stole my truck, blindfolded me, and threatened to tie me up! You're taking me to an undisclosed location, and you lied about your trip to Utah! That goes for you too, Kaelynn. You are both out of my trust circle!"

Nash laughed. "Epic, dude. Epic. Close your eyes, and take a nap."

I turned to look at him, but all I could see was blackness. "Take a nap? Seriously?"

"Epic."

My head dropped against the seat, and I closed my eyes. "I hate you, Nash."

Thirty-Four

MORGAN

I STARED AT myself in the mirror as Blake talked to me while Charlie attempted to put my hair up in what she called an elegant messy bun. I still wasn't sure there was such a thing, but apparently there was.

Blake was currently giving me his correct birthdate, which I already knew, of course.

"Oh shit. I'm so sorry, Blake. I'm committing it to memory right now. Listen, I've got to go; my next patient is here. But I hope y'all have fun with whatever it is you're doing! Just don't let them miss their flight! I love you!"

I hung up and set my phone down.

My eyes met Charlie's, and we both laughed. "Do you think he knows?"

"No. He bought it. He thinks I'm at work," I replied with a smile.

"You don't think he would suspect you would have your calls forwarded?"

"Nope. He thought it was a surprise birthday party at first, but now he truly sounds confused. Poor guy, I sort of feel bad he thinks I didn't know when his birthday is."

"He'll get over it the moment he sees you."

I focused back on myself in the mirror. Chewing on my lip, I prayed I wasn't doing the wrong thing.

"Do you think he'll be mad?" I asked.

"I wasn't mad when Tucker did it for me. I was over the moon."

"I wish Terri and Jim could have been here," I said.

Charlie leaned down and put her face next to mine. "I know how much you wanted them here."

Terri and Jim had taken a family vacation with Jim's parents to Europe. They were supposed to be back two days ago, but Jim had jumped off a wall in Rome and landed wrong. He broke his ankle and ended up needing surgery. They missed their flights back and wouldn't be heading home for another week.

"What terrible luck," I said.

Charlie went back to putting small white flowers in my hair.

"There. I think we're done. Do you like it?" Charlie asked with a wide smile on her face.

"I love it. I can't believe I'm doing this. I am surprising Blake with a wedding."

There was a knock on the door that caused me to jump. Charlie called out, "Come in!"

I looked through the mirror and saw Rick.

"Everything is ready down in the cave. I think you should get dressed so we can start making our way down nice and slow."

With a nod, I smiled. "Thank you so much, Rick, for helping me do this all so last minute."

"It's my pleasure."

It had been so last minute that even my parents weren't there. It was the only day we could get the cave with the busy summer season. My folks were on vacation, Blake's father was at a medical conference, and Dustin had gone out of town with his girlfriend to her brother's wedding.

"It's time to get dressed!" Charlie called out. "Kaelynn called, and they're thirty minutes out! Apparently Blake is livid and is accusing them of driving around in circles to throw him off."

I laughed as Charlie approached with the bag that held my dress in it.

Twenty minutes later I stood in front of the mirror in Rick's office, staring at myself in my wedding dress.

My. Wedding. Dress.

I smiled and met Charlie's gaze in the mirror.

"Morgan, you look beautiful."

I lifted my gown and revealed the special-order sneakers Charlie had gotten me. They were covered in crystals.

"Thank you for these. They're perfect!"

We giggled. I turned around and looked at the room we were in. Rick had transformed his office into a dressing room for us. When Kaelynn and Nash got here with Blake, he would use this room to change into the tux I had brought.

With a sigh, I said, "Well, it's almost time. I really hope Blake doesn't get upset."

Charlie kissed me on the forehead. "He's going to so happy that you were so excited to marry him you made it happen. And in a place that means something to him."

I nodded as the nerves settled in slightly.

"Come on, let's get going so we don't risk Blake seeing you."

I nodded. "Are the bouquets already down there?"

"Yep. Between Tucker and Rick, everything has been taken care of. "Are you ready? Nervous at all?" Rick asked.

"I'm not the least bit nervous."

They both raised a brow.

"Okay, I am a little nervous. Mostly because I'm worried about Blake's reaction."

Charlie wrapped her arm around mine, and we made our way through the lobby toward the cave.

"It's normal to be nervous. This whole relationship has been a whirlwind for you both. But I see the way Blake looks at you. I saw it months ago that night at the dinner party at my house. The man is head over heels in love with you. You're wearing his ring."

I focused on the beautiful diamond ring on my finger. It had been Blake's mother's ring, and it meant so much to him—and now to me.

"I can't wait to be his wife."

Giggling like two high school girls, we lifted our dresses and made our way to the cave entrance where Rick waited to let us in and walk us down.

"I don't think we've ever done a wedding where the groom walks down to the bride!" he said with excitement in his voice.

"First time for everything, Rick!" Charlie said as I took in deep breaths. My excitement and nerves were beginning to comingle, and I wasn't sure which one would win.

When I walked into the cave's main cavern, I gasped at the sight before me. Rick and Tucker had candles and small bouquets of flowers placed around the cavern, and the lights the most breathtaking shadows. It was so romantic looking I was overcome with emotion.

"I'm speechless. I remembered it being beautiful down here, but this is . . . it's so . . ."

My eyes burned with the threat of tears.

Charlie wrapped her arm around me. "Do not cry. I'm already stressing about your hair down here in this cave! I can't deal with makeup issues!"

Laughing, I dabbed at the corners of my eyes.

Tucker gave me a hug. "Are you happy with everything?"

I looked around the large open area of the cave, taking it all in. At the end of the open cavern was an archway that was covered in the most beautiful array of flowers I had ever seen. Candles outlined the area where Blake and I would stand and exchange our vows.

"It's all so beautiful. You guys did such a great job."

Glancing over to Charlie, Tucker's smile grew wide. "I wish Rick and I could take the credit, but Charlie and Kaelynn came here a week ago and took pictures. They got with the florist and worked out all the details.

I turned to face Charlie. "Y'all did that for me?"

She nodded.

Now the tears did come, and there was nothing I could do to stop them.

"No! No, no, no! Do not cry! Hanky! Stat!" Charlie cried out.

"They're here!" Rick said as he rushed past the three of us and headed out of the cave. Right then the pastor from the church I had grown up in made his way into the cavern with one of the park employees.

"Well, I have to say I've married people in some pretty cool places, but a cave is the first for me." He wore a smile, but it dropped when he saw me crying.

"Morgan, sweetheart."

"I'm okay, honestly. I feel so loved right now."

Pastor Cole wrapped me up in his arms. "You are loved, my dear. Now, take a deep breath."

I did as he said.

Charlie had magically pulled a compact from somewhere in her dress and was dabbing it around my eyes.

"Thank God for waterproof mascara," she said.

"Amen," Pastor Cole added.

The park employee cleared her throat. "I'm going to go on up to walk your other bridal party member down."

"Thank you so much," I said, pulling myself together. This was it. Kaelynn was on her way down, and Blake would be right behind her.

What if this was too fast? We hadn't even talked about the wedding yet. Hadn't set a date. Maybe he wanted a long engagement. Or a big wedding. I hadn't even thought that it might be important to Blake to have his father and brother here. Then I remembered the night of our engagement. Blake wanted to run off and elope. The memory calmed my nerves some.

"I can't wait to see Blake's face when sees you!" Charlie said, excitement filling her voice as she and Tucker exchanged a loving glance.

My hand came up to my throat as I tried to smile and ignore my racing heart.

Oh no. What have I done?

Thirty-Five

BLAKE

NASH WAS LEADING me into a building as Kaelynn whispered something to someone behind me.

"Nash, I'm going to go on in," she said a moment later.

"Okay, I'll see you in a few."

"What in the hell is going on, Nash? I'm tired of this game."

A door shut, and the blindfold came off.

Glancing around the room, I pulled my brows in when I saw Rick. "Rick?"

"Blake," he replied.

I turned and looked at Nash. He was smiling from ear to ear. "You're surprising me with a cave tour? Kaelynn can't do a tour. She's pregnant."

Nash laughed. "Dude, we're going on a different sort of adventure."

Now my interested was piqued. "All right. I'm listening."

"I need you to get dressed."

Glancing down to the jeans and T-shirt I had on, I lifted my gaze back to Nash. "I am dressed."

"In this." He held up a bag. "Your tux is in here."

I laughed. "My tux? What in the hell kind of adventure are we going on?"

"One where your future bride is waiting down in the caves for you to marry her."

Tilting my head, I let out a disbelieving chuckle. "What did you say?"

Nash placed his hand on my shoulder and said, "Morgan made all the arrangements for the two of you to get married today. Down in the caves."

My mouth dropped open. "Married? Today?"

For the first time since my blindfold had come off, Nash's smile faltered.

"You do want to marry my sister, don't you?"

"Of course I want to marry her. I wouldn't have asked her if I didn't. It's just, I wasn't expecting to marry her *today*."

Nash took a step back. "I see. Well, this is a bit awkward, because she's down there with Kaelynn, Charlie, Tucker, and the pastor of our church, waiting to marry you."

My hand jerked through my hair, and I started to pace across the office.

Morgan had planned a wedding. A wedding.

"I think I'm going to step outside for a minute or two," Rick said, hitting me on the back and then walking out the door, quietly shutting it behind him.

Nash tossed the suit bag onto the chair and folded his arms across his chest. I could feel the heat of his stare on me, but I needed a moment to process everything.

"Listen, if you don't want to marry her—"

"I do want to marry her, Nash."

"Fine. Then you don't want to marry her today. I'm not going to be the one to go down there and break my little sister's heart. You're going to have to do that."

Stopping my pace, I faced him. "What?"

Nash looked pissed, and I couldn't blame him. I was sure it looked like I wasn't wanting to marry Morgan, when in fact I was trying to figure out what to do about the wedding plans I had quietly started making for us.

"You are going to have to go down there and tell her you don't want to marry her today."

I laughed. "Nash, hold on a second. Give me a moment to process all of this. You just told me I'm getting married."

"And if you really wanted to marry her like you said, you'd be jumping into the tux and running down there."

"And I will. Dude, I've been talking to a wedding planner up in Canada. I wanted to take Morgan to Canada this fall to a hotel I went to growing up as a kid. They decorate up for Christmas—they go all out, with trees everywhere—and I had this great idea about getting married surrounded by trees and lights. I know how much she loves Christmas, and I figured she would love it. I thought maybe we would have a small ceremony up there. About the only thing we've talked about is we want it to be small. Close friends and family only."

Nash stood there staring at me. "You were planning a wedding already?"

"Yes. I wanted to do something special for her. This place has a special place in my heart, and it's like someone puked Christmas all over it just for her. Then she did this for me."

"Are you upset?"

The back of my eyes burned with the threat of tears. "Upset? God no. I'm stunned, actually."

"Stunned?"

"Nash, your sister is the most selfless person I've ever met. She knows how much caving means to me, why I started doing it in the first place, and she's doing this for me." I hit my chest as my voice shook. "She's doing this for me. This should be her day."

Nash placed his hand on my shoulder and gave it a squeeze. "She's doing it for you because she loves you, Blake."

My chest ached in the most beautiful way. No words would ever be able to say how much I loved Morgan. None.

"I love her, Nash. I honestly have loved her from the first moment I saw her."

He smiled. "Then get that tux on, and let's get down there."

"What about Canada?"

His smile grew wider. "Make that your honeymoon and surprise her with a second ceremony. Just for the two of you."

I nodded. "That's a damn good idea."

"Well, I tend to have those pretty often. Isn't that why you went into business with me?"

Laughing, I pulled him in for a hug.

"Come on, let's get you hitched."

⁓⁂⁓

NASH, RICK, AND I made our way down to the entrance of the cave. My hands were shaking so badly I had to stop for a moment and get my emotions under control. Rick and Nash waited patiently for me before we made our way down. Rick pulled up his walkie-talkie. "ETA, one minute."

"You ready?" Nash asked before we came up to the entrance of the large cavern room where I would be getting married.

"Never been more ready."

The moment I saw her, I felt the tears building in my eyes. Morgan smiled, and everything else faded away. All I saw was this beautiful vision in white waiting for me. Her gown hugged every curve of her body. Her hair was up with little pieces hanging down to frame her gorgeous face. I could practically see her blue eyes sparkling as she watched me approach. She was stunning, and she took my breath away. I walked to her, silently praying with each step that my legs wouldn't give out.

When I finally made it to her, she giggled. "Surprise!"

Leaning in, I kissed her on the lips. "You got me, you little sneak."

"I owed you one."

"It looks beautiful down here."

Morgan nodded. "I thought it would be the perfect place for us to start our life together."

Cupping the side of her face with my hand, I replied, "I agree. Thank you."

Pastor Cole, whom I had met a few times when I went to church with Morgan and her family, cleared his throat. "Are we ready to begin?"

"Yes," Morgan and I said together.

For the next ten minutes or so, I stood there, holding the hands of the only woman I had ever loved. The woman I knew my mother would have adored. The woman who would someday bring me my own children to love. The woman I would spend the rest of my life keeping safe and happy.

"You may now kiss your bride," Pastor Cole said.

The moment was perfect.

I cupped Morgan's face in my hands and leaned down. Before I kissed her, I whispered, "I love you, Mrs. Greene."

Tears slipped free and slowly made trails down her cheeks.

"I love you too, Mr. Greene."

Thirty-Six

MORGAN
FOUR MONTHS LATER—OCTOBER

KAELYNN PLACED HER daughter, Emma, into my arms and took a step back. I tried to understand this intense feeling that was racing through my body as I stared down at the sleeping baby.

"What's it like being a dad?" Blake asked Nash.

"It's the most amazing thing in the world. I mean, I thought I was happy when Kaelynn and I got married. Along came Emma Rose, and I honestly feel like my life is complete now. I am the happiest son of a bitch on the planet."

I grinned as I looked up and caught Kaelynn gazing at her husband with a look of pure love. Then I looked over to Blake, who was now watching me as I held Emma. He smiled, and my stomach jumped. It amazed me how this man could still make me feel like a lovesick girl with just his smile or a simple touch of his hand.

"She's so beautiful. I cannot believe I'm an aunt. It hasn't really sunk in yet!" I said before leaning in and smelling Emma once more. She smelled like a lavender cloud.

"Want to hold her, Blake?" Kaelynn asked.

"I'd love to hold her. She needs to start bonding with her favorite uncle."

Nash laughed. "Dude, between you, Jim, and Tucker, this kid is not going to want for anything."

"What? I limited myself to one gift." Blake said as Kaelynn placed Emma into his arms. The moment he started talking baby talk to Emma, my ovaries went into overdrive. A signal was sent to my brain that screamed I wanted a baby. Sooner rather than later.

Kaelynn must have sensed it, because she whispered, "Does that make you want one?"

I nodded. "Yes. It's like babies let out some secret magic dust the moment you hold them. A magic that says, 'Go now and reproduce so I have a cousin my age to play with.'"

We giggled. Blake didn't notice the whispering. He was to tied up in rocking Emma back and forth in his arms.

"She's so beautiful," he said, running his finger over her soft cheek.

I stared at Blake as he stood there, completely lost to a little girl who only weighed seven pounds and two ounces.

"If she has Blake this smitten, I can't imagine what it's like for Nash," I said with a wide grin.

"Oh, she has me wrapped around her little finger already," my brother admitted. "I swear I almost cry every time she looks up at me with those big blue eyes."

Blake laughed. "Pussy."

"Language around the baby!" Kaelynn said.

Nash and Blake both turned to Kaelynn and stared at her.

"Kaelynn, I seriously doubt your child understands bad words. Besides, Nash swore earlier, and you didn't say anything."

She placed her hands on her hips. "Well, if you get used to saying bad words around her now, you'll do it when she is older. So no bad words, Uncle Blake. That goes for Daddy too."

Emma opened her mouth and yawned, causing both Nash and Blake to gush over her. The two of them showered her with attention.

I followed Kaelynn into the kitchen as Nash and Blake discussed what Emma's first sport would be.

"Wow. The power that little girl holds over those two is unbelievable."

Kaelynn nodded. "Tell me about it. She has no idea now, but I believe she will never be able to do wrong in Nash's eyes. Do you know I found him standing over her bassinet the other night just staring at her? I asked him what he was doing and he said he wanted to be near her, in case she needed him."

I put my hand to my heart and sighed. "That is the sweetest thing ever."

She smiled and replied, "I know. I nearly melted into a puddle on the floor I swooned so hard. I see why people have babies back to back. I get turned on just watching him with her. I'll be cleared for sex again in six weeks, and I am counting down."

Snarling, I said, "Too much information. Ugh."

With a shrug, she replied, "It's true. There is something very sexy about a man loving on a baby."

I peeked back out into the living room. Nash was asking for Emma back, and Blake wouldn't give her to him.

"Or two men arguing over a baby."

Kaelynn turned to look at them.

"Dear God. You better have sex with that man the moment you can."

I giggled. "Trust me. I intend to."

Kaelynn and Nash took turns giving me a kiss and hug goodbye.

"We'll be back in a few days to visit," I said as I waved at them before slipping into Blake's Audi.

The moment we pulled away, I turned to him. "We need to have sex. Soon. Like, maybe you could pull over somewhere."

He looked at me like I had lost my mind. Then he laughed.

"No, Blake, I'm serious. I'm horny as hell. I think the baby gives off some sort of hormone that women of childbearing age absorb. I need you. Now."

Still looking forward as he drove, a smirk spread across my handsome husband's face. "So you need to be fucked?"

"Yes. Please. Quickly."

"Morgan, where in the hell do you want me to go?"

I looked around. "A side road?"

Blake laughed. "A side road? I guess we can add that to the list of places we've made love."

Heat radiated through my chest, and I was left breathless. I loved that he had referred to all of our times together as making love. That was exactly what it was, each and every time.

"I love you."

The words spilled from my lips without even a thought.

Blake pulled over to the side of the road and put his car in park. He turned to me, taking my hand in his. When he brought it up to his mouth and kissed it, I nearly melted on the spot.

"I love you more, Morgan. Tell me what's on your mind."

I chewed on my lip and looked down at our hands. "It was just seeing you with Emma. It turned me on."

His finger went to my chin and lifted it so our eyes met. "And?"

"And I think I want to start trying for a baby. Unless you think it's too soon."

The way he smiled had me daring to hope he wanted that too.

"I don't think it's too soon. I was going to surprise you with this, but I can't keep it to myself anymore. It's time we went our honeymoon. You know how I told you to keep that week in November free?"

I nodded.

"I'm taking you to Canada. There's a hotel there that we used to go to every year. I loved it there, and it was one of my mother's favorite places. I want to take you."

"Blake, I would love to go."

He winked. "Good, because I already bought the plane tickets and booked the hotel."

Laughing, I unbuckled and leaned over so I could kiss him.

"Do you have any idea how happy you make me?"

"I hope really happy."

"Really, *really* happy."

He winked and kissed me on the nose. "Two reallys? Damn, I'm doing something right."

"Yes, you are. Now let's go home so you can make love to me."

"What about the starting the family thing? Should we start now?

What about your practice?"

I swallowed hard. "I've been thinking about how it would work with my practice. There's a girl I went to school with who's also a wonderful painter. She has been working for a nonprofit and is ready to leave and start building up her own practice. The thing is, she only wants to work part-time. I'm still not carrying a fulltime load, but my practice is growing. I think bringing her on and having her start would be perfect. Once the baby came, I could work the days I want to, and Natalie could work when she wants."

"You've talked to her about this?"

I looked down sheepishly. "I wasn't trying to plan something behind your back, I swear."

"I know that."

Glancing back up to meet his gaze, I blew out a breath. "You're growing your business with Nash, and I truly love what I'm doing. But I also want to be there with the baby, so I think for now I would like to keep working on my practice and maybe in a few years consider pulling back even more."

"You wouldn't give it up, would you?"

"No. I don't think so. I love it. But I see what an amazing job Charlie does balancing work and motherhood. I know I could do that too, but I'd like to leave the door open for possibly just being mommy and wife."

Blake placed his hand on the side of my face. His thumb swept lightly over my cheek. "You know I will support you in whatever you decide to do. Even if you want to change one of the rooms in your office to a nursery and hire a nanny so the baby can be there while you work."

I stared at him, letting his words sink in fully. "You would do that?"

"Of course I would. There isn't anything I wouldn't do for you, Morgan."

"Thank you for loving me like you do, Blake."

His mouth curved up into a gentle smile. "This is just the beginning, princess."

Thirty-Seven

BLAKE
ONE MONTH LATER

MY HANDS WERE sweating as we got out of the rented SUV and headed into the hotel. My nerves had been shot the last week while I tried to plan everything and keep it from Morgan, all while acting like this was just a delayed honeymoon.

"Blake, this is beautiful! Everything is decorated for Christmas!"

The excitement in Morgan's voice eased some of my nerves. I pulled out my phone and sent Kaelynn a text.

> Me: *You arranged for the dress to be here, right?*

She responded almost instantly.

> Kaelynn: *OMG! YES! And the shoes. Will you stop worrying! It's going to be beautiful, Blake. She's going to be over the moon.*

I let out a sigh of relief.

Why in the hell am I so nervous? It isn't like we aren't married already.

> Me: *Thank you, Kaelynn. I couldn't have done this without you.*
>
> Kaelynn: *No, you couldn't have! Have fun!*

As we walked up to the check in, Morgan spun around in a circle, taking everything in.

"Hello, are you checking in?"

"Yes, for Blake Greene."

The woman smiled bigger, taking a second to look at Morgan and then me.

"Yes, Mr. Greene. Thank you so much for staying at the Fairmont. We have you booked in our Royal Suite."

Morgan walked up next to me. "That sounds fancy!"

The clerk gave Morgan a polite smile. "It's one of our grandest suites. You'll be very comfortable there."

"Thank you so much," I said, wrapping my arm around Morgan's waist as we waited for the check-in process to finish up.

"Here is your room key. All of your requests have been taken care of as well, Mr. Greene."

Smiling, I replied, "Thank you so much. And the packages that were sent?"

I could feel Morgan looking at me.

"They're in your suite as requested."

"Thank you."

"It's a pleasure seeing you again, sir."

As we walked toward the elevator, Morgan pulled me to a stop.

"Do you own the hotel too?"

I laughed. "No! Why do you think that?"

"All your requests, your packages. Sir. I'm having a déjà vu. You're not going to pull me into a dark corner and make out with me, are you?"

"I believe we did a little more than make out."

Her cheeks flushed. "Yes, we did."

Although I wasn't an owner, what Morgan didn't know was my father owned 50 percent of the hotel. When it had gone up for sale a few years back, he and another business partner bought it.

"Come on, let's get up to our room and get settled. You'll love the suite. It's the same one my family and I always stay in when we come here."

As we stepped onto the elevator, she reached for my hand. "When was the last time you were here?"

"Maybe three years or so ago. Dad has always tried to make time for the three of us to come up as much as possible. I think it's his way of staying close to Mom. Keeping the memories alive."

"That's so sweet. Does Dustin come up here on his own too?"

"No. This is actually the first time I've been here without Dad and Dustin."

"Really?"

"Yep."

She squeezed my hand. "Thank you for bringing me."

We got off on the top floor and made our way to the suite. When we walked in, Morgan gasped.

"Blake! This is not a room! This is a small apartment. How big is this place?"

Laughing, I gave the bellhop a tip and shut the door.

"I don't know. I've never asked."

Morgan squealed when she saw the Christmas tree.

"Blake! They have a tree in here!"

"Per my request."

She spun around and stared at me, her mouth agape. "Oh my gosh. You had them put a tree in here for me?"

"I know how much you love Christmastime."

Her eyes filled with tears, but she fought to hold them back. Rushing over to me, she threw herself into my arms. Our mouths crushed together in a hot and needy kiss.

"Make love to me."

"Your wish is my command."

It didn't take us long to shed our layers of clothing. I grabbed the blanket from the back of the sofa and spread it out in front of the gas fireplace along with a few throw pillows. The staff had already started the fire and turned on the Christmas tree.

Morgan laid back as I lowered myself over her warm body. Her legs wrapped around me, pulling me to her as I positioned myself at her entrance.

"No foreplay this evening, Mrs. Greene?"

"We have plenty of time for that over the next week, right now I need you inside me."

"Let me make you come first."

Moving my hand between us, I found her sweet spot and rubbed it while I teased her with my cock.

"Blake," she gasped, lifting her hips in anticipation. "Oh God. Blake. Blake!"

She shattered into an orgasm as I pushed inside her.

"Yes," she cried out, wrapping her arms and legs around me, holding on to me as if she thought I might leave her.

Never.

"Morgan, you feel so good."

Her hips moved with mine, and it didn't take long before she was squeezing around me, coming again.

"I'm going to come," I whispered against her ear, spilling myself into her and wondering if this would be the time she got pregnant.

Leaning over on my elbows, I dragged in a few deep breaths as Morgan looked up at me.

"Why does it always feel like the first time?"

I rubbed my nose with hers. "I don't know, but my goal on this trip is to get you pregnant."

Her cheeks flushed, and she wore the most beautiful smile.

"Right now though, it's time to get up and into a shower. We have somewhere to be at nine."

Morgan's smile faded as she let me help her up.

"Where?"

"It's a surprise," I said as I scooped her up into my arms and carried her up the winding staircase to the bathroom.

"Oh my goodness. Blake, this place is amazing."

"It is. And it's ours for the week."

Setting her down in the large bathroom, I turned on the water to the shower.

"If it were up to me, we wouldn't leave this suite. I would stay naked the entire time."

Lifting my brows, I replied, "As tempting as that sounds, I have too many places I want to show you. Let's get cleaned up."

After cleaning up in record time, I slipped out of the shower while Morgan washed her hair. I wrapped the towel around my waist and walked into the bedroom. When I opened the closet, I couldn't help the way my chest squeezed at the sight before me.

Fighting back the emotion, I reached out and touched the satin fabric. Attached to the hanger was a note. Taking it off, I read it.

Blake,

I know your mother is with you and Morgan this week, and I know she would be honored to have Morgan wear her dress. I want you to surround yourself with all the amazing memories we made up on that mountain. Take Morgan to Scoops and Hoops for their famous chocolate fudge brownies. Be sure to stop and eat at Bernies□you know how much your mother loved their hamburgers. And remember Mom□s rule: you have to eat in the hotel restaurant at least once.

I also want you and Morgan to make new memories, Son, but never forget the ones we made there as a family. Simply add to your stockpile.

Someday I hope we□ll all being heading up there with your own children to make a whole new set of memories.

Congratulations, Blake. Kiss Morgan for me.

I love you, Son.

Dad.

I folded the note and set it on the dresser next to me. Looking back at the gown, I drew in a shaking breath and closed my eyes.

"I miss you, Mom, but I know you're here with me."

The sound of the water turned off, alerting me that Morgan was finished. I took out my mother's wedding dress and shut the closet doors some, hanging it over the top of one. I opened my suitcase and took out the pair of Jimmy Choos Charlie insisted I buy for Morgan. The small black pouch my father had delivered along with the wedding dress sat on the bed. I opened it and took out the pearl necklace and diamond drop earrings I had bought specifically for this day.

"There is a view from every window! I mean, everywhere I look I see—"

Morgan stopped talking when she walked into the bedroom. There was a large set of windows behind me, showcasing yet another view.

"Wow. Look at that sunset! Look at those colors!"

I smiled and walked up to her. "Will you close your eyes for me?"

She did as I asked.

"Another surprise?" she asked, a slight giggle slipping through.

"Yes," I replied, guiding her over to stand in front of the dress.

Leaning down, I placed my mouth at her ear and whispered, "Open your eyes, princess."

The moment she did, she leaned back against me, her hands coming up to her mouth.

"Will you do me the honor of marrying me again this evening?"

Morgan stood there, staring at the dress. Then her body started to shake, and I knew she was crying. Turning her to face me, I gently pulled her hands away from her mouth.

"Happy tears?"

Her chin trembled as she said, "Blake, that's your mother's gown."

Shock hit me as I took a step back. "How did you know that?"

"You have their wedding picture on your mantel. I've looked at a million times. I know that dress."

I looked past her to the dress, and I smiled before focusing back on Morgan.

"Well, aren't you a perceptive little thing?"

She shook her head. "I never even thought you might want me to wear her dress for our wedding. I'm so sorry."

"What? God, no, Morgan. The day we got married I told Nash I was already looking at possibly coming here during the holidays to get married. I hadn't mentioned it to you yet. I know how much you love Christmastime, and in my mind, I imagined you getting married surrounded by snow-covered mountains, with lights and tress everywhere."

"Oh Blake," Morgan said.

Shit. I wasn't making this any better.

"I loved our wedding, Morgan. I loved that you did that for me, in a place that had meaning behind it. Now I want to do same for you. I want to give you the wedding you dreamed about when you were a little girl."

Her eyes widened in shock. "How do you know?"

Smiling, I pulled her to me. "Kaelynn told me that when you were little, you dreamed of getting married with snow falling all around you and Christmas trees everywhere. You selfishly gave up your wedding for me, so now I'm giving it back to you. It was my father's idea to have you wear Mom's dress."

Another tear slipped free. Lifting my hand, I wiped it away with my thumb.

"So, will you do me the honor?"

She laughed and let out a sob at the same time. "Yes! I'd marry you a hundred times if you asked me to."

Kissing her softly on the lips, I took a step back. "I have a wedding present for you."

"What? Blake, you've already—"

I placed my finger to her lips and shook my head. "Let's get dressed, and then I'll give it to you."

Morgan turned and looked at the dress. "I'll need help."

"I'll help you."

Morgan threw herself into me, wrapping her arms tightly around my neck.

"Why do you do all these amazing things for me?"

Pulling her tighter against me I replied, "Because I love you, Morgan Greene."

She pushed back and then did a few happy little hops and spins. "Oh my gosh! I need to do my hair! And put makeup on!"

Then she disappeared.

Exactly one hour and twenty minutes later, I put the pearls around her neck as she stood in front of the mirror in my mother's gown. It looked beautiful on her and fit her like a glove—again, thanks to Kaelynn for giving my father the measurements from Morgan's June wedding gown.

"One more thing."

Her hands were on her stomach as she watched me in the mirror. "Blake, the necklace is enough. I never even knew there was a such a thing as blue pearls. I love how they make my eyes—"

She stopped talking when I opened the next jewelry box.

"Are those?" her eyes snapped up to meet my gaze.

"Blue diamonds."

Morgan's hand slapped over her mouth as she said, "Blue diamonds!"

"They are rare and precious, just like my wife."

Morgan cupped my face in her hands and lifted up to kiss me.

"Blake Greene, you are precious. More precious than any rare gem, and you are mine."

The knock on the suite door pulled my attention away. Stepping back, I asked, "How do I look? My tux okay?"

"You look so handsome I'm already looking forward to slowly peeling it back off of you."

Wiggling my brows, I kissed her and then headed out of the room quickly to answer the door. Opening it, I saw Greg, the manager of the hotel, standing there with a wide smile on his face.

"Mr. Greene, we are ready for you and your wife."

"Perfect. The flowers?"

"Ready."

"The trees?"

"All lit up like you asked."

Turning, I saw Morgan descending the stairs. I could not believe this stunning creature was mine.

I cleared my throat and said, "My God. She takes my breath away."

"She is very beautiful, indeed. You are a lucky man, sir."

Without taking my eyes off of her, I nodded. "Yes, I am."

"So, are we ready?" Morgan asked, a hint of pink on her cheeks.

The blue diamonds and pearls made her eyes stand out even more against the white satin dress. She was the most stunning thing I had ever laid eyes on.

"Is it possible to fall in love all over again, Greg?" I asked.

"I believe it is indeed possible, sir."

Morgan winked and took my offered arm.

"Where are we going?" she asked as I grabbed the key to the suite and we followed Greg.

"To your winter wonderland, my lady."

Morgan smiled. "I feel like a princess."

"You look like a queen."

Leaning in closer, she spoke so only I could hear her. "If you're trying to get lucky, you already had that in the bag with the Jimmy Choos."

I tossed my head back in laughter. I was going to have to thank Charlie for that one.

Soon we were being whisked down the elevator and through the lobby of the hotel. People stopped and stared at Morgan as we walked by.

"Congratulations," one couple said as we passed them.

"Thank you," Morgan and I answered at the same time.

We stopped at the door, and the same girl who checked us in stood there with a white blanket for Morgan.

"You'll need this, Mrs. Greene."

Morgan looked up at me. "What in the world are you up to?"

"You'll see."

As we walked out of the hotel, a horse drawn carriage waited for us. The slight amount of snow that was falling made it look even more romantic. That one was on mother nature.

"Blake! Oh my gosh! You didn't!" Morgan said, rushing ahead of me and walking right up to the horse.

"It seems your wife is rather taken with horses, sir," Greg stated.

"I guess so."

"Mrs. Greene," I said, holding out my hand for her.

"Mr. Greene."

Once we were both in the carriage, I pulled her to me and draped the wool blanket over us. The ride to the area where we would be renewing our vows wasn't far. And thank goodness, because it was freezing out.

As we turned the corner, Morgan gripped my arm.

"Blake Greene! What have you done?"

The sight before us was exactly how I had hoped it would be. A clear tent was set up, and all you could see were Christmas trees and lights strung up everywhere inside it.

"I remembered when I was younger, there was a wedding here. They had a clear tent set up so you could still see the mountains. I knew it would be dark out, but with the moon full, you can see the mountains perfectly tonight."

Morgan wiped a tear away.

"I don't have words. It's all so beautiful."

The carriage came to a stop, and I helped Morgan out by lifting her. I gathered up the dress, and we walked down the blue carpet and into the tent.

"It's warm in here!" she exclaimed.

"Thank God, my balls were freezing."

Hitting me on the arm, Morgan rolled her eyes.

"I've never seen . . . this is . . . I can't believe . . ."

Morgan walked further into the tent and spun in a circle, taking in every single detail. I loved that she did that. When she was excited or trying to take a scene in, she spun around in a circle.

She walked up to one tree and lightly touched the ornaments.

"This must have cost you a small fortune, Blake. You shouldn't have."

"I should have. Is it like you envisioned when you were little?"

Her eyes sparkled from the cast of all the lights surrounding us.

"It's everything and more. Thank you."

Leaning in, I kissed her on the lips. "Let's renew our vows, shall we?"

Thirty-Eight

MORGAN

I WAS IN a wonderland of sparkles and snow, with a light shower falling as Blake and I renewed our vows. It was just the two of us surrounded by Christmas trees that were decorated so beautifully I almost felt as if I were in a dream. He'd made everything perfect. Right down to my bouquet of anemones and stephanotis. The red and white in the flowers paired with the greenery to make a gorgeous bouquet. My mind was swirling as I tried to figure out how in the world I could save it and bring it back to Texas. I needed to take a picture of it so I could paint it.

After we renewed our vows, a photographer took a million pictures of us in the heated tent. I needed a picture with each of the trees, and Blake was so patient as we took photo after photo. Not every woman was lucky enough to have two amazing weddings. I wanted to have not only my memories but pictures to show our children what an amazing father they had.

"Ready to head back up to the hotel?" Blake asked in a deep, seductive voice. My insides trembled thinking about his hands touching my body. Those perfect lips placing soft kisses over my sensitive, exposed skin.

"Yes," I replied in a voice that said I was as eager as he was to get back to our suite.

Blake walked me back to the awaiting carriage, the same white blanket wrapped tightly around me.

"Have I told you how beautiful you look?" he asked as I snuggled up next to him in the seat.

"About a dozen times, but I don't mind."

"I have one more wedding gift for you."

Looking up at him, I smiled. "Another one? How could you possibly top all of this?"

He winked. "I've saved the best for last."

Once we returned to the hotel, Blake asked if I wanted to go to the bar for a celebratory drink. That was the last thing on my mind.

With a shake of my head, I answered, "I think I'd like to go up to our suite."

He frowned. "Are you okay?"

"Yes! I'm more than okay."

"Tired from all the excitement?"

With a chuckle, I replied, "No, just the opposite. I'm flying high. I want to be alone with you, that's all."

"That I can arrange."

We rode up in the elevator in silence. I could feel the sexual energy bouncing around in the elevator, and I knew Blake felt it too. He was already removing the tie on his tux and unbuttoning the first few buttons of his shirt.

Once we were in the room, I pulled him to me. Our mouths collided, and we both moaned.

"God, I love you so much."

Smiling against his lips, I replied, "I love you more."

"Impossible."

Taking my hand in his, he led me over to the large table, where a set of plans was laid out.

"When did you do this?" I asked.

"I have my ways."

Lifting a brow, I was beginning to think Blake had more pull at this hotel than he was letting on. Dresses being delivered, plans being laid out on the dining room table . . . I was going to have to press him for more, but right now I was too curious about the plans.

The title across the top read, "Morgan and Blake Greene."

"This is the first draft of the house I'm designing for us."

My hand went up to my mouth as I squealed in excitement. "Blake! Let me see!"

He lifted the first page, and I gasped. Drawn out on the paper was a beautiful, two-story, ranch-style house. There was a wraparound porch that looked like it went completely around the entire house.

"Does that porch go all the way around the house?"

"Yes."

"I love that, Blake!"

He grinned. "Here's the back. I'm thinking we can find some land with a view. I can see us sitting on the porch at night, maybe even in a porch swing, watching the sunset."

I watched him as he talked. He looked so happy envisioning our future home. My hand went to my stomach to settle the rolling sensation in there. If he thought he was saving the best wedding gift for last, I had my own surprise for him.

"That sounds wonderful," I said as Blake turned the page.

"Here's the downstairs. If you want the kitchen bigger, I can make it bigger."

My eyes burned as I fought to hold back my tears.

"It's perfect," I managed to say.

"It opens up into the family room. I know it was important to you to have that open space. I put a fireplace in the family room because I figured that would be where we would be most of the time. The formal living room doesn't have one, but if you want one—"

"No. I love it just how you designed it."

My fingers were at my lips as I took it all in.

"Here is the master bedroom. I put floor-to-ceiling windows so we can take advantage of the view."

I nodded, no longer able to speak from being so overwhelmed and nervous.

"I put a nook off to the side of the bedroom here so you could set up an area for painting if you wanted."

A single tear slipped free, and I quickly wiped it away. Blake was so focused on the plans, he wasn't paying attention to me.

I drew in a deep breath and slowly let it out then said, "But first we could use it as a place to put the baby. So he or she is closer to us."

"That's a great idea. Then there's another room next to ours that I thought we could both use as an office."

I smiled. My goodness. He wasn't going to make this easy.

"I love that idea. *Or* it could be used as a nursery for the baby, since it looks like all the other bedrooms are upstairs."

Blake nodded. "We could do that. There are four bedrooms upstairs, we can make one into an office and . . ."

He stopped talking and turned to look at me. My hand was over my stomach, and I was smiling like a silly schoolgirl.

"You keep mentioning a baby."

"I do."

"Morgan?" his voice cracked with emotion, and I nodded again.

"I believe I saved the best wedding present for last, Mr. Greene."

His eyes widened, and his face broke into a brilliant smile.

"Are you pregnant?"

A tear slipped free, and I somehow managed to answer, "Yes."

Blake placed his hand over his heart and started to cry. I swooned on the spot and had to reach for a chair to keep my legs from giving out.

"You're pregnant?"

"Yes."

He reached for me, pulled me into his arms, and spun us around.

"You're pregnant!" he cried out with joy.

When he stopped and slowly put me down, he used his thumbs to wipe away my tears while I did the same to him.

"You're going to be a daddy, Blake."

Drawing me back to him, he kissed me. It was the most magical kiss we had shared yet. I could feel his love, happiness, and excitement pouring into me.

He slowly drew back and leaned his forehead to mine.

"Morgan," he softly spoke, his thumb caressing my cheek. "I've never been so happy in my entire life. How far along?"

"Not very far. I haven't been feeling well, and I took a pregnancy test yesterday at my office. I'm guessing it happened pretty quickly since I just stopped taking my birth control last month."

He cupped my face in his hands and stared into my eyes.

"You and this baby of ours mean the world to me. I swear on my life I will love you both until the day I die."

I sobbed and attempted to speak, but nothing came out. I had never imagined I would be so happy. To know what it felt like to have someone love and adore me so intensely I felt like I couldn't breathe without him. Nothing else in the world mattered except for him, the child I was carrying, and our love.

"I'm going to make love to you now."

"Yes," I said softly before he kissed me again.

Carrying me up the steps, Blake slowly undressed me, taking his time as he worshiped every inch of my body, taking extra time to kiss my stomach and tell our child how much he already loved him or her.

Then with one more kiss to my lips, we were lost to each other. It was only the three of us. Forever and always.

THE END.

Don't miss Kelly Elliott's *Seduce Me*,
the first book in the *Austin Singles* series!

Turn the page for an excerpt

One

CHARLESTON

HE STOOD ACROSS the room and talked to Angie Reynolds like he had no idea he had shaken my entire world this past weekend. Maybe he did know. The truth was, he'd never know the real reason behind my leaving without saying a word to him. I gave him nothing. Not even, "Hey, thanks for the most incredible weekend of my life."

The only thing I did leave him was a letter because I didn't have the guts to be honest with him.

When his eyes drifted over the room, I looked away before he could see me watching him. I swore my lips still tingled from his kisses. Closing my eyes, I tried like hell to push the feelings away.

I cannot fall for Tucker Middleton.

Who was I kidding? I'd already fallen for him a long time ago.

Peeking toward him again, my breath caught while watching his hand run through his brown hair. My stomach tugged with that familiar desire that Tucker always pulled out of me.

I was struck by Tucker the first moment I ever laid my eyes on him. I turned into a complete mess. He made me feel things I'd never felt before, and that rattled me even more.

My father's voice played in the back of my head over and over. A constant reminder of why I couldn't give in to my feelings for Tucker.

"Charleston, do not be bothered with these boys in college. Focus on your future. Your future is with CMI. You can fall in love later."

When Tucker invited two friends of ours and me to his parents' lake house in Marble Falls, I was foolish enough to think I could resist him.

Yeah, I couldn't have been more wrong. I spent more time in his bed than on the lake.

My eyes closed. I could feel his scourging touch even now. Those magical fingers lightly running over my body. Deliciously soft lips against mine. His hands exploring every inch of my body.

Stop. This. Now. Charlie.

Drawing in a deep breath, I exhaled and glanced around the room. I pressed the beer bottle to my lips and finished it off. It didn't matter how much I drank; I'd never be able to forget the way his body felt. The way he pulled out my first ever orgasm and forever rocked my world.

Ugh, think of something else!

Taking another look around, I found him again. This time he was talking to Lily, my best friend and his sister. My gaze dropped to his soft plump lips. The things he whispered into my ear would replay in my mind for the rest of my life ... making me feel a high like I'd never felt before.

And therein lies the problem.

I need to stay focused. With Tucker, I cannot focus for shit.

Someday I would be taking over my father's billion-dollar global consulting firm. The last thing I could afford was a distraction. And boy howdy, was Tucker Middleton a distraction.

Feeling someone bump my shoulder, I glanced to my right to see Lily standing there.

Geesh. I was so lost in thought I hadn't even seen her walk over here.

Note to self: Don't daydream about Tucker.

"So, what happened between you and Tucker last weekend?" My heart stopped. With Lily being Tucker's sister, I had no clue what all he told her.

"Why?"

Looking between me and Tucker, who stood across the room, she focused back in on me. "Because he's been pissed ever since he got back. He said something to Nash about you being the biggest bitch he'd ever met. Then he told him if he never talked to you again, he wouldn't lose any sleep over it."

Ouch. I deserved that.

Snapping my head back over to Tucker, I saw he was now talking to a group of guys. I would never admit I was happy to see Angie had moved on and left Tucker alone.

"So . . . are you going to tell me what happened?"

My cheeks heated as I looked at her.

"Oh. My. God. Did y'all sleep together?"

When I didn't answer, she yanked at my arm. "Charlie, wait. I've never seen that look in your eyes before." She gasped then slapped her hand up to her mouth before dropping it again and saying, "You like him!"

With a curt laugh, I rolled my eyes and said, "Please. I do not like Tucker."

Lie. I think I'm in love with him.

She lifted her brow. "But y'all slept together?"

I shrugged. "Maybe."

Grabbing me, she pulled me down the hall and into the bathroom. "Okay, I'm so confused. I know Tucker has the hots for you, but I didn't think you liked him. I mean, you get all weird around him and all but . . ." She gasped again. "Oh no."

My eyes filled with tears, and I quickly looked away. "Charlie, what happened? He acts like he can't stand you now."

I instantly felt sick. "What did he say?"

"Pretty much the same thing he told Nash. That you were cold hearted and didn't care about anyone but yourself. He just told me he didn't care if you ever hung out with us again."

Squaring off my shoulders, I took in a deep breath as I tried to bury the sting of his words. I deserved them, though. "Well then, that's for the best. Takes the awkwardness away from the situation."

Narrowing her deadpan stare, she asked, "What . . . situation?"

How did I tell my best friend I was in love with her brother, had the most amazing weekend of my life with sex that was mind blowing, and then snuck out Sunday morning without so much as a word? Well. There was the note I left, which is probably why he hates me.

"Um . . . well . . . we, ah . . . things got a little . . . you know . . ."

Shaking her head, she responded. "No. I don't know, and you're babbling." Her brows pulled in. "You never babble."

I jumped and pointed at her, causing her to shriek. "See! That's the problem. Your brother brings out this whole other side of me, and I can't think straight when I'm around him. I trip on shit and say the stupidest things. You'd never know I was going to run a huge corporation someday by the way I act when he's near me."

The smile that spread over her face made my stomach drop.

"Oh. My. God. You *really* like him."

I frantically nodded my head. "Yes. No. Oh God, I don't know. No! I don't like him. I cannot like him. We had an amazing weekend with the best sex of my life, but it's over. I told him in my note I wanted to forget it ever happened and that it was best if we were just friends."

Swallowing hard, I looked away as I chewed on my lip. Oh, how I tried to talk myself out of kissing him that first night. We were both a little drunk, and damn it if he didn't look hot as hell in his stupid Dallas Cowboys baseball hat turned backward. *Do guys have any idea how hot that makes them look?*

For the last three years I fought my feelings for Tucker. I had a moment of weakness. Okay, it was more than a moment. It was three days' worth of moments of weakness.

"Friends? So you're saying you're not attracted to my brother?"

Attracted? Pffttt. Boy, was she off. I had fallen for Tucker the first time he grabbed my hand and walked me into a movie theater with our little group of friends. To him it was a friendly gesture . . . to me it made my entire body come to life. I knew then he was going to be my kryptonite.

Innocent touches here and there I could handle, but this past weekend took everything to a DEFCON level 5. All I heard the entire weekend were sirens going off in my head. Not to mention my father's voice warning me to stay focused and not get involved with what could only amount to a fling. After all, college relationships never lasted, he said. It didn't matter he had met my mother in college and married her. Or that they had been happily married for thirty years. He made me promise I wouldn't date and that I would solely focus on school.

I had kept my promise too. Kept it as long as my heart would allow.

Well, until last Thursday night when I let my betraying bitch of a body control me.

But Tucker was different. So very different. He made me want things I never desired before. He was a weakness I couldn't afford to have in my life. Not if I wanted to pursue my dreams. Well, my father's dreams.

"Hello? Earth to Charlie? Are you even listening to me?"

I shook my head to clear my thoughts. "Sorry. Listen, I messed up this past weekend. Things got a little hot and heavy with Tucker. It was a mistake that I . . . that I . . . regret."

I wonder if that sounded convincing to her? It sure as shit didn't to me.

Her mouth damn near dropped to the ground. "Wait, did you say you told him you wished it never happened in the note? The note you left him, Charlie?" Her eyes nearly popped out of her head.

Damn. This is where the shit is going to hit the fan.

"I, um . . . well. I left super early."

The look of disappointment on her face about killed me. I knew if I had waited for Tucker to wake up, I wouldn't have been able to leave. I would have found myself wrapped up in him another day. And that would have turned into another night, which would ultimately turn into more days and nights. There was no way I would have been able to look him in the eyes and say it was a mistake we were together because deep down in my heart, it was exactly what I had been wanting. There wasn't one ounce of regret in my body over the time we spent together, but my mind was flooded with all the whys and hows of why we could never be more than friends.

My blank stare was answer enough.

She closed her eyes for a brief moment before glaring at me with pure anger in her irises. "So, let me get this straight. Y'all made love, you led him on, then got up and left without so much as saying goodbye?"

The way she said it made me feel like such a slut, and truly the world's biggest bitch. Tucker was right when he told Nash I was a bitch. In fact, he was being a tad bit generous in his assessment of me.

Note to self. Sleeping with a guy and then getting up and leaving without so much as a thank you for the multiple orgasms is a bitch move. A total bitch move.

I didn't like the way she looked at me. Anger quickly raced through me. It was the only choice I had. "We didn't make love, Lily. Don't try to romanticize it. We *fucked*. He wanted me; I wanted to see what it would be like with him. Itches scratched. End of story."

Lily slowly shook her head. "You know it was more than that, Charlie. I see it in your eyes. You're just too damn scared to admit it. Maybe next time you want to get laid, go find some asshole who won't care when you get up and leave. Someone who will actually slap your ass on the way out the door. Tucker had feelings for you. How could you do this to him? How could you lead him on all weekend and then leave him high and dry and say it was a mistake?"

My chest squeezed thinking Tucker might no longer have feelings for me. That if he had feelings for me, I'd crushed any chance of ever being more than what we are right now. The thought that I had ruined a friendship I valued so much for a few hours of pleasure was fracturing my already broken heart. I had to keep telling myself it was for the best; it was the only way I'd be able to put one foot in front of the other around him.

Forcing myself to keep a steady voice, I replied, "Tucker wanted in my pants as much as I wanted in his, Lily. I can't help it if he thought there was going to be something more out of it. There were no promises made between us; it was just two adults doing adult things with no strings attached. Plain and simple."

Her head jerked back and she wore a shocked expression before letting out a scoff. "Wow, Charlie. You really *are* a bitch. A heartless bitch with no feelings at all. You've mastered that at the ripe old age of twenty-one. You're going to make a great addition to your father's company with that attitude."

With that, my best friend spun around on her heels and stormed out the door. I couldn't even be mad at her because every single word she said was true.

All of it.

Want more Kelly Elliott?

Check out her *Cowboys & Angels* series . . .